LECKEY

KV-355-426

CROWNBIRD

CROWNBIRD

Kit Thackeray

PETER DAVIES : LONDON

Peter Davies Ltd
15 Queen Street, Mayfair, London W1X 8BE
LONDON   MELBOURNE   TORONTO
JOHANNESBURG   AUCKLAND

Copyright © 1976 Christopher Thackeray
First published in Great Britain 1976

432 16512 6

Printed in Great Britain by
Willmer Brothers Limited, Birkenhead

To my Mother and Father, my best friends; and to the memory of Richard Chipperfield, tragically killed in Uganda in April 1975. He read an early draft of this book and said that it would make good in-flight reading if there was absolutely nothing else available. Like many others, I shall miss him. He said little, knew a lot, and loved Africa above all.

Prologue

The army drove into the outskirts of the village just before dawn. The sun was almost up, and the noise of the heavy engines disrupted the early morning quiet and silenced the local cockerel. The vehicles formed a curved line across the path that led to the main road, and the shadowy figures of the soldiers spread unseen between the huts. As the first red tongues of sunlight licked the sky, a whistle blew. Within seconds, the small mud dwellings were ablaze, and the air filled with screams. As the villagers ran about, confused and terrified, the soldiers clubbed them down with gun butts, or knifed them. Soon the ground was covered with bodies, many still writhing and moaning, hands held pointlessly across gashes through which blood pumped out on to the beaten orange earth. Groups of soldiers began binding some of the men and manhandling them into the lorries. Through the smoke a young girl ran blindly, pursued by an askari. She leapt through a debris of bodies and charred wood, jumping obstacles, her breasts bouncing as she ran. She had almost reached the long grass that surrounded the clearing when a rope tethering one of the village goats brought her to the ground. The animal bucked wildly, but its high scream of terror was cut off abruptly by a heavy blow from a panga. When the girl picked herself up, she was encircled by four men. She turned this way and that as they closed in, sobbing and gasping for breath, her urine coursing on to the gorund, nostrils flared, then they were on her, tearing at her garments, and she collapsed under them.

On Karuma bridge, some thirty miles down the road, an old man watched the approach of the small convoy. Behind him were parked three vehicles, a lorry, a Land Rover and a black Mercedes. At either end of the bridge armed guards stood im-

1

mobile, and the only sound was the roar of the Nile as countless tons of water swept over Karuma Falls, passed under their feet, and accelerated down into Gorogong rapids. The lorries stopped on the bridge, and the soldiers began to drag the captured men to the side of the road. Some of them were unconscious and had to be propped up against the low parapet; they lay there limply, unseeing, the lucky ones. At last there were thirty-one men lined up by the roadside. Behind them clouds of spume and spray filled the air as the great river thundered on its way across Africa. A door opened in the Mercedes and a man stepped out, tall, immaculate in the uniform of a colonel. He looked down at the water and up at the sky, but he addressed the old man.

'The river is to our country as we are to the world, M'zee. It pays us a fleeting visit and then moves on to unknown lands. If it dries in the sands of Egypt or sinks in the marshes of the Sudd, we do not know of it.' He glanced along the road to where the prisoners slumped in various attitudes of despair, and then the river drew his eyes downwards. When he spoke again his voice was almost a whisper.

'The man from the village cannot know where the waters lead unless he travels with them.'

The old man said nothing, but stood looking out into the distance. Purple clouds were massing down river, to the west, and the sunlit water danced against the darkening sky. Omuria continued, his voice raised again the noise.

'This morning has been the warning that I promised you. The Acholis gave Kalaba life, and so I give you this today, as a reminder that I will not rest until he is dead, and those that sympathise with him. Tell the people in the villages what has happened here, what you have seen with your own eyes. It is I who have the power now, M'zee, Kalaba has gone.'

The noise of the Bren was barely audible. Like targets at a fairground the figures crumpled and fell. Some lifted and over-balanced, dropping into the water thirty feet beneath. One man fled along the bridge until bullets caught him, and when he dropped his legs went on trying to run. The last shots were fired, and the soldiers tipped the bodies that remained into the river. They disappeared instantly in the brown flood, and then the convoy started to move out. Soon the vehicles were small on

2

the winding road that ran up from the gorge. On the bridge, the old man pulled his cloak tightly round his thin body and started the long walk home. Beneath his feet, the first heavy drops of rain diluted the fresh blood until it could no longer be seen.

Chapter One

The big man crouched in the meagre shadow of his pick-up and squinted at the shimmering distance. Sweat coursed down his face, revealing riverbeds of tanned skin under the red dust, stung his eyes, and was finally absorbed by an already sodden neckscarf. The flat drone of insects emphasized the heat of late afternoon. It was the hottest day so far in a hot month, without a cloud in sight; just storks, circling, watching, signwriting the sky. Not that they were ever too far away to notice when you died; very little kicked off out here without them seeing. He shifted slightly, an ant panicked among the hairs on his leg and jabbed at the first skin it could find: Sam Gould just scratched and waited.

He was looking at a small herd of topi, browsing distantly, miraged by the heat. It moved slowly, almost imperceptibly nearer, blind to the danger so close at hand. In his father's day you could drive through game out here for mile after mile, as far as the eye could see. Now it sometimes took a day-long search to find a herd of two hundred. Gould's face was a deep mahogany and his pale blue eyes seemed perpetually strained to focus the searing infinity of African horizons, narrowed to slits against a sun that bleached hair and cracked lips. From beneath the battered brim of an old bush hat, he scanned the plains. This place was called Kopenek, a huge area of scrub and thorn, west of the mountains that separated Uganda from Kenya. From time to time, inexplicably, small kopjes stood out of the plains like erupting pimples on neglected skin. But nearer to, they proved to be huge pyramids of orange rock, jumbled, brash and impossible, against the blue of the sky. Sometimes there were not many rocks but one, coming sheer out of the earth to

4

a height of four hundred feet, several miles in girth. Their natural caves and fissures provided homes for great and small alike: the hyrax and the leopard lived there, and birds of prey made their crude nests on inaccessible outcrops. From those promontories, Africa took on a different perspective. Its vastness, rumoured before, became a reality.

The topi were closer now, and Gould brought the ten-fifties tight into his eyes. Africa leapt towards him, almost near enough to touch. Over the years, these man-made eyes had helped reveal her secret ways, the comings and goings of her many children. He had seen birth, migration, sudden death; scenes of infinite gentleness and ruthless extermination; the cowardice of the strong, and the magnificent, futile bravery of the gentle weak: but it was all in the game. Only man broke the rules. The topi grazed peacefully. In among their number two males acted as sentinels, using old anthills as their lookout posts. Further off, another group of hartebeeste, this time kongoni, grazed fitfully in the yellowing light. Gould shifted his weight. 'Twenty minutes,' he thought. 'Another twenty minutes should do it.'

'Kopenek Reserve—No shooting without Permit.' In a way, sadly, it was a joke. The whole park-reserve system seemed doomed before it began. Mankind had driven the game further from its habitats, and parks had merely prolonged the end, concentrating animals into areas of land that could not support them. Gould had a profound mistrust of the average African. To them, everything that walked, crawled or flew was just 'nyama'—the Swahili word that meant both 'game' and 'meat'. Past incidents came easily to mind: the army officer whose sorties to machine-gun buffalo along the Victoria Nile had earned him such popularity with his men. Gould had seen it, time and time again. The tripod, the unearthly stuttering roar, black thumbs on the worn twin grips of an ex-British army Vickers. Huge animals lumbering, turning, bellowing, their herd disrupted, legs cut off, teeth, faces, horns smashed, pulped, blood and offal sluicing from the crashing blows delivered by an enemy that they could neither see nor evade. Then silence. The inevitable vultures. And marabous. But first, before any of these, the African. For fifty miles either side of that same stretch of river the land was deforested. Dead trees stretched from horizon to horizon, ring-barked by elephant in such numbers that only heavy and persistent culling of the herds could ensure the continued existence of the remainder. They knew, these elephant, where the park boundary was, and came in their thousands for its tenuous sanctuary.

Gould shook his head as he picked his way through the past. He had returned to Uganda at the age of seventeen, after five years at school in England. His father had died, leaving him a little money and a bungalow near Lake Victoria; later he'd joined the Game Department to track down the adventure that he'd always hoped would be synonymous with the word 'Africa'. As an assistant warden he had travelled all over the country, helping to fulfil two main functions: protecting people from animals, and protecting animals from people. The irony of the situation had failed to impress him; in those days he had been young and zealous, unable to see the certain end to which the practised methods of 'guarding the national heritage' must eventually lead. His years in the game department taught him many things, but they did not make him wealthy. In 1958 he left his job, and it was two years later that a letter appeared in the ministry post: Samuel Gould, age twenty-two, applying for a license to hunt professionally.

When all the papers came, he sat down and sorted them through. There were twenty-one sections, and a would-be hunter had to prove proficiency in them all. The first page listed the general headings, those at the end of the list having more to do with clients than animals. Or perhaps it amounted to the same thing:

19. *Social Ability.* General knowledge of LITERATURE, SPORTS, POLITICS and RELIGION.

20. *Entertainment.* Experience, differentiation between clients, campfire drinks, atmosphere; and ETIQUETTE.

21. *Appearances.* Physically reasonably fit, free from apparent disease.

Criterion: 'If I were a client, would I accept him/her as my professional hunter?'

But there was nothing there he hadn't done or couldn't learn, and by the end of the year the formalities were completed and the money paid. He remained a white hunter for almost two years, until a growing dislike for the majority of his customers, and the absurdity of constant slaughter, erupted into a loathing

6

of commissioned hunting that made it impossible to go on. And, at the same time, an event occurred that was to radically alter the lives of everyone living in the state—Uhuru.

But all that was a decade of yesterdays ago. Today there was work to be done, work that was both specialized and dangerous. His business was to catch animals alive, for export to the game-parks that were sprouting like mushrooms in Europe and America. He would never discuss the ethics of what he did, but he knew with a rare certainty that one day the balloon would go up in East Africa, and then the game would die, shot out of existence even faster than in so-called peacetime.

Here in Karamoja no one knew a thing about politics, least of all the Karamojong, who spent their time amassing vast herds of cattle at the expense of some other tribe. They were proud people, but an anachronism in newly-awakened Africa, despised and feared as savages, a scareword mothers used to keep their kids in line. Gould remembered a day six months past. Two Karamojong had crossed the Greek river into Sabei. They were naked as always, although word had been sent out that they must wear clothes if they wanted to travel south. An army patrol had stopped them, taken them into the bush. It was one of Gould's men who had found the skeletons. The wrists were tied with cord, and the bones that the scavengers had left were shattered. Gould remembered the skulls: their perfect teeth, marred by a gap where the two front ones in the lower jaws had been extracted. It was an ancient custom, protection against lockjaw starving or asphyxiating the victim. He had fingered the skull thoughtfully while his men chatted and laughed. To this day the sightless sockets reproved him with the eloquence of the violently dead.

The Karamojong lived for his cattle. It was said that when dying they would call not for a wife or mother, but for their favourite cow, and often during the excitement of a cattle raid tribesmen screamed a bull's name as a war cry. They were primitive, tough, fighting the odds every day of their lives, snaring protected animals by the score and shooting them with bow and arrow. They went nowhere without their spears, and carried finger knives and wrist blades, making it almost impossible for an assailant to come to grips. They lived out on the plains in low dwellings that so merged with the environment that one could

7

stumble into such a village before realizing it was there. They valued their cattle, their land, their right to do as they wished here on the plains of their ancestors. They despised the strange and alien habit of covering their bodies. They were as indigenous to Karamoja as the animals they poached—but how could you define poaching to men such as these?

Gould got to his feet and looked down into the back of the pickup. Two pairs of eyes returned the look, and he repressed a smile. Bunduki and Panga were his right-hand men, a murderous pair of individuals, tough and resourceful, living for danger and the status it brought them. The name 'bunduki' meant gun, and a panga was a kind of machete. It was anyone's guess where the names had come from.

'Tayari, baba?' Gould addressed Bunduki.

'Tayari, bwana.'

The three men started to dress for action, in helmets, goggles, leather jackets and gauntlets. The herd had stopped some two hundred yards distant. The pickup had an open back, and no roof over the cab. Strong uprights rose to above waist height from the four corners of the truck, and a heavy wooden rail had been fitted all round from upright to upright. The front rail was wrapped in strips of foam and blankets. Bunduki would stand in the right hand corner, looking high over Gould's head, holding a long bamboo pole with a rope noose. His job was to neck-rope the animal, and then pull sharply on the pole so the rope would come out of a wire clip at the end of the bamboo. The other end of the rope was fixed to the vehicle. Panga placed his huge hands on the rail either side of Bunduki, and pinned him tightly to the wood. The word was almost go. Gould waved back towards the thicker bush, and then got into the cab. A hundred yards away, a support vehicle carrying a large wooden box was almost invisible under an acacia.

The raucous four-litre engine shattered the silence, and swarms of insects rose into the air. Clouds of red dust churned from under the rear wheels, and Gould engaged second gear at a speed of twenty miles an hour. The metal radiator guard smashed through thorn trees and scrub, as the truck dodged madly through a series of sun-baked ant-hills, some higher than the vehicle itself. The topi, splitting into groups, hit their top speed almost immediately, and Gould had learned to his cost that hartebeeste

8

could run faster and longer than any other cloven-hoofed animal. And they didn't run blind. They had it all worked out. Zig-zag from ant-hill to ant-hill, but always make for the heavy bush, the thick stuff where even Gould must admit defeat.

The cab was full of whistling thorn, and swarming with red ants. Gould swung hard left to avoid a crater, and the Toyota leant on the front offside wheel before it came round, screaming in protest, and straightened up. Ahead, moving rhythmically, were three topi, travelling deceptively fast with their peculiar gait; bouncing, not running, all four feet leaving the ground at once, heads moving up and down, puffs of dust from their flashing hooves. Gould cut a corner through two large silverthorns and the broken stumps screeched briefly on the sump guard. In the back, Bunduki heard the engine note drop as Gould went into top: they were now doing fifty over virgin territory and overhauling the topi fast. Suddenly, they were alongside; he lowered the loop in readiness, both hands free, his body pinioned by Panga's colossal arms. Just as suddenly the animal dipped its right shoulder, rounded a termite mound, and was gone. They were now travelling in roughly opposite directions, but not for long. Gould double declutched violently and dropped a gear; wrenching the wheel hard right, he stamped on the throttle, spinning the truck in its own length. Releasing the wheel, the steering righted, and the truck shot away, back end swinging wildly, in renewed pursuit. Way back, half obscured by dust, the support vehicle moved to intercept the fleeing animal.

The topi's pace had barely slackened. Already it was five hundred yards distant, running alone, a trail of red dust marking its passage. Gould felt renewed admiration for the unknown forces that had constructed this creature. By all the rules in the book it should collapse, trip, turn at bay. But it never would. The long-legged giraffe could only be safely chased for two minutes, after which time they were likely to lie down and die. The eland, with its powerful shoulders, would decelerate from gallop to trot in no time at all. But the frail hartebeeste, with its diminutive horns and long, tragicomic face, legs like matchsticks and brown, sad eyes—they ran with the heart of a lion until they either escaped or were caught.

The storks and vultures wheeled closer, sensing a kill. Below them, in the arid tableau of thorn and dust, both vehicles were

9

converging across the topi's path, a metal vee closing a gap it could never reach in time. The noose went out, scooping low over the bush, Bunduki reaching far out into space. The animal raced on in a narrow corridor with a truck on either side. It neither slowed nor stopped, but ran, waiting for a way out, an opening, a mistake. The noose moved slowly over its back towards its head. Suddenly the topi stopped. Straight-legged, it appeared to turn in mid-air. When it hit the ground, it was already moving in almost the opposite direction. But in turning it had leapt through the noose, which was now loosely around its rear haunches. Bunduki yanked on the pole screaming 'Simama!', and as Gould trod on the brakes in compliance, the rope jerked tight round the animal's body. The two vehicles skidded to a halt side by side, and eight men leapt to the ground.

'Toa sanduku! Haraka!' Gould yelled, and while four of the watu undid the ropes and dragged the box onto the ground, he joined the others in their headlong rush to the far end of the rope. The bucking animal was securely held by the horns, and Gould tucked himself close to its left flank and held its shoulders. The object of the chase now became a reality, a warm, furry, wriggling she-topi in beautiful condition. Her skin was deep brown, with the distinctive areas of dark grey on both haunches, and her breath smelt of Africa—the grasses, the herds and the heat. It was the work of moments to manhandle her into the box, and to lift it, with its sidebars, onto the truck. The words of an old jingle came to mind, about a gnu in a zoo that was sick of being mistaken for other animals. But it eluded him, and the chatter of the men didn't help. He took a long pull from a canvas water-bottle and climbed up in to the cab. The two trucks moved off through the thorn.

Listen to the night, Gould. Listen to the night creatures of Africa. How could you ever leave again? How could you sleep in the silence, or with the roar of traffic in your ears? His camp was situated near Greek river, now hardly more than a muddy creek. As he sat outside the small grass banda that served him as an office, he faced the plains that stretched to the foot of Mount Kadam. It was a silhouette now, the mountain, distinctive as ever with its sheer sides and perfectly flat top. Gould had always meant to climb it, to clamber through the lower forests and

10

out onto the pink candy buttresses that changed their texture and colour every hour of the day. But he never had. Perhaps it was enough just to look.

A figure materialized at his side, teeth flashing white in the near-darkness.

'Voulez quelqu'chose, M'sieu?'

Gould chuckled to himself. The legacy of colonialism had him sitting here, an Englishman in South Karamoja, speaking bad French with a Watutsi from Zaire! His was probably the only camp east of the Nile that could boast genuine French-style cuisine.

'Oui, Zappiel, du thé.'

When the tea came, he held the mug tightly, letting its warmth seep into his fingers. Steam rose, and condensed on his face like a fine dew, leaving it cold in the night air. It was over half a century since his grandfather had come out here, soon after the Great War. Things must have been different then. He remembered his own childhood in Jinja, walking the endless golf course with his father, understanding little of the conversation that flowed around him. And then afterwards in the clubhouse, the terrifying Great Dane that had really been as docile as a sheep. And darts. The first time one actually hit the board and stayed there. Memories flooded in, and Gould rocked back in his chair, looking at the stars: familiar patterns winked back, the Seven Sisters, Orion the hunter and the Plough, right down on the horizon. At school in England no one had ever believed him when he explained that in Africa all the constellations lay on their sides. Although he knew it to be a fact, the reason had not been that obvious, and as a boy he'd never been able to explain the phenomenon to his own, or anyone else's, satisfaction. It was all a long way away and a long time ago. And but for one single event, he might never have gone there at all.

When he was eleven, his mother died of childbirth, leaving a frail six-pound boy behind her like an afterthought. The house had seemed different after that, as if its very soul had fled. At first, it was almost unbearable, and soon the little things that his mother had done became apparent through neglect. On the verandah, a giant begonia withered for lack of water, and the clematis climbed tendril by tendril along a tortuous route into the garden, there to re-root and survive. In the house, Kahindo,

11

the ageing African nanny, was as much overcome by grief as anyone. For hours she sat in her cramped quarters at the back of the kitchen, and her soft crying filled the air with melancholy. After three days she gave notice and left, carrying her worldly goods, wrapped in a sheet, on her head. An ancient bus, full of Africans and their livestock, carried her noisily away towards Fort Portal in a cloud of blue-black smoke. With her going, something else of value faded from the already empty house.

It was after the funeral that his father had driven him to a promontory overlooking the Nile as it flowed out of Lake Victoria. It was evening, and hippos were edging nearer the bank, ready to leave the cool of the water for a night's foraging along the riverside. The sun reddened the landscape, and the huge animals broke surface amid a shower of golden droplets, their yawning jaws black, toothy silhouettes. Father and son sat together in the evening light. The words, when they came, were quiet, though emotion was never far under the surface.

'Samuel, it's time we had a talk. Perhaps now is a good moment.'

His father looked old and drawn. In a matter of days he seemed to have shrunk in stature, and his eyes gazed unfocused about him, seeing only memories.

'Things have changed now that your mother's ... now. I'm going to sell our house, because it's not the same there any more, and now I've got to think what's to become of you.'

A terrified sense of anticipation filled the boy's mind as he listened. 'I can stay with you, Dad,' he wanted to say, 'I can travel the plantations like you do, and meet the people at Mbarara and Chambura. You can teach me what to do, for later, when I'm older.' But the sounds wouldn't come, and he just sat there, looking up at his father's face. After the silence, words came with a rush.

'You've learned a lot of things at school, Samuel, history and geography and the like. Well, how would you like to find out about all those things for yourself? Your grandfather came from England, and your mother's people all live over there. You could go to a nice school in the country, and meet a lot of other boys your own age. Teach them a thing or two, I shouldn't be surprised.'

The sentences fell slowly down, till their meaning penetrated the soft shell that housed all his secret thoughts. To leave Africa! To go away and live in one of the pictures from the geography book, England with the endless chimneys, and little houses huddling in the cold, grey under slate roofs and a slate-grey sky. He felt his father's arm round his shoulder, but it no longer carried the reassurance that he needed. Even the voice seemed different.

'It's not just you, Samuel. You've got a baby brother now, and he needs a woman's care. I'm arranging for you both to live with your Aunt Rosemary. You'll like her, and she'll like you.'

But he knew with conviction that he wouldn't like her, or England, or anything ever again. Suddenly accumulated anguish broke over him like a torrent, destroying all reason. With sobs racking his body, he wrenched open the car door and half fell, half jumped, into the African night. He ran blindly, tripping and stumbling, the sounds of the big river and his heart thumping loud in his ears. Somewhere in the distance behind him a voice called his name, echoing in the darkness. And then the ground dropped away under his feet, and he was falling, taking with him a shower of earth and rubble, until his body hit the stream bed, and blackness shut out the moon.

Gould ran a finger over the thin white ridge that skirted his hairline. All those years, and the scar was still there. He hadn't even avoided the boat trip to Southampton from Mombasa—the fall had gained him just five stitches and four days in bed. Soon everything started to happen at once. Tickets were arranged, and Mrs Squires, wife of one of the plantation managers, moved into the spare room. It was she who would look after Samuel and the baby during the four-week voyage to England.

The train from Kampala to Mombasa left the station in a huge cloud of white steam. From the relative luxury of a first-class carriage, Samuel and his father watched the hills of the town fade from sight. Secretly, though scarcely wanting to admit it, he was feeling the first stirrings of excitement at the coming journey. Puffing with the effort, the train slowly wound its way towards the border with Kenya. At the frontier, travel documents were checked by uniformed officials, while those African children who had managed to slip unnoticed through the station railings ran from carriage to carriage with pieces of sugar cane, pineapple and baked corn.

13

Then they were in Kenya, and twilight fell on the land. Samuel was asleep in his bunk when the train passed a tiny station; a single red lamp lit two words painted white on a brown board: Equator Halt. In the darkness, a tall African urged his cows to cross the track, and watched as the lights of the guard's van faded into the distance, and the train, with its slumbering cargo, headed down into the great rift.

Mombasa was a place for greetings and farewells. Ships came into Kilindini harbour from all over the world, on their way to Europe and the Far East. As the liners disgorged their passengers, laughing groups of people chattered and kissed on the quayside. But soon the crowds drifted away, and there was a period of peace, without even the cries of the gulls so familiar to those who have berthed in colder ports. Then the crowds came back. But this time the atmosphere was different, and the faces showed the change. When the gangplanks were raised, and hawsers let go fore and aft, the people on the dockside waved handkerchiefs and also used them to wipe the slow creep of tears from their eyes. The big ship's departure was cruelly slow to those who were left behind. When the tugs had her pointing straight out into the Indian Ocean, Samuel's father turned quickly away and walked towards his taxi, waiting behind the customs shed of godown thirteen. Two miles away, at the other end of the Kilindini road, lay the Manor hotel. He was not a great drinker, but, by God, he was going to have one now.

Samuel watched his father turn away and found he couldn't swallow. His eyes followed the tiny figure out of sight, walking stiffly, a distant marionette. 'You'll be out here again before you know it. For the summer holidays. And next time we might see about an aeroplane.' Summer? It had always been summer in Africa, as long as he could remember.

The shore was receding now, water a deep ink-blue under the bows. Salt spray curled into the air like chips of shattered crystal, and Nyali beach showed a strip of coral white, fringed by curving palms. Behind the ship, a line was already out from one of the crew decks, and a lure skimmed the water to tempt sailfish or marlin. But the school of porpoise playing leapfrog with the fishing tackle would never take the bait. Some said they knew exactly what it was for, and would stand on their tails and watch as fish after fish was pulled in. Later Samuel heard that

14

a big fish had been caught, a blue marlin, before the liner had picked up too much speed. Desperately seeking freedom, it had jack-knifed its way across the surface of the ocean, trying to throw the hook. But the crew were not sporting men, and the line had a breaking strain of over five hundred pounds. Eventually exhausted, it had been dragged in and gaffed with a special tool made for such occasions in the ship's workshops.

'Weighed a hundred and fifty pounds,' the cabin boy confided to Samuel. 'Only a baby really.'

And after that Africa became, like so many other things, just a poignant memory.

Aunt Rosemary was an ample woman to whom looking after children was a vocation. It never seemed to occur to her that her own offspring were now fully grown, and she continued to treat one and all as if they were still at school, running her domain from the large kitchen which was the centre of the household. Aunt Rosemary was married, it was generally assumed, to Uncle Fred, and together they farmed one hundred and sixty acres of dark brown Merioneth soil. The farm was in a small valley near Llandderfel, where the tough upland heather that covered the Berwyn foothills reluctantly gave way to the lush blue-green grass of pasture and paddock. Up on the moors, groups of shaggy ponies sheltered from the wind beneath the stone walls that wound their way over the hills. In the winter they came down into the valleys, to eat the scatterings of hay that farmers knew would help them through the cold.

When Samuel, Mrs Squires and the baby arrived in Wrexham, it was far from being winter time. An ancient taxi carried them into the country, up a steeply winding road that led west towards Bala. Occasionally, a gateway allowed a glimpse of the countryside otherwise obscured by the steeply-banked hedgerows. Sometimes the foliage was so dense that the sky disappeared overhead, and the way ahead became a twisting tunnel through a world of dead leaves and tree roots. At the bottom of a long descent, just where it seemed that the road would never rise again, lay a small, hump-backed bridge over the clear, dark waters of a mountain stream; beyond this, on the left hand side of the lane, clumps of cow parsley almost obscured a sign: Steep Hill Farm. Backfiring energetically, the old taxi chugged through the gate, and entered a copse through which the faint outline of farm buildings could just be seen.

And that had been the beginning of his five years in England, time that had gone fast in the holidays and slowly during the long school terms. He remembered with an inward shudder the gaunt buildings of Abbotts, tucked beneath the wind-chased crags off the road from Corwen to Llangollen. The costly public school education that turned a blind eye to a multitude of sins. The headmaster had been called Halland, a small man with a prominent chin. On Fridays, when choir practice finished in the assembly hall, it had been his delight to take a stiff drink before visiting the little top dormitories where the new boarders slept. His visits were well-known and dreaded. The cry of 'Cave! The Head!' sent boys scuttling wet out of showers and baths, up the wooden-floored corridors to their beds. Somehow, pathetically, it seemed safe under the blankets with just your eyes peeping out, waiting for the footsteps in the passage and the tall figure to stoop and enter the dormitory. The prefect on duty grinned amusedly at the unsolicited activity some ten minutes before lights-out. He was still grinning when Halland's bulk filled the doorway.

'Good evening, Taylor. Has something amusing happened?'

'Good evening, Sir. No Sir, nothing.'

'I see.' Halland surveyed the two rows of iron bedsteads that lined the room, ten in number, and what he did see was that one of them, even allowing for the slight frame of an eleven-year-old boy, was empty. 'Whose bed is that, Taylor?'

The prefect consulted a list, ran his fingers down the names; the boys were very new.

'Gould, Sir.'

In the corridor outside, Samuel heard his name and knew that there was now no way in which he could reach the anonymity of his bed without passing the two men. A diminutive figure in overlarge flannel pyjamas, he walked into the dormitory. What followed was something that all the boys had come to accept passively, without question, during the first few weeks of term. In the small, self-sufficient kingdom of a boarding school there was even an inverted code of honour to protect those who perpetrated the strange acts that the environment encouraged. In a detached way Samuel lay on his bed, and felt the large

16

hands undo the buttons of his pyjama top. Whisky fumes fanned his face and he felt the man's jowls, covered with a day's growth, rubbing on his chest and stomach, fingers working into the crevices between his ribs until breathing became almost impossible. Rasping, Halland had called it, bringing—just on Fridays after choir—his own special brand of nausea to the new boys. And yet such was the man's authority that nothing was ever said.

It was only towards the end of term that school became bearable, stripping beds and packing trunks symbolic acts that preceded the holidays. The rules slackened slightly, and there was an air of camaraderie as if everyone could afford to be nice to everyone else now that there were only a few hours left to go. Then school was over and the holidays started, as full of promise as a misty dawn. In the summer the days were long and physical, an endless cycle of cows and sheep, barley and wheat. The work never ended. There were tractors to be driven and horses to be exercised, and sometimes, after a long, hot day, heady cider from the cold musty cellar that lay beneath the house. Uncle Fred spoke little, and sometimes not at all. His economy with words did nothing to undermine his position, it just meant that what he did say was usually quite important, and people listened. And if ever there was a word of reprimand or criticism, he would do it privately, taking the man aside, so that it was always a personal thing, between the two of them.

To begin with, the letters from Uganda came regularly, talking of things that made Samuel long to return. The Curry's tame eland had calved, bananas he had seen planted were bearing their first fruit, Mr Van Weinand had caught an 190-pound Nile perch near Gorogong. Then the flow of post slowed, and eventually came to an almost total standstill. From the first Fred treated him like his own, and on the farm none of the post-war food restrictions seemed to matter. While city dwellers existed as best they could on ration books, supplemented by the black market, the farming fraternity was never short of the occasional cheese or a side of bacon.

It was at sixteen that another single event helped decide his future: he was summarily expelled from school.

It was a day that Gould could laugh at now: at the time it had been far from funny. The waiting had been worst, outside the sombre oak of Halland's study door, with the overwhelming

17

urge to shit that those sort of moments seemed to generate.

'Enter!'

Samuel opened the door, walked into the room. Behind his desk the headmaster looked like a witch-doctor about to read the bones. One wall was dedicated to group photographs, row upon row of rugby XV's, cricket XI's and fives teams. A glass cabinet, poised upon frail legs, contained a number of inscribed silver cups and in a special rack, suspended within easy reach of the desk, were five canes of differing lengths and thicknesses. Through the leaded panes of the tall gothic windows, Samuel could see the valley, and beyond it the clouds scudding over the high tors.

'Ah, Gould, yes.' Halland appeared to consult some notes on the matter in hand, then pushed them aside and removed his glasses. His eyes met Samuel's across the desk. 'It appears that you have finally disgraced both yourself and your school simultaneously, boy. As I understand it, Matron and a friend from Shrewsbury were walking this afternoon on the footpath that goes from Hut Cross up onto the table. Along that path, this side of the wood, there are two dutch barns. Painted orange, I seem to recall. In the normal course of events, Matron would not have left the path, but this afternoon a sudden shower sent her and her escort hurrying for shelter. After the shower they were on the point of leaving, when an interesting object came to light—to be precise—your scarf. Lying in the hay. And on looking up she beheld yourself and a young lady from the High School. Also lying in the hay. What exactly you had been doing there I am about to find out.'

Samuel considered what he should say. There were two sides to every story, but in this case only one that would carry any weight. He'd met the girl only twice before, also on Saturday afternoons, but during First XV rugby matches. It was the only place where the boys could ever see the girls from the High School, unless you counted those rare occasions when there was a dance, and then if you weren't in the sixth you had to climb on the science lab roof and look through the high windows of the assembly hall to watch the proceedings. At the rugby matches there was always a crowd, and it was surprising the number of people who actually seemed to like the game. The girl was called Alexandra, and her mother was very wealthy. She was fifteen. On Saturday afternoons, when the rugby fixture was away, both schools were turned out for a compulsory walk. They walked in the country that lay either to the east or the west of the main road; one week Abbotts would go east, and the following week the High School.

Samuel had worked himself into such a state waiting for the girl that by the time she arrived he'd chewed all the fingernails off his left hand. The right hand nails stayed intact because they were needed in an attempt to master his latest acquisition—an old guitar.

'I thought maybe you weren't coming.'

The girl was dark, pretty, cheeks flushed from the walk. 'I nearly didn't—I mean, I feel so obvious in this ghastly uniform.'

The High School dress was a dark chocolate brown with hat, shoes and stockings to match. A gold hatband carried the school motto in Latin: 'Through Virtue we Achieve.'

Samuel cleared his throat. 'Well, it's not so bad as mine, you know. That's why I've turned the jacket inside out.'

Boys from Abbotts were even easier to spot, looking rather like giant beetles with red and black shells roaming the countryside. There was an uncomfortable silence. Suddenly the girl opened her bag.

'Would you like some chocolate? I brought a whole lot that Mother sent me.'

Samuel took it gratefully. The sounds of tearing paper and chewing broke the silence, and conversation began to flow, this way and that, about people at the schools and teachers and home life. Soon it seemed that they had known each other for years, and not just a small part of a Saturday afternoon. He kissed her, and her breath was sweet and warm on his face. With the kiss the last tension fell away, and he felt like laughing with relief. She opened her eyes, and he saw that they were brown like hazel, with long curling lashes. And then the eyes widened in alarm.

'Someone's coming!'

Samuel scooped up the remains of the chocolate, and the girl's bag. 'Quick! Up there!'

The barn was big, and where they had been sitting sunlight filtered in through the trees outside. But towards each end of the building the bales had been stacked to a height of twenty feet or more, and it was dark. They had barely reached their

19

perch when two figures ran laughing into the building, a stray shaft of wintry sunlight spotlighting their faces. Above them in the sunbeam's brightness clouds of glinting dust drifted back and forth like aimless insects. The woman took off her coat and shook it. Drops of water caught the light.

'Just in time! It's more like April than April!'

Her voice carried well in the confines of the barn, and Samuel felt the bottom drop out of his stomach. The girl looked at him inquiringly; putting his mouth close to her ear, he hissed: 'Jesus! It's Matron.'

Wedged together, they peered down through the hay bales at the couple beneath them. They stood close, the man's hands pulling their bodies together. He stooped, kissing her throat and neck. Her hair hung loose in a way that Samuel had never seen it before, and her face was relaxed. Without the stern expression and the white uniform she looked younger, softer, more female. He heard her voice, lower now, the words a muttered whisper.

'Darling we musn't, not here. Supposing someone comes?'

But the man made no reply save to pull her blouse out of her skirt and run his hands up the skin of her back. At this she seemed to sag, and the coat dropped forgotten onto the loose hay. Then they were of one mind, each hurrying to undo the buttons of the other. Samuel watched as first one breast, then the other, appeared in the dappled light, and a distorted moaning filled the air as the man cupped them in his hands and flicked his tongue back and forth across the nipples. Then he was behind her, his hands working at the fastener of her skirt, pushing everything she wore in a great tangled bundle over her hips. Samuel felt a terrific embarrassment at the noises she was making; somehow they were infinitely private, and he wanted to get out but he couldn't move, and his eyes wouldn't look at anything but the scene below, where the questions that had tantalized him for three years were being explicitly answered by practical demonstration. He didn't dare to look at the girl beside him. What could he say to her? God, now the man was getting completely undressed, how could they do it, surely it wasn't that warm? Samuel felt his mouth open and close, his tongue as dry as the ubiquitous hay. Then the girl's breath came hot in his ear.

'Samuel! They're going to do it! Here!'

He half turned to say something and saw her face, flushed in the twilight. Clumsily he kissed her, and slid his hand under her skirt and over the smooth skin of her thighs. Gently, he eased his fingers under the elastic of her knickers and probed her flesh. It was moist and warm. A whistling sigh escaped her lips, and he froze. Every term for three years he had fantasized about a moment such as this, and now he was in a barn with not one but two women who between them could probably hit the right note to bring the place down. He moved slightly, and the girl scissored her legs, holding his hand in place. Beneath them, the matron of Abbotts had abandoned herself entirely to ecstasy. She was almost completely hidden from view except for her legs and arms, which thrashed uncontrollably, her fingers digging up great handfuls of hay, and then jettisoning them with jerky movements of her hands. And gradually, under the spellbound gaze of the two watchers, and the deep driving rhythm of the man, she began calling 'Yes, Oh . . . yes!!' until the words fell away to nothing, and the two bodies rolled over and lay still. Samuel was amazed to see that she was crying.

And that had been almost, but not quite, all. After twenty minutes they had got dressed, and she had bent to pick up her coat. With it, another garment had come to light. A school scarf. Samuel felt ice crawl up his back as she searched for the corner that carried his name tag, a school regulation to identify missing clothing. Slowly she raised her eyes until it appeared that she was looking directly at him.

'Gould.' It was a statement of fact.

Samuel lay as if dead. His heartbeats were deafening.

'Samuel Gould! I know you're up there, and you have five seconds in which to show yourself!'

And that had been that. Although he'd told her that he'd just been asleep, and hadn't even known she was there, the lie was evident in his face, and then the girl had stood up as well just as he was saying that he was alone . . .

His mind jerked back to the present. Halland was speaking again.

'I'm going to start at the beginning, and what I want is a straight answer to my questions. Either "yes" or "no". Firstly, did you kiss the girl?'

Samuel licked his lips. 'Yes, Sir.'

'Did you put your hand under her clothing?'

21

Even as he stood there Samuel could feel an awareness in the fingers that had probed the mysteries of Alexandra: they were tingling. He looked Halland in the eyes and formed his reply: 'No, Sir.'

'I must warn you, Gould, that the girl is in the sanatorium, and will shortly be examined by a doctor. So think carefully before you reply. Now, do you really expect me to believe that the two of you lay in the hay in a barn and did not—how shall I put it?—touch each other?'

By now the boy had lost his feeling of trepidation. In its place a slow anger was building.

'We were just keeping quiet, Sir.'

'I see. And why was that?'

Samuel felt his mouth forming words that he hadn't meant to say. 'If you get the doctor to examine Matron, then perhaps you'll find out. Sir.'

Halland came out of the chair like a sprinter, and caught hold of the boy's ears, shaking his head violently this way and that. He was beside himself with rage, and Samuel felt as though he was being torn to pieces, so he reached up and caught hold of the man's wrists. They were facing each other like wrestlers planning the next move when the phone rang. Abruptly, Halland released his grip and returned to his seat. One hand reached for the phone.

'Halland here.' A pause. 'No, Doctor, go ahead.' He listened to the brief message in silence, then there was a snick as he replaced the receiver on its rest. For a moment the ticking of an unseen clock dominated the room.

'The Doctor tells me, Gould, that the girl probably did not commit intercourse this afternoon, but that if she had it wouldn't have been the first time.'

Samuel tried to ignore the pain in his ears and concentrate on the implications.

'Obviously the pair of you have been duping the authorities of our respective establishments for some considerable time, and I shall write to your guardians and suggest that they remove you from the premises forthwith, giving my reasons.'

So it was to be the grand order of the boot. Somehow, now it had happened, it was a great relief, and the urge to protest his innocence and deny the accusations faded. After all, who

22

cared? If Halland thought that leaving this place was a punishment, that was his problem. Outside his mind the unctuous voice rolled on.

'This might be the way the primitives of Uganda behave, but I can assure you that it is not the custom in England. Now, you may go.'

And with an overwhelming sense of freedom, Samuel went.

Steep Hill Farm was full of unseasonal activity, and the countryside shone in the pale sunlight. Samuel arrived at midday in the old taxi, and Fred said was he well? and yes, he'd got the letter, but he didn't have a mind to talk about it just then, but he and Rosemary would talk it all over after supper. And with that, he drove off on a tractor. At four o'clock Samuel went with Rosemary to collect his brother from the nursery school in the village. Rosemary was quiet, and Samuel supposed that it was because of his expulsion. Five-year-old Andrew was unaffected by atmospheres, and burbled happily along beside them. It was only after supper, when the last dishes had been cleared away, that Rosemary and Fred told him, in the best way they could manage, that his father had died of a stroke in Kampala, leaving in his will a little money and a small bungalow on the lake. A variety of letters and documents had accompanied this information. Not only the sympathetic but stereotyped company letter which spoke in terms of 'many years of faithful service', but also a surprising number of letters from people half forgotten, which began, 'Dear Samuel, you may not remember us, it has been a long time . . .'. It had been easy to forget at the age of eleven. But now it was all coming back, the smells, the sounds, the moist air, the heat of Africa. Sleeping naked under a single sheet, sucking the sweet pips of the passion fruit from their flaking, crinkled skins. And suddenly, he knew what he wanted more than anything.

Outside his grass office on the plains of Karamoja the man Gould opened his eyes, and the pictures of his youth fled. Nearby, the river gurgled thickly, and the cicadas were shrill. Across the clearing, around the edge of the animal compounds, an oil lamp traced a wandering path through the darkness, carried by the invisible hand of the night guard. Gould stretched, and rose to his feet. His neck ached from the unnatural position in which

23

he had dozed off. 'Must be getting old,' he muttered, and made off towards his bed. From the nearest enclosure a giraffe watched him disappear, and then carried on where she had left off, quietly chewing the cud.

It was early morning.

Flat on his belly, Gould crawled towards the ridge. The upper branches of a thorn tree were just visible on the far side of the rise. Behind him, several yard to his right, Panga was following, shiny with sweat, a .458 slung over his shoulder. Gould was carrying a dart gun and a belt containing a number of flighted darts in individual containers, each of which he had painstakingly assembled the night before. There was, in his opinion, no good cause for using dart guns except where other methods failed. The disadvantages were many: the guns were inaccurate and their range limited. Too far away and you might hit a fair sized animal anywhere, even in the eye. That was assuming the one you particularly wanted would stand still and ignore you, which was unlikely. Then again, you needed different drugs for different species, and you had to be careful to prime the darts with the right amount of dope, and that meant guessing the body weight of the animal you were after. With four- or five-year-old elephant, one animal that you sometimes could drive relatively close to and dart, the results were often disastrous. When the young animal started to go down, the rest of the herd, far from disappearing, would congregate and mill around, stamping, trumpeting and ready for war. Gould had decided that getting to the drugged animal then was a job for the mad or courageous, but not for him.

But the object of the exercise now was leopard, and that was a little different. This was cat country, and for leopard particularly the foothills that rose out of the plains provided the perfect base for their nocturnal hunting trips. Gould had heard their coughing quite near to his own animal compounds on several occasions, but even in the dark only a desperate cat would strike at creatures so near to the strong, rancid smell of man. Gould had baited the tree that they were slowly approaching with a calf the previous day. A few bloody tit-bits scattered around the trunk would ensure that various creatures stopped by—but only a specialized few would be able to climb to the free meal that

24

hung in the branches. Cautiously, the two men peered through the grasses. But it was no leopard that caused Gould to jump to his feet and start towards the tree. A lone Karomojong, tall and naked, was easing the weight of the calf onto his shoulders. Straightening his legs, he picked up his hunting spear, longer than his body, and set off with easy strides into the bush. Gould was never quite sure what happened next.

'Hey!! . . .' His cry was still in air as the tribesman reacted. The calf dropped from his shoulders as he spun, the spear already in flight. For a moment their eyes locked across the clearing. The long, black body that had moved so fast froze in the position of release: arm, hand and fingers pointing in a line, the last irrevocable stage of a lifelong reflex. And then the man was gone, and the spear struck.

Gould looked down to see his intestines bulging through the lips of a foot-long gash. For an endless second his mind registered the brilliant hues of his own chemistry. How often had he seen the same bright colours lose their lustre, dimming, scarlet to black, under a white sun? But those colours had not been his, they had belonged to the victims of a day in the life of Africa, where death was neither the beginning nor the end, only the means. He watched as his own hands gently cupped the bluish coils of gut. Blood flowed darkly over a lip of grey muscle, yellow fat and tanned skin. Then came the realization. His knees gave, and he was on the ground, retching violently, stomach and bowels voiding their contents in huge racking spasms that jerked him to and fro.

'The pain is good,' a voice kept saying. 'When you stop hurting you stop living.' But the voice was wrong, so wrong, and the pain was unbearable, every shallow, rapid breath like a knife thrust. Panga picked him up and the heat of the day turned to cold and sweat iced his skin. Shivering, he watched as the clearing receded and the world faded from sight.

The Land Cruiser left Greek River at eight a.m. and passed through the village of Chepsicunya at seventy miles per hour. In the back crouched four Africans, each with one arm holding the rail and one holding Gould. He lay on a rough bed of majani and foam rubber, covered by a sheet. A light froth flecked his mouth, and his face was grey. At the wheel Panga, clad in his catching gear, completely failed to slow down for a herd of cows and goats being driven slowly across the road in front of him. Head and hazard lights flashing, the Toyota's solid radiator guard carved a swathe through animals and herdsmen alike. There was a series of heavy jolts and some screams. By 8.45 a.m. the Toyota pulled into the car park of Mbale's Aga Khan Hospital. Skidding on the gravel, it crashed into the back of a Mercedes saloon, and came to a final halt.

Gould, or what was left of him, had arrived.

Chapter Two

Evening, and noisy with frogs.

Flemming lay on his back in a tent somewhere near the Kenya-Tanzania border. Above his head a chik-chak waited motionless for unsuspecting insects, while on the far side of the tent a young African girl crouched on supple limbs and swept the groundsheet with a small handbrush. Flemming scratched his balls absent-mindedly, and watched her at work. She was naked except for a small band of red cloth that circled her hips, and it seemed probable that even this would go sooner or later in a breeze or just during the daily conflict with gravity. Flemming could see the attraction in spite of himself. Her skin was dark and smooth, the colour of plain chocolate, and at the age of thirteen she had breasts that swelled out firmly from her body whatever position she was in. There wasn't much hair on her head, and even less elsewhere, but one of her sisters had obviously spent much time splitting what hair there was into small bunches, twisting, knotting and waxing them: the result was not dissimilar to a World War Two mine, with spines sticking out all over the place. Flemming had been amazed in his first-ever camp when the local headman sent a procession of young girls to his office, each carrying a bundle of possessions. Being unable to work out what they were after with his limited Swahili, he yelled for Benedict, the cook.

'Ask 'em what they want.'

The cook looked at the girls for a few seconds, and then back to Flemming; he had wrestled with an Australian accent, and lost.

'Flamin' oath, man! Can't you understand English? Ask-'em-why-they're-here-and-where-they're-from.'

27

'Ndio, bwana. Munakaa wapi? Munataka nini?'

The girls giggled among themselves. The eldest answered: 'Sisi nakaa kwa shambani, sisi nataka fanya kazi.' She looked at the ground, traced patterns in the dust with her foot. Then, as an afterthought: 'Mimi nasema kingereza kidogo.'

'They are coming from the village, bwana—she says she is knowing some English. I think they want to work for you.'

Flemming looked at the girls; they were very young, whatever they'd come for.

'What can you do?'

'Dhobi, bwana—wash and cleaning.'

In the end he'd just retained the eldest, and even then he'd been blind to some of her various talents. But one night it all became clear. He was ready for bed, and had switched off the little Honda generator that gave out juice for the camp. By the light of the moon he walked the few yards from the office to his tent. Loosening the mosquito net, he sat on the edge of his bed and leaned back. It was than that his hand sank into something damp and warm. With a reflexive speed he left the bed. Two prodigious bounds and a terrified grunt saw him through the door, and yelling for Benedict. Chattering Africans crowded behind him as he cautiously re-entered the tent armed with a torch and, for good measure, a loaded thirty-o-six. Lying on the bed, pinned in the torch beam, lay the young 'washer and cleaner'. A moment's silence barely preceded howls of laughter. In a matter of seconds the whole camp had collapsed in mirth; thighs were slapped with great vigour and it seemed likely that many would expire, asphyxiated with merriment. The young bwana had lost a lot of face.

Flemming pushed a sandy mop of hair back from his forehead; the memory caused him to grin wryly. Only a few months had passed, but it all seemed to have happened a lifetime ago. He had first come out here on an anthropological survey, full of professionalism, convinced that it would be he, and he alone, who would pull from this endless, burning landscape the final, conclusive proof of an African genesis. But such achievements had been destined for others, and Flemming's interests had taken a sudden geological turn. He hadn't even accepted the young girl's tacit offer to provide distraction during the lonelier hours of the night, realizing it was a mistake to judge her actions by his own standards or those of a modern society. She was just behaving naturally, and would know nothing of the way sex and its connotations had, in one form or another, come to motivate so much of the white man's world.

She finished sweeping the floor and looked up, waiting as ever for some sign of encouragement. Her teeth and the whites of her eyes stood out in the gloom, and Flemming found himself thinking of all the endearing little patches of pink that were the same colour as his own skin, her palms and nails, the soles of her feet, the inside of her mouth when she laughed, and her tongue ... but he made no move. The girl dropped her gaze, and said nothing as she stood up, but her scent tickled the air round Flemming's nose as he watched her out of the tent.

Around the camp the frogs stopped their noise, as they had started it some time before, in perfect unison. But the silence of the African night was louder than ever.

The first stones had been brought to him by a Masai. Flemming had looked at them as they lay in the man's palm. A chunk of rose quartz, some chips of agate. Perhaps the red one was ruby, but the chances were it was garnet. And several others that he didn't recognize. He wondered where they had been found, and if they were of any value. The Masai covered huge tracts of land in the course of their nomadic wanderings, and these gems might have come from anywhere in four thousand square miles, and that was a lot of bush. The first glimmerings of a day-dream came into his head, and out of nowhere he could see baskets full of jewels from every corner of the borderlands, all converging on his camp, borne by the wandering tribes. Boyhood memories of Prester John flashed before his eyes, the riches, the power. Only a considerable mental effort brought him back to the present. The Masai still stood there, immobile. In his hands the dusty stones did not look like the precursors to an empire. Flemming fished in his pocket for five East African shillings.

Akbar Bahri ran a hardware business in Nairobi. Steady streams of customers filed in and out of his premises on Koinange Street, but few of them left with buckets or spades. His office was at the back of the shop, down a narrow and ill-defined path between hanging bundles of dusty brooms, mountains of nails and tin baths. Somewhere a fan marked time, wafting the distinctive

29

smells of the ironmongery business into every corner: sacking, paint and paper. In the office itself the outside world seemed remote. On a huge desk four telephones, each a different colour, vied for position, and behind them, liked a wizened spider at the centre of his web, sat Bahri.

Flemming was ill-prepared for the blast of cold that met him as he entered. His shirt, damp with sweat, shed 30 degrees in as many seconds, and three separate air conditioning units hissed at him venomously, maintaining near-arctic conditions. The room was thickly carpeted, but functional. A hide table bore a pile of current magazines, *Time*, *National Geographic*, *La Chine*. On the wall, an original Shepherd captured to perfection a moment in the life of an elephant. The man behind the desk was small, neat, moustached. It had taken time to get to see him at all, Flemming reflected. Not the sort of joker you popped in to visit on the way home. And the desk! Talk about a pose, Christ, he can just about see over it.

Bahri replaced the red receiver. So this was the Australian, Flemming. They all seemed to be young, these people from Australia, and look the same. Even the women were typecast. And their voices! Briefly, Bahri wondered what happened to old Australians, then he leant forward and punched a button on the desk.

'Bring tea.' To Flemming: 'You do take tea, Mr Flemming?'

'Too right! It's like a freeze-box in here, Mr Bahri.'

'I'm not a well man. The cold numbs the affliction.' He smiled faintly, toyed with a fat gold Sheaffer. The question was how much the Australian ought to be told. There was no doubt that he had the perfect set-up. Wandering tribesmen stopped briefly, as they had often done, at the camp of an accredited anthropologist. Valuable merchandise changes hands for an initial cost that is negligible. Respected scientist then visits Nairobi periodically for stores. It was simple, the perfect cover. Flemming must be paid enough to keep him eager, but not enough to arouse his suspicions.

The tea came, carried by a young Kamba girl. Bahri watched Flemming's eyes as they followed the girl's retreating legs. The two men drank. Opening a small ebony case, Bahri produced a tray of cut stones. Slowly he arranged them in an order, moving

30

them back and forth, with deference, as if they were alive. At last he spoke.

'The stones you left with my assistant on your last visit to Nairobi are worth over 4,000 shillings.' A gesture of his hand brushed away Flemming's whistle of approval. 'You will appreciate that they have only just begun what is to be a long journey. In the course of their travels, they will rise in value many times, and large amounts will be involved. But you may well make the largest percentage of all—to invest five shillings and reap a harvest of four thousand must surely be to your taste.' He paused, gestured to the table. 'You see before you the stones that are of interest to me.' A small ruby appeared magically between his thumb and forefinger. Revolving, it caught the light like burgundy through cut glass. The ruby disappeared. In its place 'Fire opal. Not so valuable, but always in demand.' The third was aquamarine, the fourth a sapphire. Flemming watched, mesmerized.

The last stone held no striking hues. Bahri's long fingers played around its edges before he picked it up. Within its stony heart pale fires of lambent green danced to the ancient song of greed.

Bahri's voice was almost unemotional. 'A type of nephrite. Quite rare, actually. There is a growing demand in the East because of a similarity to certain antique jades. Most of the stuff that comes out of China today is the colour of lettuce. But here we have a stone that in a period setting would convince all'—his eyes met Flemming's—'save the expert.'

Flemming was gone. In his place was another man like Bahri, his black eyes, moustache and hair suggesting obscure origins, a small town perhaps, beset by the desert, on the long road from Sivas to Kabul.

'You saw on the monitor?'

The visitor nodded. 'The money will keep him happy—we can't afford to have him taking stones elsewhere. In any case, he believes we're interested in almost anything that sparkles, and your story about antique jade was really quite original.' He smoothed his hair, fingers tanned and weighted with rings. 'He knows his position is vulnerable. Sooner or later we should hear from Mihel, and then . . .' Unfinished, the words hung in the air.

Bahri's chair was moving backwards. With a slight hum and

31

a click it stopped, turned, and came out from behind the desk. The lower half of his body, a twisted travesty of what had once been legs, was hidden by a blanket. At arm's length the two men faced each other.

'I have heard. Today.' Bahri's hand held an envelope, post-marked Washington D.C.: the letter he extracted was in Arabic. In the muted distance, jammed traffic growled resentfully. 'This is from the Institute. The stone is old, incredibly old. And unique.' His voice thickened with emotion. 'The diamond is harder, but in terms of intrinsic worth—it will be priceless.' The slight body stiffened. 'I have lived my life for a moment such as this. Since I was a child I have dreamt, longed and schemed for this day. A cripple needs compensation every hour of his life. To ease the bitterness. To occupy the mind. And so now I am com-mited—we must find the source, and find it quickly. There can be no turning back.' He stopped, eyes cast down towards his withered limbs. 'Before the days when the great dhows plied their trade from beyond the gulf to Zanzibar, my people came from Karmen. We will call the stone Karmenite, in remembrance of our origins.'

The months that followed his meeting with Bahri were busy ones for Flemming. The word went out over the entire region that the Mzungu at Mount Chalbi would give many shillings for coloured stones, and details of the latest transactions were discussed at markets, round camp-fires, none admitting he had sold for less than his neighbour. And from time to time, in among the quartz and the garnet that arrived in camp, Flemming found sapphires and small rubies, and, on even rarer occasions, the pale green stone whose name he did not know. At first he knew little of the gems he sought. But gradually, he began to look forward more and more to the arrival of a new batch, hunting through the pile for something unusual, exclaiming with pleasure at each find. He bought books, studied and compared, carried out simple tests, and began to understand the compulsions that have always existed for those who prise their wealth from the rocky clutches of the earth. But nowhere could he find a picture, a description, a mention of the fifth stone in Bahri's list: it was as if it had never existed.

After four months of dealing, Flemming was hooked. He

32

found himself looking at the sides of the rift valley, recognizing different strata. Paddling beneath the waterfalls that dropped cold and clear from the Nguruman Escarpment, he sought some of the answers to the riddle of a continent. The upheaval that had created the great rift valley defied imagination. The world had split apart and healed again, to leave a scar spanning fifty degrees of latitude, from the Jordan valley to the Shiré tributary of the Zambesi. At times it reached a width of sixty miles and huge cliffs, mountains and valleys had formed. High on the ancient plateaux there was mist and rain and plenty to drink for all. The surplus water formed streams of exquisite clarity which tumbled into the arid distance. Over the centuries they had worn deep into the rock, loosening its secrets and carrying them away. Deep pools formed beneath waterfalls, delaying their flight, and thick foliage sprung up, hiding them from view. And it was in one such pool that Flemming made his discovery.

It was a snake that pointed the way. It crossed the path in front of them, tapering until it disappeared from sight. Flemming stopped. The fifteen-foot python was gone, and there was nothing to show it had ever passed by. High to the right and left of the narrow defile the land rose steeply, clad in a tangled mantle of foliage, and cactus-like euphorbia stood out plainly, giving the whole scene a Mexican flavour. Flemming was puzzled. The abundance of greenery all around suggested water, and plenty of it. But there was no sound, only the heavy drone of insects. A hand touched his arm, and he looked round. In the past few weeks he had come to depend more and more on the man standing behind him. He had appeared one morning from nowhere looking for a job, which was normal enough in Africa, but his name had a classical ring to it: Deo Gracias. Jesus, but the Catholics certainly extracted their pound of flesh! Okay, who wouldn't be grateful to the good Fathers and their orphanage for a start in life? But to expect someone to carry a name like that around for the next half-century was unreal. And in Latin! Funny thing was, the joker seemed quite pleased about it all. Certainly a name like that would be a hit on the cocktail circuit back home in Peppermint Grove.

'Bwana, tutapita kwa njia hii, chini.' He pointed in the direction just taken by the snake. Flemming's hesitation was slight.

'Okay, sport, you lead the way.' Quietly, the two men headed

33

down the incline into an area of dense bush. Ten minutes brought them to the edge of a small fissure, some twelve feet deep. Its floor was rock strewn and narrow. Silently, they slithered down into the cooler air. The narrow defile dropped sharply away, and soon the sky was only a thin strip above them. With the light went the sounds of the bush, to be replaced by the echoing noise of their own passage. Soon it was necessary to use a torch, its thin, yellow beam revealing a confusion of rocks and boulders lying wetly on the steeply plunging floor. Flemming coughed loudly, reassuringly, in the blackness, and stumbled on.

The rocky convolutions at the end of the tunnel had formed a light trap and beyond that lay open space. The two men stood breathless on the edge of a sickening drop, ending some thousand feet below in the tangled treetop garden of a great forest. Emerging from the rock, hundreds of feet beneath them, a white ribbon of water writhed on down into the greenery. Some miles distant that steppe, too, dropped away sheer to the floor of the rift valley. So that was that. Flemming was not sure what he had been expecting, but certainly not this. A current of air blowing along the face of the cliff caressed his face damply. Damp? They weren't underground now. He held his palm to the wind—there was no mistake, it was loaded with spray. Spray from where? To pick up moisture the wind must be blowing through falling water. His eyes cast around. The entrance to the tunnel came into the light obliquely. It was impossible to see to the right, where a shoulder of rock jutted out over the abyss beneath. To the left he could see a vertical rocky profile some fifty yards distant. And that was all.

'Bwana.'

Flemming turned to find that Deo Gracias had disappeared.

'Niko hapa chini.' The voice came from the ground. The African was flat on his back, head over the drop, looking up. Above their heads, the cliff face appeared to level off slightly to a mere sixty degrees. There was foliage up there, and roots. In effect, the tunnel was like a jagged end of pipe sticking out from a wall. The decision to be taken was simple: was it better to return through the tunnel, and try to relocate the spot from the surface, or, better still—Flemming looked down—forget the whole thing altogether? His face dampened as more spray drifted

34

down on the wind. Of course, there was another option open to them—straight up and over.

Getting onto the African's shoulders at the edge of such a drop was terrifying. Flemming remembered working on high-rise development projects during University vacations back in Australia. Some jokers used to stroll around up there like cats. He'd never gone near a floor that had less than two walls in place. He had now reached the point of no return. With his feet on the African's shoulders he could reach up to a height of twelve feet. Exploring with his hands, he found and gripped the trunks of two leafy shrubs. Head thrown back, he could see them against the sky, already quivering under the strain. Supposing they gave way? Supposing ... But another part of his brain told him that he was already tiring. With a little hop, legs swinging wildly, he pulled himself slowly up, until his chin was level with his arms. Releasing his grip with one hand, he grabbed for another bush, and its thorns bit into his flesh. Loose earth and stones cascaded over the drop. Little by little, he inched upwards until he could swing his legs on to the ledge. Birds, alarmed and noisy, launched themselves into space. Flemming lay crouched close to the ground, exhausted. Behind, the ground curved steeply up, covered in greenery. From the angle at which he lay it was impossible to judge how severe the incline was that he must climb.

'Bwana.' The voice came disembodied, from somewhere beneath him. Flemming peered down over the edge to where Deo Gracias stood, gazing up. The folly of what he had done brought a burning stream of bile into his mouth. Before, he had intended to haul the African up after him, but it was now obvious that he might have to return the same way, possibly tie his belt to a root and lower himself back down. Then he'd need all the help he could get.

'Ngoja hapa, mate. I'm going up. Mimi ju. Got it?'

'Ndio, bwana.' A look of relief crossed the black face as he realized that he was not expected to follow. Above him, Flemming's body disappeared from sight.

The going was not difficult. He found himself on top of a spur that jutted out from the escarpment. At first, it seemed that the slope led directly to the foot of a towering cliff, but slowly the incline lessened and at last levelled out completely. The bush

35

became thick, with moist tangled vegetation growing in places above head height. Suddenly it dawned on Flemming that he was walking in under a colossal overhang. From a distance the cliff face had seemed to rise out of the spot where he was standing. Now, looking up, the rock was sheer above him, and deep in shadow the roof of what appeared to be a gigantic cavern stretched into the mountain side. Some fifty yards further on Flemming stopped dead, the sound of water in his ears. Silently, the dripping foliage closed behind him, while to the front lay a scene that was almost unreal. The ground dropped away sharply to a small emerald lake, catching and enhancing the colours of the rich greenery in which it was set. The lake formed the floor of a huge abscess in the mountain, totally cut off from the outer world except by the hazardous path from the cave mouth. It was only now, in mid-afternoon, that the sinking sun could shine through the rocky, horizontal slit that formed the entrance. Its rays, yellow-gold in the gloom, illuminated not only the lake but the source that fed it, a single cascade of silver water, twisting and glinting as it fell out of the black rock one hundred feet above. Here the wind played strange tricks, the entrance acting as a venturi with gusts swirling in great spirals carrying white jewelled droplets from the waterfall. It would be impossible to know of the existence of this place from the outside. The escarpment top overhung it, and the plains beneath were impossibly distant. Even an aircraft would never travel close enough to spot it, even assuming it was at the right height in the right place at about three in the afternoon. Flemming started down to the lakeside; it had been a day of superlatives and he was beginning to feel the strain. The cold air chilled him, its moisture soaking his clothes. The place was eerie, strange fungoid growths squelching obscenely underfoot. The high walls of the cavern were papered with areas of multi-coloured lichen, separated by gullies that ran with liquid. Dark rows of bats hung upside down from the rock, but the air circulated too freely for any smell except the clean, cold purity of the water. Flemming stood beside it, mesmerized. Now and again, spatterings of stone splashed down from above, and beneath his feet water gurgled and echoed as it ran into a natural overflow. Possibly it was this water that he had seen from the tunnel mouth, coming out of the cliff below and plunging into the distant trees. Cutting a

36

stick he tested the depth: three feet near the bank, and getting deeper quite quickly. A lot of water. Gingerly, he lowered himself over the edge and crouched down to try to get a handful of sediment or stone from the bottom. Within seconds he was shivering violently but not altogether from the icy water. The two pieces of stone in his hand were familiar. Straight from the lake bed they glistened in the sunlight, sometimes green, sometimes yellow. One piece was shaped like a lemon quarter, but the rind wasn't soft, and the jagged crystals that adhered to it were not edible. Flemming looked around. He was the only one who knew. The only one. The words bounced back and forth inside his skull. He must find out the real worth of the stones in this lake. But who to trust? Certainly not Bahri. Keep him happy with bits and pieces, and in the meantime try to arrange his own pipeline for getting the stuff out. The source must remain a secret, his secret. If only he could find a way.

Suddenly it was colder still, and the sun was falling below the lip of the rock at the entrance. Flemming looked around, breaking out of his reverie. A secret jewelled wonderland that only existed in colour for three hours a day. Just long enough for the plants to photosynthesize, and then back to a monochrome existence, the cold and gloomy grays of near darkness. Selecting one of the gems, he tucked it into his pocket. The other made a slight plopping noise as it sank beneath the water. At the top of the rise Flemming came into the welcome sunlight. It fired the tremendous vista with its warmth, bathing the escarpment in gold. Still shivering, he hurried towards his last ordeal of the day.

High on a knoll lay a large pile of white painted stones. They could be seen for miles, similar mounds stretching the length of the Kenya-Tanzania border, making it easy to tell by aerial survey in which country a site was located. Flemming and Deo Gracias crouched beneath the stones, fiddling with a large spray. The African hummed 'Waltzing Matilda', a tune he had picked up from the Australian. He was constantly flat, and Flemming was beginning to hate Matilda more with each passing day. To stop the noise he spoke.

'Is it going to work, tiger, that's what I want to know.'

The African stopped humming, right on 'billabong' if he'd

37

known the words. A puzzled expression appeared on his face.

'Aw, forget it, at least you've stopped the music.' Flemming smiled at the man, and got a big answering grin in return. 'Mzuri, eh?'

'Ndio, bwana, mzuri.'

Flemming was pretty sure that Deo Gracias knew a lot more English than he let on, but the man refused to be drawn, and so Flemming had started to make a serious attempt to get to grips with Swahili. It was working out pretty well. Bush Swahili was a simple language that could convey meaning even when spoken by an Australian. Now the African was pumping vigorously up and down on the handle that protruded from the top of the machine. It got harder and harder to move as the pressure built up, and seemed likely to explode. Flemming motioned him to stop, and lifted the whole outfit on to the man's back. Together they approached the border marker.

Two hours later, the pile had changed completely. It was half the height it had been, many of the smaller rocks having been scattered in all directions over the knoll. But the main difference was in their colour: gone was the bright irridescent white, and in its place a drab green matched perfectly the colour of the surrounding bush.

Some time later, six and half miles to the south-east, a similar scene was being enacted. It had been no mean feat to assemble such a pile of assorted masonry, let alone arrange it into a rough pyramid. But now the work was done, and Flemming could feel well pleased as he watched the last touches being added to a new coat of matt white paint.

Flemming was moving camp. Permission had been given for him to carry on his research from a new base almost on the border. A government inspector had already ascertained that the new location was in Kenya. In fact, Flemming had taken him to a good lunch before driving him to Wilson Airport to board the Skymaster that was used for this sort of straightforward reconnaissance. The Australian talked animatedly for most of the flight, holding the man's attention. From time to time he replenished their glasses. Beneath them, intermittent piles of white stones stood out minutely against the greeny-brown bush like

38

the sporadic droppings of a giant bird. It had been too easy Flemming thought.

The atmosphere in Bahri's office had changed little: if anything the air was colder than it had ever been. The small man's face was pale under the brown pigmentation of his skin. Across the desk, the other man, Salim, sat in the same chair as before.

'So what is he doing now? By the prophet! I ask you to bring information of one man, for which task you are provided with unlimited funds. Are your people so stupid that they find themselves unequal to the work? If that is the case, it raises doubts about the intelligence of the man who hired them.' The black eyes stared across the room, unwinking.

Salim shifted uneasily in his chair. His tented fingers flexed up and down to an inner rhythm. He chose his words with care.

'It is my belief that he has discovered the source, at least a source of the stone. I also believe that he knows its worth. There have been letters, phone calls.' He paused, raised his hands, palms upwards, to the ceiling. 'And the new camp. It must be for a reason.'

Bahri sat immobile in his chair, eyes now fixed on an abitrary point somewhere on the wall opposite. 'He probably thinks it's topaz, or chrysoberyl because of the green. We must make him an offer.'

Salim dropped his hands. 'And what if he heats a piece? Or does an S.G.? He's not a stupid African. He has books, and he can draw conclusions. It's not difficult to determine specific gravity and when he comes up with 3.57 he'll know he's not dealing with pumice stone.'

'Where exactly is the new camp?'

'It is near to nowhere except the border. An area of thick forest on a plateau halfway up the high escarpment. I can see no reason why he is where he is—unless it is near a source.'

Bahri's eyes shifted fractionally towards Salim. 'Can you be sure that he intends to . . . go into business . . . on his own?'

'The Australian has been going for long safaris into the hills. He has developed a keen interest in geology. The last time he came to see us he didn't even quibble about the price. Most uncharacteristic. And what did he bring? Taka-taka. Rubbish.'

He shrugged his heavy shoulders, ticking the points off on his fingers. 'What more do you want me to say?'

'Does he travel alone?'

'No, with one of his men.'

'An African?'

'Kikuyu.'

Bahri's fingers drummed the desk-top. 'Perhaps we could talk to this man. Find out where they go. But I am forced to agree with you, his attitude has changed, and so must ours. Arrange to follow Flemming wherever he goes. Sooner or later he must return to whatever it is that he is trying to hide. When he does we will review the situation. Maybe arrange an accident of some description.' His shoulders shrugged, as if apologizing for their frailty. 'After all, Africa is such a big place.'

On the other other side of town from Koinange Street, Deo Gracias had been buying stores for Flemming's camp. Then he drove through a narrow wrought-iron gateway off the Haile Selassie Avenue in to a small walled courtyard. On one side a smart town house, three storeys high, was hung with white and purple bougainvillea. From a flagpole above the door the Kenya flag drooped in the still air and beneath its limp cloth an armed sentry stood to attention. Deo Gracias flipped open a pass and disappeared in to the building. The sentry relaxed while above him on the first floor a venetian blind snicked shut.

It was early evening when the Land Rover pulled out of Nairobi on the Uhuru Highway. Turning right at the Langata roundabout, it headed towards the Ngong hills and the long, dusty track south towards Tanzania.

The skull did its best to glare reproachfully with sightless sockets. Flemming turned it slowly in his hands. Not the rarest of specimens, he reflected: baboon, circa last year. But bones might well provide the answer. Bones laced with gemstones could well solve the main problem: export. Carefully packed, carefully labelled. Anthropological Specimens. Fragile. Handle with Care. Addressed to himself at an academic address in England. Docks always overloaded, struggling to recover from the last strike. And thence to London, one of the world's centres for almost every illegal

40

enterprise imaginable. Tomorrow he would make a return visit to the cavern and prepare the route.

Late the previous evening Deo Gracias had arrived back from Nairobi with some of the equipment necessary to make the trip easier. It wasn't difficult to get climbing gear in this part of the world, there was always some party or other setting off to kill themselves in the Rewenzoris, or flog their way up Mount Kenya. Flemming had bought a quantity of light nylon rope, a hammer, pitons and a grappling iron. Not enough to humble Everest, but sufficient for the task in hand.

The strain of living with a secret was beginning to show on Flemming's face. Blue shadows pillowed his eyes, bloodshot from lack of sleep. Every night he tossed and turned, living prematurely the kind of life that limitless wealth could bring. Always a material person, his fantasies now ran wild, and the night hours passed in a confusion of large cars and country estates. Each morning found him drained, feverish and irritable with the men.

There was also the problem of Deo Gracias. The man was intelligent, and had spent at least some time in a Catholic mission. And yet he rarely said anything in English, a language that Flemming was now convinced he spoke. How much did the man know, and how much more did he guess? After the journey through the tunnel Flemming had come to treat him almost as an accomplice, yet the arrangement was tacit: neither man had ever spoken to the other about anything except the mundane. Did the African realize why they had spent a day in the bush painting stones? Christ, he must! But when Flemming had asked him to keep quiet about anything that happened while the two of them were on their own in the boondocks, Deo Gracias had shown no surprise at all. It seemed that he had kept faith, mixing little with the others, and even cooking his own food, sitting alone in the darkness over a small fire. Of course, he was getting four times the standard rate of pay, but four times a very little did not necessarily make a lot. It occurred to Flemming that perhaps he ought to get more.

By 11 o'clock the next morning the two men had reached the escarpment, leaving their Land Rover hidden in dense bush high up on a ridge. Heavily laden with backpacks, they forced a path through the greenery and lowered themselves carefully down

41

into the fissure that led to the tunnel. Soon the darkness enveloped them completely, and they disappeared from sight.

Twenty minutes later they emerged and Flemming tied a bowline through the ring at the end of the grappling iron; knotted loops at intervals in the rope would serve as foot holes. All seemed ready.

'Righto, my old rafiki, watch your head!'

Standing as near the edge of the drop as was possible, he swung the iron round his head and released it. Dislodged stones cascaded down as the hooks landed in the earth above. Flemming tugged sharply, and the iron promptly dropped out of the sky, and nearly knocked him over the edge.

'Shit!'

The third throw saw the iron securely hooked around something as yet unseen on the slope above. Flemming gingerly put his entire weight on the thin rope, which stretched and creaked alarmingly. But it held. Slowly at first, and then with increased confidence, he climbed up and disappeared. Once on top he released the iron and lowered it down to Deo Gracias who hooked the packs on to it. With the gear safely up, Flemming extracted the hammer and two pitons and drove them firmly into flaws in the rock. Fastening the rope to them, he slung the end over the edge and in a matter of seconds the tall African was sitting beside him. Leaving the ladder where it was, they turned and headed up towards the cliff face.

Four men emerged cautiously into the sunlight at the mouth of the tunnel, blinking in the unaccustomed brightness. Keeping close to the safety of the rock face, they peered out into the void. It was not at all obvious where the Australian had gone. From where the four stood, reluctant to lose the feel of hard rock against their backs, the rope was invisible, several yards to the left. At a casual glance all four men looked the same. Dark skinned, but not black, with straight jet hair, strangely semitic noses and finely drawn lips. Arabic origin, perhaps browner. The sort of men you could see any day from Lamu to Zanzibar, along the length of the coast. One of them moved forward, looked down, as if he half expected to see Flemming floating into the distance on home-made wings. But there was nothing, just the emptiness and the birds flying below. It was as he turned that

42

his eyes spotted the rope, followed it up, unbelieving, to where it disappeared over the rim. Moving to it, he fingered the nylon thoughtfully. Motioning one of the men to stay behind, he reached up and placed both hands high on one of the loops. With a quick glance upwards and even quicker one down, he began to climb smoothly, hand over hand, towards the top.

Four miles away, at the foot of the escarpment, a cluster of drab green vehicles lay grouped beneath the thorn trees. A tall officer, wearing a major's tabs, finished talking on the radio, handed the transceiver back to the operator. His eyes travelled slowly up the escarpment where it reared high over the plains. So they were all up there, he mused. Six men. Perhaps even now talking, trying to find a point of agreement, a way to share the spoils. But the major doubted it. It was such a long drop from the top of the escarpment. And Africa was such a big place.

The cavern was in almost total darkness when Flemming got there. He stood looking down towards the small lake, and cast a sideways glance at Deo Gracias. The African was almost speechless, his eyes huge rounds in the dark face, pupils black buttons in the dim light. The place had lost none of its fascination. It was good to get back up here and find things just the same. Crouching on a slab of rock he began to undo the packs, taking out a couple of cans of corned beef and a water bottle.

'Pretty good place, hey?' said Flemming and caught the man's involuntary nod before he could feign incomprehension. 'Well, if you don't want to talk English, don't. Here, have some Beefex.' He lobbed one of the cans into the air and the African caught it deftly. The water bottle seemed a bit ridiculous now, with gallons of the stuff all round them, but at least it wasn't going to give anyone the shits. The Beefex was dry and not quite salty enough, but the two men ate it wolfishly with slabs of bread, and butter from a can. There was a silence between them. 'God knows, that's no novelty,' Flemming thought. His Swahili was adequate now, but not colloquial. Anyway, Africa was a place where silence was friendly and acceptable, too many words intrusive. The Australian had thought long and hard before deciding that it would be impossible for him to manage on his own. Deo Gracias must have guessed after the first trip that

43

something important lay above and beyond the tunnel entrance. Anyhow, he was here now, for better or worse. The two men finished the meat with deep draughts from the bottle, and for Flemming a salt tablet. He then got out a large torch, a small satchel, a reinforced plastic helmet and a pair of crude, home-made tongs. The first creeping shafts of sun were beginning to move into the cavern, illuminating the clouds of spray and making silhouettes of the bushes at the entrance. Flemming sat at the water's edge, put on the helmet, and swung his legs over the side. He hoped to take samples from various parts of the bottom to try to get an idea of what was where under the water. Tentatively, he stepped away from the side. The water got slowly deeper until it was up to his waist. He advanced slowly towards the middle, picking up stones with the tongs and putting them into the satchel. Cold spray from the fall blew in clouds across the surface of the pool, irridescent as they crossed the almost tangible shafts of sunlight. Flemming turned back towards the bank, away from the noise of the water. Then he stopped abruptly. Two men stood behind Deo Gracias, each with drawn pistols. One of the men leaned forward slightly, called in a voice more casual than the occasion demanded:

'Please keep your hands in sight Mr Flemming, and come out of there slowly.'

Flemming waded out of the pool.

'We're impressed, Mr Flemming. My employer suspected that you might have unearthed something of value, but this'—he gestured with his free hand, the dark eyes never leaving Flemming—'is rather more spectacular than we had imagined.' The man was raising his voice slightly to compete with the water, but the English was carefully pronounced.

Flemming looked at Deo Gracias. The African was standing immobile, face cast down towards the ground. Suddenly the number of ways to overpower the two armed men seemed very few. And maybe there were more outside. Why had he been so stupid as to underestimate Bahri? The man was not a fool, but he'd treated him like one.

'So what happens now?'

'Before we go into that we'll just take a look in the little bag. Just throw it towards us. Gently.'

The bag landed with a dull sound on the rock. The second

44

man appraised one of the samples. There was a quick conversation in an unknown tongue, then the tall man nodded and addressed Flemming.

'As you probably know, this stone is not of a common type.' He smiled thinly. 'It would be truer to say that it is like no other type at all. In a word, a unique find.' The words reverberated slightly round the lichen-covered walls. 'And you might have gone down in history—had the circumstances been different. But you were greedy, Mr Flemming, as are most of us, and now no one will hear of you again in connection with rare stones, or for that matter, anything else.'

Flemming felt a heaviness in his hands and feet. He was aware that time was running out fast, but seemed unable to move. Here they stood, speaking the unlikely dialogue from a 'B' feature but incredibly it was all taking place. Then another voice broke into his thoughts, assertive, vaguely familiar.

'Do you realize what will happen if you fire that gun in here, Salim?' It was Deo Gracias, speaking perfect English. Events were moving too fast for Flemming. What the hell was going on? The African was inching slowly towards the muzzle of a 9 mm. automatic. The tall man recoiled visibly at the mention of his name. Both guns swung swiftly on to the approaching African.

'How do you know my name?'

Deo Gracias was smiling now, apparently at ease, his feet sliding almost imperceptibly across the ground. 'We've known about you for nearly two years, Salim. Your subordinates and superiors. Everything about you. Asian parasites who drain away the wealth from our country, wealth it can ill-afford to lose.' The feet grated as they slid forward, dragging like a cripple's. 'And if you use a gun in here, we'll all be dead and buried in seconds.'

Salim was backing up, the other man slightly behind him, his eyes stabbing quick glances at Flemming's helmet and the roof of the cavern, weighing the truth of the African's words. Flemming tensed ready to move, knuckles white round the bone handle of a puma skinning knife. Suddenly the cavern erupted into violence and movement. Deo Gracias' body dipped as a shot tore into it from point-blank range. Flemming's hand jerked the knife into the open, and he launched himself at Salim, but his foot slipped on the wet rock and he fell forward, supporting his weight on his left hand. A shot tore over his right shoulder,

45

and then he was up again and felt the knife sink to the hilt in the man's bowels. Even skewered on a six-inch blade the Asian fought desperately, trying to bring the gun up into Flemming's stomach. Four yards away Deo Gracias and the other Asian were locked together, the African's yellow shirt washed orange with blood. Two more shots rang out hollowly, and Flemming felt Salim go slack in his arms. A dull rumbling filled the air and he looked up to see a broad section of rock pull slowly away from the roof and drop towards the water. Flemming let go the limp body, turning towards Deo Gracias. As in slow motion he saw a third Asian moving round the rocky ledge towards him, gun in hand, and watched as a moving wall of displaced water clutched first at his feet, then at his legs. The man was slowly overwhelmed, gathered completely by the advancing wave as it smashed forward into the rocky recesses of the cavern. Flemming braced himself as the water spread towards him. For a brief second he kept his balance, and then he was under, tumbling over and over until it was impossible to say which way was up. Noises came dully from far away, but the Australian had had too many near misses at the hands of the ocean to panic now, and he forced himself to stay limp as he was tossed this way and that. He could hear his heart pounding in his ears and the first feelings of tightness across his chest. Something hard smashed into his left shoulder, radiating dizzying shafts of pain. Then his numbed fingers clutched at a rock, and the water was gone.

Inside the cavern rock and rubble cascaded down from the roof, filling the air with dirt. Water sluiced everywhere mixing with the fallen earth to form a thick mud. Flemming, dazed, began to pick his way round the extremities of the cavern, making for the entrance. Of the intruders there was no trace. He was half-way out when he came across two bodies flung up against a pile of debris. The first was one of the Asians, though it was impossible to say which. The gun was still clenched tight in his right fist, but the corpse was headless, smashed by falling rocks. The other man was Deo Gracias. He lay with one arm outflung, the other doubled back in an impossible position behind him. Half his lower jaw was shot away, the flesh washed pink and clean by the water. Flemming gagged, bile hot in his throat. As he looked down, the eyelids flickered in the remnants of the black face. Slowly the eyes opened, struggled to focus. In the abating thunder of falling rubble Flemming wondered briefly who he was, this man who had apparently been pulling the strings. And then out of pity he knew he had to acknowledge the man's mute appeal for help. Overcoming his revulsion, he bent quickly, slung the limp, ruined body over his shoulders and moved painfully with his burden towards the open air.

As the first belching clouds of dust squeezed their way out of the cliff face, a helicopter rose like a giant locust from the plains. Clawing for height, it rose in a steep banking turn until the thorn trees were left far below. The major leaned towards the European pilot.

'Where the hell have you been? We should have been up there ten minutes ago.' They could see the fourth Asian was ascending the spur towards the cavern.

'Sorry, major.' The pilot grinned thinly across the cab. 'Would you believe it wouldn't start?'

Deftly, he hovered above the spur: from the side of the craft a ladder flopped out and down. It had scarcely unrolled when the first soldier swung out into the air, closely followed by five others. The man stopped for a fraction of a second before turning and working his way back down to the top of Flemming's rope ladder. Sporadic fire followed him, but he was already out of sight on the incline. In the helicopter, the major ignored the Sterling slung round his shoulder and clipped a full magazine into the belly of an SLR. The wind along the cliff buffeted them, and the pilot backed off until he was a hundred yards out from the rock face.

'How close can you go?' Protectively, the major cradled the gun in his arms. The helicopter was steady again, hovering motionless.

'This is about it, major. A gust of wind in the wrong place up here and you don't have a lot of room to get out of trouble.'

The Asian had reached the rope now, his face showing as a small light patch, repeatedly looking up and back as his feet explored for the first knot. The sound of the first five shots was almost lost in the general clamour. The man on the rope nearly lost his grip as the bullets chipped into the rock around his head, but then his threshing legs steadied, and he slipped the last three

47

feet down to the ledge. Deliberately, the major allowed his searching feet to find their first slight contact with the ground before his black forefinger squeezed the trigger. Once. Twice. Three times. Two dark spots appeared on the man's back, and a thick dark gush of blood sprang from his neck. Like a deflated toy, the body fell back into space, and the two men watched as it disappeared from view.

The soldiers had found Flemming just in time, almost at the end of his resources. Quickly, the wounded African was winched into the helicopter, then the Australian. The soldiers followed, and within minutes the machine was a diminishing speck, sinking towards the Savannah.

'It's not up to me, Flemming.' The major picked remnants of breakfast bacon from between his teeth with a silverthorn, while all around the camp was being wrapped ready for the trip to Nairobi. 'You must count yourself lucky. Had it not been for your attempt to save one of our men I think I can promise you that the future would have been of little concern.'

Flemming realized that of all the factions involved, he had been the real amateur, the lamb among wolves. The government had been watching Bahri for two years. And Bahri, in his turn, had led them to him. Deo Gracias had been dead when the major landed, but Flemming was convinced that his last gesture to the African's remains had already paid the ultimate dividend. To the Australian much of the sequence of events was a mystery.

'Of course, there are some factors in your favour.' The major had abandoned his teeth in favour of a small, pungent cheroot. That it was only 7.30 in the morning did not deter him in the least. 'Your evidence against Bahri will be conclusive.' He slid the end of the cigar between his lips and sucked it thoughtfully. 'It could almost be said that you cooperated with us. Possibly your ... professional reputation ... could remain untarnished.' Abruptly he got up and walked towards the waiting trucks. A stream of orders came drifting back across the clearing.

Flemming sat dejectedly in the canvas chair. He'd had untold wealth within his grasp. Now it was gone, leaving bitterness and rancour in its wake. A lifetime's anticlimax faced him: perhaps it would have been better to die up there in preference to spending the next half-century with nothing but empty memories.

And who would believe him? Where could you tell a story like that without the nudges and winks that said 'another Aussie bullshit artist'? Slowly he got to his feet and walked towards the waiting trucks.

The sun was just rising over the rim of the high escarpment when the small convoy got under way. Everything was normal for the start of a hot African day. Grudgingly, the distant engine noise gave way to the drone of insects.

Chapter Three

Soon Tsa Lee, re-christened 'Charlie' by his American school friends, said goodbye to his home and family three years before Singapore, under Lee Kuan Yew, seceded from Malaysia and became independent, and four years before the confrontation with Indonesia was finally settled and Dr Subandrio, Madame Dewi and President Soekarno became names of the past. He went by British India steamer to Madras, train to Bombay and then by boat again via the Seychelles to Mombasa. It was a long-winded route, but untraceable, and his father had said it was the only thing to do. He travelled light with just one suitcase and the fine-honed ability for unarmed combat that had indirectly led him on this journey halfway round the globe. Bemused, he had watched from the stern as Singapore slid into the sea. It would be a long time before he saw his home again.

Charlie adapted quickly to his new life in East Africa. The climate was similar, the national language English and there was already a small but thriving Chinese community. He worked for his mother's cousin, an elderly man, who ran a small establishment called the Monsoon club in a good position looking west to the mainland. In no time at all, Singapore seemed impossibly distant, and the reason for his sudden departure dimmed in his mind to insignificance.

Like much of the violence in life, the affair had started as nothing, a matter from which all concerned could have walked away unscathed. The Flying Fish was a clip joint not far from Boogie Street in the heart of Singapore's red light. The road outside catered for every type of perversion the oriental mind could conceive; perfumed joss hung heavy in the moist air and beggars squatted close to the buildings on either side, their disfigurements displayed to the best advantage, for pity's sake. Their faces half obscured by conical hats, vendors tended the flickering fires of their cooking carts, and skewered satay crackled in the flames, ready to dip in bubbling bowls of peanut sauce. Young boys touted for their sisters or their brothers or themselves. Girls, some of which were boys, sat on high stools, their cheongsams split to the waist and nothing remarkable showing in the way of underwear. It was all there to be seen, to be believed. Dope to smoke, eat or mainline. Things to do or have done. Till the small hours the bicycle rickshaws and taxis brought the punters in. Many were sailors, and had dreamt of this night for scores of nights in a narrow, rolling bunk. Others, the more adventurous tourists, were determined to get the best or the worst out of the city's infamous nightlife. And sometimes there were embassy people, for a stroll around the quarter was as much a part of the Singapore scene as tea under the slow-moving fans of the Raffles hotel.

Charlie and his friend, Stephen Ling, fitted none of these categories. They had taken to exploring the city during their last year at school, finding the incredible nocturnal activity of the red light as strange and alien as any doctor from Massachusetts on a round-the-world trip. But it was all part of growing up. No one troubled them, they were too obviously locals, and though they never bought any of the various goods for sale, rarely an hour went by without some incident, absurd, tragic or ugly that shed a little light on the myriad facets of the human psyche.

The singer was just finishing her routine as Charlie came out of the toilets. The heavy smell of perfume, alcohol and cigarette smoke enveloped him, and he started to make his way round the edge of the tiny dance floor to where Stephen sat. During his absence, he noticed, two of the girls from the chorus of the Penang club had joined them. They didn't start work till 12.30 and Charlie had met these two, Mei and Suki, some weeks previously. Once the two boys had gone with them to a depressing room somewhere near the Rex cinema, but after half an hour perched on one of the narrow beds sipping tea they had exchanged glances and tacitly agreed to ease their way out of the situation. Still, the girls were pretty, and nicely put together. Charlie was not averse to slipping his hand into the warmth between Mei's thighs in the darkness under the table, and she always opened

51

her legs to allow him better access, chattering and laughing while her natural juices welled as if nothing out of the ordinary was happening. But he had been aware for some time that the fact that she responded well to various basic stimuli would never make her intelligent.

As it was, Charlie never reached his table. A babble of raised voices came from his left, and a man leapt to his feet into the passageway. He was well-dressed, with a dark oriental face, Cambodian perhaps, or Vietnamese. Beer had spilt all down the front of his suit, and more was slopping from the glass in his hand. Charlie cannoned right into him, and the man fell over backwards and sat comically on the floor. A howl of laughter went up. Charlie reached down and proffered a hand, but the man knocked it violently out of the way and scrambled to his feet. His face had gone blue-white in the low lighting of the club and the hubbub of conversation died away. A group of American sailors on the other side of the floor turned to face the action.

'Is that guy mad, or is he . . . ?'

'Sock it to him, baby!'

'Ten bucks says the kid goes through the ceiling!'

The man pushed the waiter aside who was trying ineffectually to wipe his suit, and came right out in English.

'You stupid young bastard, why the hell you don't watch where you're going?'

Charlie knew suddenly that there was going to be trouble. Over the man's shoulder he saw Stephen's face, and the two girls. They seemed a long way away. Unconsciously, his feet slid apart to a distance of about twenty inches, toes turned slightly in towards each other, knees bent. It was called the position of the horse. Now the weight of his body, as it angled backwards was all on the big muscles at the back of his thighs.

'Sir, it was you who fell into my path.'

The man broke into a swift discourse in his native tongue, and threw his glass to the floor. There was a hush over the room. Charlie kept his eyes on the other man's face and waited.

The signal, when it came, was a tensing of the neck. Charlie sensed the blow coming and turned from the waist. His left hand, open palmed, deflected the man's forearm into empty space. At the same time, in pure instinct, he countered. His own blow

52

started with the elbow of his right arm in line with his sternum. His fist snapped forward a maximum of six inches, and when his arm straightened the flat surface of his knuckles flicked upwards making an angle of forty-five degrees between the top of the forearm and the base of the thumb. The blow was too quick for the eye to follow, and looked too simple to hurt. It was part of an infighting technique developed by a nun some centuries before in the mountains of northern China. The power of the blow was designed to expend itself half an inch behind the struck surface and, properly delivered, carried a poundage equal to one and a half times the bodyweight of the user.

There was a ghastly crunch of splintering bone, and the man's nose simply disappeared under a gush of blood. His high scream blew droplets of red over three tables, and then, clutching his face, he fell like a dead man onto the floor.

The horrified silence seemed to last forever. The Americans were frozen in their seats. One of them exhaled softly, and the sound carried.

'Jee-sus!'

Charlie felt Stephen's arm pushing him towards the exit. He realized that he had just been standing there, and made a conscious effort to pull himself together. Behind them an uproar of sound welled up the stairs in pursuit. Once in the street they both ran straight into the maze of alleys opposite the club, making for the taxi stand at Jilek corner. Before they got there, Charlie stopped. Stephen was panting hard, and leaning forward with his hands on his knees to get his breath back. When he eventually straightened Charlie was standing by the wall of the alley looking at him.

'You'd better go home, Steve.'

Stephen nodded slowly. 'Christ, what a mess! What will you do? Why did you do it?'

Charlie shook his head wordlessly The man had come forward under his own momentum, and had actually moved into the blow. One of the basic precepts drummed into you from the word go was to immobilize your adversary at the first opportunity: sometimes there was never a second chance. But it was too late for excuses; he took a deep breath and told Stephen: 'I'm going home. If they ask you, say I ran off, and you didn't see me again. Will you do that?'

53

Stephen straightened. 'Of course I will. But don't forget, he went to strike you first. If you go to the police . . .'

Charlie looked at his watch. His mind was made up. 'No, no police. Just say nothing at all. I must ask my father what is best.'

Stephen looked over his shoulder, down into the darkened alley. 'If it was me, home is the last place I'd go. And it's the first place they'll look for you.'

Five hours later, one hundred miles north of Singapore in the small coastal town of Mersing, the first flush of pink crept along the horizon out to sea behind the archipelago—and the whole matter was out of Charlie's hands. His father had never questioned the rights and wrongs of the matter, merely expressing surprise that his son should be found in such a club in the first place. It was agreed that the boy would lie low in a small house on one of the plantations until such times as the family knew if he had been identified, and what had happened to the other man. Then his mother, looking extremely worried, had quickly packed a bag with provisions. Ten minutes later the family car was carrying Charlie and his father up the coast.

As things turned out, they had acted none too soon. The radio later that morning offered the news that a member of the Burmese Trade Delegation had been struck down during a club brawl the night before. He had choked in his own blood before help could be summoned. A youth was said to be helping police with their enquiries.

Four days after the incident in the Flying Fish, Charlie Soon boarded the coaster MV *Kuantan* with his one large suitcase, a money belt containing an assortment of United States currency, Straits dollars, and English pounds, and a wallet inside his jacket which held a variety of documents including a seaman's ticket.

He boarded the boat at Trengganu, a coastal town to the north of Mersing, and asked for the mate by name, as he had been told to. He had said his farewells the night before, so there was no-one to wave him goodbye. He left feeling that there were a hundred loose ends that ought to be tied up, but when he tried to think of one he realized that there wasn't a single thing outside his family circle that would wrench at him as he sailed away, or try to urge him back. Sitting on his bunk, he opened his father's sealed instructions; the old man had treated the whole thing like a business deal, efficiently and fast. He scanned the pages of small

54

neat writing: Madras, Bombay, Mahé. Names from a book. And his destination: Africa.

During the night the boat passed Pulau Tioman, and for a short time crossed the patch of sea visible from his parents' window. In the invisible house on shore his mother and father lay together, troubled and unable to sleep. And in his bunk Charlie lay immobile listening to the throb of the diesels.

He went to work with his mother's cousin, the elderly Mr Nam, who was seriously anaemic and refused to take anything but some old herbal cures that had been in his family for generations. They weren't making him any better, and he rapidly became totally dependent on Charlie for the running of the club. Charlie waited daily for hordes of relatives to arrive like carrion for the anticipated pickings when the old man eventually died but none appeared. Distant relations at the Bamboo restaurant became friendly, solicitous, generous with advice on business matters, but that was all. For the first time in his life Charlie knew what it felt like to have power, the power to hire and fire, the authority to audition cabaret acts and make a decision on them, to screw or not to screw the singers and dancers and strippers that hustled the meagre work along the coast. He found himself enjoying life, and imperceptibly changed the club's format to cater more for the tourists and sailors, and less for the resident population.

In 1966 old Nam died, and by then Charlie had known for six months that the club would be his. The old man's ashes were barely cooled when work started on the New Monsoon Club, and by New Year 1967 the alterations were done, a band hired and rehearsed, and an impressive list of exotic and erotic acts on the books. All this used up the majority of Charlie's cash inheritance, and so he set out to devise new ways of making money. He was twenty-three years old.

The road north from Mombasa was more or less tarmac for seventy-five miles. Then, just after Malindi, the asphalt gave way to a juddering, rutted surface of sharp stones bedded firmly in a fountain of baked orange earth. More than just a smooth ride ended at this point: it was the end, too, of the twentieth century. Thereafter, quite abruptly, the road led back in time, leaving behind the hotels, development companies and the fine white-sand beaches yet to be spoiled forever by brown silt and mica from a flooded river.

At first the country was fertile, and green grass spread itself between widely spaced palms and baobabs. Herds of humped cattle grazed peacefully among orange ant-hills, and in villages of mud and grass naked girls were pounding maize. Their mortar was a long hollowed log, their pestle a straight timber with a rounded end. The sound of the thump! thump! as the wood hit the maize carried in the air, and their shrill chanting carried too, now coming, then going on the wind. Charlie drove slowly through one such village and watched as a tall Giriama girl stretched and leaned, her body brightly, blackly moist in the sun. Her breasts quivered and swayed as she lifted and dropped the pole, turning it slightly as it struck the maize, then lifting it again, her ribs taut against her skin for just a moment until the downstroke.

Twenty-five miles from Malindi there was a right fork to Ngomeni, winding down among the mangroves to the Italian rocket station that lay, surrounded by sand dunes, close by the sea. But the main road carried straight on, and eventually Charlie turned north-west on the little-used road to Galole, Garcen, Garissa and Wajir, the last town before the five hundred mile distant Somali frontier.

The so-called road had been nothing but a sandy track for eight hours when the wheels bit on the main Nairobi-Garissa road, but the relief was short-lived. A small distance from the Garissa checkpoint, where vehicle numbers going further north were recorded, he turned left on an ill-defined track that roughly followed the western bank of the Tana river. The going was slow, the country parched and sandy, and as he coaxed the truck further into the bush the sun started to set directly ahead of him. In the last blue light of the day, after sunset, he came to his destination: the chief's camp at the tiny settlement of Mbalambala.

The proposed meeting with a man called Shenazi was not until the following day, but Charlie had come prepared for a long wait. He drove slowly down to the huts and asked if any Somalis had crossed the river that day. The locals viewed his face with suspicion, but told him that the day had been quiet and no one had crossed the water. Charlie thanked them, and drove upstream for about half a mile. There he found a clearing almost within sight of the village with a good view of the river. He ate some bread and sausages, and then walked down across the sandy shore in the moonlight and washed at the water's edge. After this he returned to the Land Rover, stretched out on a foam mattress that slotted down the centre of the floor and with a loaded rifle within easy reach, slept fitfully till first light.

'Shenazi?'

The men looked at each other, and then one of them spoke. His voice was high-pitched and seemed somehow wrong from so tall a man.

'I am Shenazi.'

Charlie felt vaguely disappointed. He had expected to meet a sort of brigand chief, and had built up all sorts of preconceived ideas as to what he would be like. Instead, he appeared to be a very typical African tribesman. But maybe that was how the man had managed to keep out of trouble for so long.

Charlie put out a hand.

'Habari gani, Mzee? I am glad that you are here.'

The African stood and proffered his hand in return. The fingers were limp and awkward in Charlie's own.

'Mzuri, bwana, mzuri. Are you here alone?'

Before Charlie could answer, a voice came from behind.

'Yes, he is alone, Mwenga, he is alone.' He turned to see a man, not much taller than himself, standing by the Rover. The man's eyes were black, and they twinkled in amusement from either side of a long straight nose. The rest of the face was almost obscured by a bushy beard, which joined up with the man's hair to form a sort of huge furry football set on powerful shoulders.

The newcomer walked forward and clapped Charlie on the shoulders. He wore a bleached khaki shirt and faded blue denim trousers. His feet were naked.

'Well, well, I am Shenazi. But it is no good to take chances. And you are Bwana Soon.'

Charlie came under the scrutiny of the other man, and felt suddenly young compared with this African powerhouse, the man, it was said, that they despaired of catching; the man it had taken him eight months to see. He answered the rhetorical question with a statement.

57

'Shenazi, you have been a difficult man to find. Now we are both here, I hope that we can do business.'

The poacher scratched his beard. 'First, my men take these cows to the chief's camp. Then we can eat and talk.' He eyed the Land Rover. 'Maybe you have some chocolate in there?'

'Only to drink,' Charlie told him. 'Drinking chocolate.'

Shenazi shrugged his shoulders, and his eyes twinkled again. He ran a pink tongue over white teeth and black lips. 'Chocolate to drink.' He broke into rapid Somali, and the men laughed. They all stood up, and Shenazi looked at Charlie and the Rover and the duom palms and the cows, and his great hairy head tilted to the left and right and his good humour embraced the world.

'Well, well,' he said. 'Chocolate to drink.'

Charlie spent two days with Shenazi and his men, and they discussed the price of ivory, and the poachers told of the incredible dangers of killing elephants and escaping unseen with the tusks while the vultures told the world at large that something big was dead. Charlie talked of the market price, of the terrible costs of transport and bribery, of customs officials and the time it had taken him to work out his plan, little by little, so that he could sit here and have something to talk about. Then they all discussed, once again, the price of ivory.

It took the full two days to prepare the ground-rules, and another meeting was planned for the next month; before the Africans left, Shenazi gestured out over the river. 'Look at my wealth,' he boasted. 'I am a rich man. I have no need to break the laws.'

Charlie asked him why then he continued to break them, and the poacher spat into the dust, the spittle rolling over a few times before it lay exhausted in the hot sun and evaporated.

'Well, well,' came the answer, and the black eyes twinkled, 'I do it to keep young.'

When Shenazi and his cattle disappeared eastwards in a cloud of their own making. Charlie Soon was committed in his mind to crossing the thin line between a straight and a crooked life. Thereafter, he would always be looking over his shoulder, and he never really learned to live with the uncertainty of what the next day would bring. But for years he organized a successful traffic in illegal ivory and rhino horn. One thing led to another, and as the post-Uhuru years increased in number, so too did the opportunities for exploiting the situation. Charlie became rich, but as his income grew, so too did his expenditure. It was only a matter of time before his life-style became remarkable. But he lasted for ten years before a situation arose that confronted him once and for all with the sad facts of how tenuous his roots in Africa really were.

At the age of thirty-two Charlie Soon sat by the pool in his club and looked dejectedly across at the mainland, a limp, buff envelope in his hands. It had all started when the British Navy left. What clubowner could possibly be expected to survive legitimately in a seaport without sailors—or at least without sailors that had any money? Then the combination of the Suez closure and the terrible inefficiency of dockland under an African administration had decimated the foreign tonnage that once called regularly at Mombasa. And what was left? Charlie rolled his eyes skywards. Coasters, and the Pakistan Steamboat Company. Two ships on the Seychelles-Calcutta run, and one of them the *State of Hariama*, renamed by a British wag the State of Paranoia. Powered by curry, and a sublime faith in the teachings of Mohammed, it was even money to sink on every trip. Then there had been a lucky break, the hefty seventeen per cent devaluation of sterling. The greedy East African community had decided not to revalue, thus leaving an even bigger discrepancy between the fixed value of their currency and its real worth. It was well known that if you tried to change Tanzanian or Ugandan shillings in Europe, they'd laugh in your face, and even the Kenyan pound sold for half price. So the black market boomed, and because of the club Charlie had an official exchange licence. On the premises he'd change money from overseas at the bank rate, then pocket it and substitute his own local cash. But that wasn't enough, so he organized a network of touts at the hotels and docks, offering a pound for a pound and nine shillings for a dollar. As more cracks appeared in the financial equity of the community, Tanzanian and Kenyan notes lost their validity on all but home soil. Now there were individuals and small firms with amounts of Tanzanian money that they couldn't use, or Ugandan money that no one wanted. Charlie saw per-

59

centages whichever way he turned; soon he was offering thirty Tanzanian shillings for a pound sterling, and his contacts with the tour operators brought the buyer's orders. Tourists were getting their holidays as cheap as half-price in Tanzania, and it wasn't long before Germans and Americans, particularly the young, made him their first port of call in Africa.

But that had been before Joseph N'lella walked into his life, by far the cleverest African that Charlie had ever met. He was an inspector at the exchange control in Nairobi, and had visited Mombasa as a tourist. Within five days he had accumulated enough evidence to put Charlie in the can for life. Charlie had tried to bribe him, and was sickened by the man's greed when he would accept nothing less than 2,000,000 shillings, nearly £120,000 at the bank rate. Now he had a house on Nyali Estate, and a motor yacht moored near the fishery steps.

Last year, the final blow had been delivered when five tons of ivory from one hundred and twenty elephants was seized at Lamu. Worse than that, the work of six years, the whole carefully planned operation no longer existed. It was fortunate that the trigger-happy bastards had left no one alive aboard the dhows to point the finger. And yet he felt that somehow, even posthumously, the finger was being pointed. Even the brief hours of this morning had brought their share of trouble. Firstly, his white stripper, the only one on the coast, had quit. No explanation, nothing, just a note saying that she wouldn't be back. And after all he'd done for the girl. Secondly, he was nearly out of noodles, bean sprouts and a variety of other Chinese fare.

Last was the buff envelope from the High Commission: 'Owing to recent events in various sections of the Commonwealth, we wish to clarify your position vis-à-vis your British passport. Could you please fill in and return the enclosed form or, if you wish to make a personal appeal, come to the above address at 11 a.m. on the morning of Wednesday the 13th.' Appeal? What were they talking about? He was being treated like a bloody Asian! The thirteenth was almost on him, and the commission was in Nairobi. His hand chopped down sharply on the table beside him and an empty glass lifted gently into the air and fell into the pool. But he'd have to go, of course; there really wasn't any choice.

At 11 a.m. on the thirteenth Charlie disembarked from an

EAA Viscount after a cramped seventy-five minutes from Mombasa to Nairobi. He had been thinking long and hard on the flight and after leaving the terminal building and haggling for a taxi to the city was still thinking, but had come to no conclusions. In town he pushed through the glass doors of the High Commission and walked towards Passport Enquiries. An attractive girl with a friendly décolleté listened to him sympathetically and read the letter.

'It's probably just a formality,' she said. 'Anyway, it's from upstairs, so if you'll excuse me, I'll just go and make some enquiries. Won't you take a seat?'

Charlie sat down in one corner of the room, as far away from an Indian woman and her six kids as he could manage. Ten minutes later the girl was back and smiling at him apologetically over her glasses.

'I'm sorry, sir, but apparently there is quite a lot we have to know. Unfortunately, the gentleman who's dealing with this isn't here at the moment, and he seems to have the file with him.'

Charlie drew himself up until his eyes were level with the girl's. 'But the letter!' He jabbed a finger down onto the paper. '11 a.m. on the thirteenth. That's today! Do you know that I came all the way from Mombasa for this, and now you tell me "Solly, the man's not here".'

It was the injustice of it all that really hurt, and for the first time in years he heard himself substituting 'l's' for 'r's'.

The girl fixed him with the standard smile of understanding. 'Look, sir, I know it's inconvenient, we're very sorry, really we are, but there's nothing that I can do about it.' She leaned forward, and Charlie found himself looking down between her breasts. 'I'll be honest with you: Mr Heron took some overdue leave at the end of last week and went up to Kitale. He's going back to England, you know. Our replacement has arrived but he won't be in till next week.' She smiled. 'All the personnel have to acclimatize when they get here, sir, government regulation.'

Charlie was getting unhappier by the minute. 'Next week! I can't stay here till then. I got things to do. Who pays for the air tickets if I keep going up and down to the coast like a bloody salesman?'

The girl appeared to reach a decision. 'If I stick my neck out

61

and make an appointment for you to see our man on Friday, the day after tomorrow, would you wait?'

Charlie thought for a moment, somewhat mollified by the girl's sincere attempt to please. 'All right,' he said at last, 'I'll wait. Friday only. No more.'

'Good,' said the girl. 'Then that's settled. I'll write you out the details on one of our cards. But do remember that he'll really be doing us all a favour. He's not officially on duty.'

Charlie grunted, slipped the card in his pocket, and thanked the girl. His eyes wandered to her bosom for a final assessment, and he tried to imagine it shaking up and down to the music, taut-nippled and naked under the purple lights of the New Monsoon. Then he was outside on the pavement. Opening his wallet he extracted the card and checked the details. They were clear enough: 11 a.m., Friday 15th, Room 105, Norfolk Hotel. A Mr McLoughlin. Humming his band's signature tune, he wandered away into the town.

62

Chapter Four

London was grey under a chill sky. In St James's, Astrakhan hats were all the rage (lambs to the slaughter) and women wore coats that would have made Pasternak homesick. Under the coats, between high boots and short skirts, lay an abundance of nylon-covered thigh, sometimes tantalizingly revealed by a gust of wind, or the act of climbing steps. Mr Priest reluctantly put down the binoculars with which he passed his spare time. Carefully he replaced them in their case. Bloody Japs. Half the size, half the weight, half the price, twice as good. Another of the countries that won the war.

The windows of his top floor office off Pall Mall framed Clarence House, set against a background of stark and naked trees. Priest, mid-brown hair, blue eyes, five foot ten, was neither more nor less engaging than the next man. He smoked—from time to time, and he drank—just once in a while. It was rather the small, intangible things that singled out Priest from his fellows. The pigment of his skin suggested that he tanned easily and often, and he walked with a sureness of step that was feline.

When asked (on those rare occasions convened to celebrate some minor departmental victory) what his function was, or how he had come to join the department, Priest was able to reply, truthfully, that it was difficult to put into words. Properly handled, this routine evasion had the advantage of making him appear modest and even slightly diffident, which he wasn't. Sometimes he would ask himself the same questions and trigger a series of soul-searching reminiscences in the quest for a sane answer. There was indeed a particular moment to which he could point and say 'That's when it all went wrong'. Nevertheless, one didn't join the department the way one might join a bank. Subtly, over a

63

period of time, influence was exerted on those unfortunate enough to have made a serious error of judgment in their chosen profession; subsequently a change of life-style often ceased to be an option and became a necessity.

Priest's father had been an officer and a gentleman. Priest, an only child, attained the former status but only for a short time. He had won a place at Sandhurst, not so much out of vocation, but because, at the time, it seemed a reasonable enough thing to do; and he surprised himself and his father by warming to the system and by doing consistently well throughout his time there. His instructors agreed that he was a cut or two above average, and it was all recorded. In 1949 he was commissioned in his father's regiment, and his father retired one year later with a distinguished record and the rank of major-general, happy to think that the family tradition was being maintained by his son.

To Priest, life seemed good. He was a man who liked to rough it, to keep fit and active, but always with the proviso that waiting for him somewhere, whether tomorrow or the next week, was the comfort of the officer's mess where life was controlled and civilized the way it ought to be.

Between 1948 and 1952 Harry Priest served in Malaya with conspicuous bravery, and by the autumn of that year had been recommended for the MC and seemed in line for an early majority. He was popular with his men, and approved of by the senior officers, many of whom had known his father. Thus it was all the sadder that soon after the regiment's return to England he committed an indiscretion which was impossible to hush up, as it happened in the middle of the officer's mess: he punched the face of one of the company commanders, a major called Bestway. No one found out from either man what Bestway had said to provoke such a violent reaction. Rumour had it that Priest had been seen leaving Colonel Hanbury's residence at a time when it was known that only his wife was at home, but who started the rumour, and whether or not it was based on fact, no one could tell.

Small talk in the mess died. Cocktails stopped moving in mid-air, and mess staff froze in their tracks. The senior officer present, a Colonel Blakely, helped to get the bloody-mouthed Bestway on to a chair.

He eyed Priest incredulously. 'Captain Priest, please confine yourself to your quarters until further notice. Captain Withers, perhaps you'd be so kind as to escort him.'

Priest turned on his heel and marched out, followed by Withers. Conversation came slowly out from hiding. Blakely called to a couple of the junior officers.

'Geeson, Park, kindly help Major Bestway along to the MO and Bellchambers, ring the sickbay and inform the duty medical orderly that Major Bestway has hurt himself and will be arriving shortly.' With that Blakely turned and left the mess.

The next morning Priest was summoned to the office of Colonel Hanbury, his commanding officer. Hanbury, like many of the other officers, didn't like Bestway, and he did like Priest. He had served under Priest's father, and saw the resemblance between father and son. But the army relied on its discipline, its long-established codes of behaviour, on and off the field of war. For those who broke the rules there was another set of rules waiting to cover the eventuality; and popularity and resourcefulness did not affect the issue.

Priest came to attention in front of Hanbury, who did not look comfortable sitting at a desk. As if aware of the fact, he levered himself to his feet.

'At ease, Harry, at ease.'

Priest relaxed slightly.

Hanbury walked behind him and began to pace the room.

'I don't want to go too deeply into the whys and wherefores,' he began. 'What's done is done, and that's that. But I am extremely surprised that an officer of your record should have allowed himself to slip in this fashion. What I have to say to you today saddens me more than you can imagine, and it'll sadden your father as well. But I've thought the matter over from every angle and there is no alternative. Major Bestway refused to comment on what it was that sparked the whole thing off, but as you can imagine he's not keen on being struck by a junior officer with half the mess and most of the staff watching, and he proposes to press charges which means, of course, a court martial.'

Hanbury walked to the window and turned. Priest tried to read some expression in the man's face but he was in silhouette, and the words just came out from somewhere in the middle of a shape, like that of a target on the ranges.

'For your own good, and the good of the regiment, I have persuaded Major Bestway that if you were to submit your resignation to me in writing and I were to forward it with a recommendation for immediate acceptance, the matter would rest there.'

Hanbury took a deep breath after this sentence, and walked back to his chair.

'You know,' he said, 'this isn't the first time that there's been a brawl in the mess of this or other regiments, and it won't be the last. Often it's two of the younger chaps, a little too much to drink, you know the sort of thing . . . then it's a reprimand and a handshake . . . but you take the biscuit. Crowded mess, mess servants, senior officer . . . and of all people least likely to lose control like that, I would have put you at the top of the list.'

There was silence, broken only by the tapping of Hanbury's pencil on the desk top. When he spoke again, his voice was slightly less official.

'Before you go, there are two more points I'd like to make.' He cleared his throat. 'I have heard this rumour about you and Sheila—' Priest coloured, and tried to cut in, but Hanbury held up his hand, '—and I want you to know that I give it no credence whatsoever. Dammit I've known you since you were a nipper and you've always been a welcome visitor to our house . . . so if that has any bearing on the matter in hand. . . .' He dropped his arm. 'The second point is this.' He waved a letter. 'Perhaps I'm being a little premature, but in the circumstances . . . the military secretary informs me that your MC has been approved. Congratulations Harry.'

The two men shook hands. And that was that. He hadn't spoken a word, one minute you were in the next you were out. The handshake wasn't even a golden one.

The men from the department found him quickly, and at first he just listened in an amused fashion, and told them he'd think about it. But after six months of kicking his heels, a strained relationship with the family, and countless interviews for jobs he didn't want, he realized he would have to take some dramatic steps to preserve his sanity. He toyed with emigrating, training soldiers in black Africa, learning to fly. But in the end he rang the number he had been given some five months earlier, and found that there were people after all who could use the talents of a professional soldier.

Nearly a quarter of a century later he was still living the same shadowy existence, just somewhat older, with a dash of grey highlighting his hair and an inexhaustible supply of cynicism that he tried too hard not to show.

The London office was not unpleasant, although the exclusive use of white paint made it seem colder than it was. Under the desk a two-kilowatt fanheater supplemented the sometimes inadequate central heating. From beyond the door came the sound of breaking crockery and raised voices. Priest was about to take the first sip of morning tea when the grey internal phone buzzed peremptorily.

'Mr Priest? He's just this minute finished. Would you like to come up now?'

A minute lift of ancient design carried Priest up to what was jestingly referred to as the Penthouse Sweet, in fact the unregistered London office of Sir Charles Sweet, KCMG, MC. The lift stopped and Priest wasted seconds expecting the doors to open automatically. A small hall in perpetual half light led past a ladies' lavatory on the left, and through a tall, narrow door of darkened glass. Priest was aware that in the lift and the short length of the corridor his movements had been monitored by a number of CCTV lenses, and that he had also been scanned by a proximitor, designed to pinpoint any metallic objects. The devices had been installed two years previously on an experimental basis and, like income tax, had never been removed. Past the darkened glass the corridor opened out into a small, brightly-lit reception area, and beneath a mahogany desk inlaid with black leather the shapely legs of Mrs Garrett demanded attention.

'Mr Priest?' Off the telephone her voice was quiet, almost pleasant. 'If you wouldn't mind?'

'Do I ever?' Pulling back his cuff he pressed his right hand on to the proffered square of impregnated padding, and then transferred the pressure to a clean white card. 'Mind, that is. That do?'

'That's fine, thank you.' The card disappeared into a slot in the wall behind her. 'You'll be pleased to know they're getting a machine for that as well.' She turned to Priest. 'Try one of these. They're new. Trichlorethylene.'

He shook the small plastic pack and opened it, extracting a

67

damp Kleenex. The black on his hand vanished under its ministrations. 'Sure it's not cyclohexane?' He quizzed her, half smiling.

'I'm only repeating what it said on the handout,' she said seriously, and looked up puzzled when he laughed. 'Would you care to take a seat? He won't be a moment.'

Priest lowered himself into a black armchair that belched asthmatically under his weight. 'Mrs Garrett, you're too serious by far; I was merely impressed by a woman remembering such a complex chemical name.'

On the desk a green light pulsed. He wondered briefly if her allure lay in the fact that he never made any headway with her on the occasions that they met. She smiled, revealing white, even teeth between pink lips.

'You may go in now.'

The room was dominated by a lifesized statue of Nelson, around whose neck was wrapped an irreverent striped woollen scarf. The principal light source was a huge skylight countersunk into the ceiling, now half-covered by a blind. Around the oak-panelled walls hung various photographs, together with a large frame containing a montage of better-class political cartoons. Sweet was pouring coffee into two enormous cups, and the room smelled good.

'Come in, Priest, come in, you'd better help yourself to sugar if you take it.'

'Thank you, sir.' Priest helped himself to two spoonfuls of moist, brown sugar; both the spoon and the sugar bowl bore the same coat of arms, a traditional mélange of knights, serpents and swords. Underfoot, the pile on the carpet gave way like new snow, only unlike snow one didn't leave a trail. Priest followed the elder man to the far end of the room, where a small projection unit was set up flush with the right-hand wall. They sat, and Priest studied the man whose next words would almost certainly presage trouble for the department, if not for him personally.

'Well, Priest, have you kept up with your Swahili?'

So it was to be East Africa. The last time had been in '64 during the mutiny, and eleven years before that his baptism under fire with the department: Mau-Mau.

'The problem is complex, and it's been difficult to decide what, if anything, we could afford to do. But now our entire footing in East Africa is threatened; companies, equipment, personnel, investments. We stand to lose the lot. And here's the reason.' He flicked a switch, and the lights dimmed. A push button panel on his desk allowed him to select any one of a previously programmed series of maps and slides from the hundreds compiled. There was a clicking as the relays tripped, and then a general map of East Africa grew in brightness on the screen in front of them.

'Three states; I'm sure you remember them well. Our problem is a combination of factors that could fester at any moment, and if that's allowed to happen no one stands to lose more than us.'

The map changed to a face. Half negroid, half Arab in aspect, it had become well known to readers of the world press: that of Colonel Omuria, self-styled liberator of the people, whose insecurity and fear of subversion had lead to the wholesale slaughter of entire villages in the cause of national security.

'Since he seized power two years ago, his actions have become more and more difficult to predict, and the way he justifies his methods is typical of penny dictators the world over: he acts in the name of God for the betterment of the people.'

Again the picture changed; a man waving to a crowd, dressed in ceremonial costume.

'His predecessor, William Kalaba, ousted in his absence, now living in exile but still planning a counter-coup. Just before he lost power he had made widescale plans to Africanize Ugandan industry. This involved proclaiming his government majority shareholders in all foreign concerns, most of which were British. So we were quite happy to see him go, and regretfully were the first to recognize the new régime. But still, that was the other lot's decision.'

Then a series of pictures came up on the screen: Omuria inspecting a parade; standing in a garden with a woman and a small girl; waving as his Mercedes nosed through a huge crowd. And the other side of the coin: a man, hooded, sagging in his bonds after the firing squad had gone to lunch; bodies being tipped from an old wooden bridge into a river; a corpse lying in its blood beneath a poster of the president.

'Things have now degenerated so far that even the simplest

69

peasant realizes he can no longer buy necessities. Nearly all sugar, for example, is commandeered by the army. Omuria has launched a tremendous campaign to point the finger at Kalaba. Barely a day passes without his claiming to have found out fresh information that proves the man's involvement, and he's come to believe his own propaganda. To provide a diversion from the internal state of the country, he now has troops massing along the southern borders, and has offered four million shillings reward for Kalaba's capture.'

Priest blinked as the lights came up. He started to speak, but Sweet waved him down.

'Yes, I know what you're going to say, how does it affect us; well, have some more coffee and I'll tell you.' He moved to the table, followed by Priest. The coffee was on a small hot-plate. 'You see, some months ago we received overtures from Kalaba. That in itself was interesting, because he's receiving Chinese help. Officially, of course, we can't intervene at all, but unofficially we'd rather like to see him back in power with our help and a debt of gratitude to pay off. And he's the only one with enough support among the tribes to make the whole thing possible. Sugar?'

Priest stirred the coffee, and watched the bubbles collect in the middle. The two men resumed their seats.

'So there's the simplified picture. We want to put the clock back two years, bearing in mind, of course, that if there's any fighting the way things are going it'll all take place in the middle of our best tea country. May even spread into the coffee as well.' The mention of coffee cued an action, and he sipped from his cup. 'It's a bit hurtful when these fellows misappropriate our loans, buy arms from the reds, and then use them to fight a war in the middle of our investments. Costs a fortune and makes us look stupid.'

Priest finished his second cup and sat forward. Obviously he hadn't been brought in here to discuss the future of a tea plantation somewhere in south-west Uganda. 'You said that was the simplified picture, sir?' he prompted.

'Yes, Priest, the whole picture is even more depressing. Let's have a look at Tanzania.' He flipped the switch again and a map of the country appeared on the screen. 'Tanzania is a big place. You can fit Uganda and Kenya into it and still have plenty over. But Uganda has the military power.' He hesitated. 'Until

70

recently, Omuria would never have dared threaten Tanzania in spite of his military strength : he didn't know where the Chinese stood, and let me tell you, there are more of them than you might imagine.' Another map appeared, marked with a long line and a series of crosses. 'That line is the proposed railway to Lusaka, being built and financed by the Chinese. And one track is already in operation. The advantages to Zambia and Tanzania are great: Zambia no longer has to send copper through Rhodesia, or use the port of Beira in what was Portuguese East. And Tanzania gets large amounts of foreign exchange, even if it is in kwachas. But the Chinese haven't stopped there. Once they had the foot in the door, all sorts of things started to happen.'

Now the pictures showed Chinese gunboats in the Pemba Channel, and Green Guards parading along Independence Avenue.

'The crosses represent Chinese-controlled military installations. They range in scope from the jungle warfare camps that trained the Frelimo guerrillas in the south, to the cross you see near the coast to the east of Songea—a fully equipped launch station to give the Africans their own weather satellite, a bit like the Italian-American operation north of Malindi in Kenya. And this with most of the world still believing that they have no established aviation industry. The point is that the Chinese would welcome an invasion—the more disruption the better. We believe that they have given Omuria a guarantee of their neutrality in the event of a confrontation. But a guarantee from them isn't worth a lot. First, they'll wait for the right moment and then move north—only it'll just look like Tanzania winning a righteous victory. Second, they'll make sure that Kalaba doesn't have a chance to get near any of his old sympathizers. Omuria probably doesn't know that Kalaba is far from being a free agent. Ostensibly, he and his men are being trained by the Chinese and equipped with Chinese weapons. But it isn't a free ride. That way they know where he is and what he's doing, and when the scrap comes you can be sure they'll be right there on the spot to pick up the pieces and fit them together to the best advantage. It's a stringalong—they know that in spite of differences in the past, Kalaba's basically occidental.' The last picture, of men bayonetting dummies, faded from sight.

71

Priest flexed his left leg, which had gone to sleep. 'Does Kalaba know the score?'

'We think he does, hence the overtures in our direction. But there'd be nothing positive, just a feeling. In all probability everything seems exactly as it should. Already the bulk of the produce on sale in Tanzanian shops is Chinese: Great Wall plum jam, nails from Canton, Double Red Horse shirts, not to mention baked beans and tuna fish. And forgive me if I sound prejudiced, but some idiot from supply sent me the ingredients for an all-red lunch and I can tell you, the stuff's inedible.'

Priest grinned inwardly at the thought of Sir Charles opening, tasting and rejecting a can of Chinese baked beans, before walking off to lunch at his club.

'Make no mistake—if they can increase their sphere of influence they will, and Kenya will be neatly pincered. I'm well aware that the East African community is a farce, but better a farce than a tragedy.'

He stood up. Sweet's interviews tended to stop as suddenly as they began. Others attended to details but he insisted on the personal touch when it came to outlining the objectives.

'So there you are, Priest. The general picture. Tomorrow you come on the operational list for the purpose of accounting. And your papers will be made out using your old rank, with a little bit of promotion for good luck. Carries a lot of weight you know, down there, that sort of thing. Marlow will fill in the gaps, starting in the morning.'

At the door, Priest turned. He had the feeling that often came after a talk with Sir Charles—a matter of great importance had been discussed, but no specific conclusions drawn.

'To be specific, sir—what in a nutshell is our principal aim?'

Sweet grimaced. 'The principal aim, Priest? To get Kalaba away from the Chinese and I don't care how it happens. You'll need him to figurehead the revolution.'

'I have got a home to go to, you know.' Priest looked ostentatiously at his watch.

Marlow snorted. 'And I suppose I haven't? Do me a favour, Mr Priest, just concentrate, we're on the home straight.'

Since the meeting with Sweet four days ago, Priest's mind had been bombarded with facts; names, numbers and statistics had

72

been hurled his way without respite, and he was beginning to wonder how many he had actually caught and how many had carried right on past him into thin air.

'Personnel,' said Marlow, and Priest dragged his eyes back to the table. 'To be brief—' he ignored Priest's muttered 'impossible' and continued, 'to be brief, you have to transport one African VIP across potentially hostile territory and deliver him to a pre-arranged rendezvous point somewhere in the Katado region. We have to give the impression that this is a private job being done by mercenaries for the four million shillings. If one of the men we use should fall into the wrong hands it's imperative he should know nothing of our involvement. What he doesn't know they can't get out of him.' Marlow paused, and pulled a buff folder towards him. 'This in itself has posed a problem: who to use? It's not like the Middle-East, and money on its own isn't always enough. One needs people that have been compromised; because they no longer have a choice, they tend to dedicate themselves more . . . wholeheartedly . . . to the project.'

Priest interrupted him rudely. 'All right, all right, get on with it.' It was always the same at base: chairbound theorists that got carried away with their personal analysis of a hypothetical situation. Then when the poor bloody traveller got to his destination he found everything totally different and had to spend a couple of days forgetting everything he'd learned. Far better to keep an open mind, and ditch the rubbish in the car to Heathrow.

Marlow pursed his lips. 'Mr Priest, I'm only trying to do my job.' He opened the folder. 'We've got three men that might interest you. If suitable, they should only know enough to enable them to carry out the mission. The motives must appear to be apolitical. Anyway, see what you think.'

Priest looked at the first synopsis card. Underneath the mug shot showing a Chinese of indeterminate years was a précis of facts useful to the British government.

Soon Tsa Lee   *Age:* 32   *Passport:* British: Restricted Entry
Charlie Soon, owner of Mombasa's least celebrated night-spot, the New Monsoon club. There was an old Monsoon club. His main problem is money. Since independence business has been bad, and the Suez closure didn't help. For some years was big with illicit ivory and horn, but last year a patrol boat captured two dhows near Lamu, loaded with the stuff. There was no one

left to talk, but rumour has it they were his. Other main source of income was currency conversion on the chini chini—the black market. He's had to make a pretty sizeable payout to stay in business.

Marlow added, 'Now he's watched all the time, but we could arrange that if you wanted him, and we've already got the boys in the HC down there to send him a worry letter about his passport, and you can be sure he'll want to keep that in these troubled times. He speaks Swahili, English, Malay—he was born in Malaya—Cantonese and Mandarin, competes when he has the money in various motoring events, and keeps fit on a mixture of unarmed combat and abstinence.'

The second card showed a European; even in black and white the tan showed. The man was good-looking, young and blond.

Flemming Murray Allan   *Age* : 29   *Passport* : Australian

This man only came to light recently. A rough diamond but he graduated from the University of Western Australia with a degree in Sociology. During military service he volunteered for a spell in Vietnam with the Australasian contingent. He saw action in the big Australasian/US air offensive at Vung Tau, stopped a bullet late in '67, and went back to Perth in '68. Continued his education and with his war record had no difficulty in getting a place on a sponsored course at UCLA. He stayed in California for three years under Professor Harvey Klein, who recommended him for a Facet Foundation grant. Flemming spent six months planning the trip. Then he went to Kenya. Apparently caught gold fever there and is now in the miltary prison at Fort Hall pending an inquiry.

'That could take years. Once again,' Marlow sighed, 'we could help him out; he's a top class swimmer and water-skier, also dives. It seems he spent the first twenty years of his life in or under the sea. And he flies a light aircraft.'

The third and last card was pink and not grey. 'We've got no hold over this chap at all. But I think you'll agree his history is interesting.'

Gould Samuel   *Age:* 36   *Passport:* British Exemption
Granted

Family went to Uganda after the First World War. He schooled in England and went back to Africa after his father died. Joined the Game Department and did a good job until late '58. Then for two years he cropped up in every central African skirmish there was—he was only twenty—and built up a nest-egg at the Banque Centrale in Zurich. He sided where it suited him and ended up involved in the Bakawanga massacre in '61.

Believed that he came to hate Africans. Tribalism made unity impossible and Gould foresaw that country after country would gain independence and go downhill. In 1960 took out a hunting licence and courted American businessmen on safari. After Uhuru did a smart about-face and started catching animals for export. Made a sound living until recently when speared by a native tribesman. Treated successfully in Uganda and Nairobi. Now in Nairobi staying with the man who used to ship his animals.

Marlow swept up the cards and put them, with the paper work, back into the folder. 'He's an interesting man. My guess is he feels he's missed out somewhere, I expect the psychiatrists have a name for it.' He closed the folder, handed it to Priest. 'One thing I forgot to mention—he's an uncanny shot. You'll find some examples in there somewhere, we got a rundown from a man who knew him in Entebbe.' There was silence. 'Well,' said Marlow. 'That's the lot. It's all yours.'

Priest took the folder and stood up. Marlow did the same, stooping awkwardly. There was no doubt about it, the man had done a tremendous job; Priest was glad he wouldn't have to pay the telex account. At the door he turned. 'It's more than I hoped for.' He glanced down at the folder. 'You've done a lot in a short time. Thanks.'

Behind him, Marlow's face suffused with pleasure. 'Thank you, Mr Priest,' he said. 'We always try to do our best.' But Priest was already outside in the corridor. 'That's what we're here for,' said Marlow to the closed door.

The 747 came sweeping low towards Embakasi. Herds of wilde-beeste and gazelle in the game reserve beneath took no notice as the huge shadow flickered among them. Priest gazed towards the town as the plane lost height. The name 'Nairobi' had come from a Masai phrase meaning 'fresh water' and the first time he'd landed there the plane had been a Comet, and the airport on the other side of the Mombasa road. The wheels touched, the giant craft shuddered and slowed. A metallic female voice was still hoping they'd had a pleasant flight when Priest stood up and made for the door. Outside, it was 7 a.m. and chilly, and the early morning had a clarity and bite that started a good feeling going way down in the lungs. Priest breathed very deeply three times and felt his head clear.

A young man from the high commission button-holed him just inside the glass doors of the terminal.

'Major Priest? My name's McLoughlin. Have a good flight, sir? Good, good. Won't you come this way?'

Things had changed a lot in ten years, Priest thought. It's lost its rustic appeal, you no longer feel that you've landed somewhere slightly outpost-ish. It was funny how modern airports were the same the world over, plastic, like Hilton hotels. Now Embakasi was just an embryo version of Heathrow or Kennedy. Priest had travelled with a small suitcase in the aircraft, and had put nothing in the hold. McLoughlin steered him through immigration, and led the way to a black Rover 3500, parked nearby. 'Norfolk Hotel,' he instructed the driver, and the car slid forward onto the road.

'We've put you in the Norfolk as requested, sir.' He hesitated. 'London said that's where you used to stay before.'

Priest smiled: 'I expect it's gone up since those days.' He glanced at McLoughlin. 'How long have you been out here?'

'Eight months, sir.'

'Like it?'

'Beats London any day.'

Priest looked out of the window. They were on the start of the Uhuru Highway, a dual carriageway that skirted the centre of the town. Uhuru. Free-dom. Well, Nairobi didn't look too bad on it. A car overtook them fast on the inside and Priest remembered how the local whites explained the name of this road: 'Uhuru means freedom to drive on the left or right,' went the anecdote. 'That's important if you're a coon and have a bit of difficulty telling the difference.' Now they were turning left past the university and the Norfolk appeared on the right-hand side. Many people preferred hotels that were slap in the middle of town, but for Priest's money this one was the answer, and it looked just the same. The car stopped, and a Kamba with gapped teeth opened the door. McLoughlin already had the room key, and the two men left the car and walked through the foyer and out the other side onto a large, sunny lawn. On their left a big aviary sported rollers, weavers, widow birds. To the right, a double storey of rooms stretched, alpine-style with wooden-railed balconies, the length of the grass.

McLoughlin stopped just inside the room. 'Well, I'll leave you to freshen up, sir. If there's anything you need, don't hesitate to call me on this number.' He handed over a card. 'I take it you won't be coming to the HC?'

Priest pushed open the bathroom door, and went in. His voice echoed slightly and there was the sound of running water. 'No, I won't. Just tell Johnny Gable that he's on for dinner tonight. Someone told me that Lavorini's is good. Nine p.m. And arrange an aircraft for tomorrow morning, early. Something high-wing and slow. Cessna 172 would do the job. I want to take some photographs.'

Priest had fallen asleep. When he awoke it was midday, and he felt wonderful. From a supine position he reached for the white bedside phone and dialled a Kabete number. It hardly seemed possible after all this time, but the name was in the book. An African answered the phone.

'Memsahib is'i in the garden. Please hold on.' The accented English gave him an idea, and he waited impatiently until he could hear footsteps approaching the phone. A husky voice, slightly out of breath, said:

'Hello? Katherine Abbott speaking.'

Priest cleared his throat: 'Why, jambo dere Miz Abbott, dis is de ministry. I is afraid dat-i your resident's permit-i has not-i been extended.'

There was silence on the other end of the phone, then the voice said, 'Is this some kind of joke?'

Priest changed the receiver to his other ear. 'You could say that, Katie. It's Harry Priest here.'

There was a pause followed by a gasp from the other end of the line. 'Harry! But it can't be! Why, you've never written and it's been—'

'Over nine years?' he interrupted. 'Yes, I know. How are you? And how's Jim?'

The woman's voice broke slightly. 'Of course, you don't know,

77

how could you?' And very quietly: 'He's been dead for almost a year.'

Priest rolled over sharply onto one elbow. The phone slipped to the floor. He'd shared a lot of fraught moments with Jim Abbott before his marriage to Katie. No one had been more irresponsible or footloose, but she'd caught him anyway, and invested herself in his energy and enthusiasm. They'd started a small tour agency. Within two years the loans were paid off, and a year later they moved to Kitisuru. That was the last Priest had seen of them, when Katie was twenty-three. He'd never written because he never wrote to anyone. Life was sad enough without invoking the past all the time, and that's what letters did. He wanted to ask how Jim died, and did you have any kids? But that could come later.

'I'm sorry, Katie. And sorry that I didn't know.'

Her voice picked up again. 'Where are you, Harry? And when can I see you?'

Priest smiled. 'How about a steak by the Norfolk pool?' He looked at his watch. 'Can you make it by one?'

Priest knew that she'd arrived when the three men at the next table turned their heads in unison, as if controlled remotely by unseen strings. He looked round, and started to his feet; the girl he remembered was gone, and in her place walked a lovely woman. She stopped in front of him and kissed him on the cheek.

'Harry! I'd recognize that ugly face anywhere!'

He pulled back a chair for her, and glowered at the three men over her shoulder, forcing them back to their food. Then he beckoned a waiter and sat down.

'Now tell me why you're here,' she demanded, eyes bright. 'I want to know everything.'

He held up a restraining hand. 'First things first. Food for the body and lubrication for the tongue.' He appraised her swiftly. 'You're as thin as a rake.' It was a blatant lie: she stood about five foot six, and was wearing a two-piece yellow outfit that she filled to perfection. Between its top and bottom halves six inches of tanned midriff showed firm and flat.

The food came, and soon they were deep in conversation.

'You're so white, Harry!' she laughed, so they changed and lay in the sun where red-flowered hibiscus bushes kept out the wind. Then they swam. In the water her black hair floated round her face like a fine weed, and the material of her bikini took on a pinkly transparent look; she laughed again when she saw him looking at her.

'Harry, you really haven't changed at all!'

He pulled her under, and it was as if the last ten years had never happened. Sometimes he wished he could live them all over again, missing out Cyprus and Moscow and Laos and Chile and substituting them all for a woman like this and a cottage in the country. But it was a pipedream, and not how the game was played.

As the sun slanted down over the town, they picked up their things and walked slowly back to his room. He felt sad; how many times must he say the things that he had to say now? Inside the door she leaned against him, and her hair fell in damp tresses on his chest.

'Katie, nothing's easy. Not even this.' He put his hands on her shoulders. 'I lead a disjointed life at the best of times—you haven't seen me for ten years and you might not see me again for another ten.' She looked up at him and he thought 'Go on, Superman, roll out the clichés and don't forget the bit about what a chance she's taking, because that's super-honest, which makes it all even easier.'

But he couldn't, not with her. Tomorrow he'd be gone, and she'd be left with the memory of what a first-class shit Harry Priest was. It would have been better if he'd let sleeping dogs lie. But then he hadn't known that Jim was dead . . .

'Harry, I don't know what you were going to say, but please don't. I'm not a girl any more, and since Jim died it's been the longest year of my life. I've tried to with other men, the hunters and the pilots, I've been fair game all right . . . but there's no one, no one that's half the man he was . . . my body works away until I'm trembling just thinking about it, but inside my mind is asking "What will you feel like afterwards?" and they never make it inside for that last drink.' She moved back slightly, and held him at arms' length. 'But you are different, Harry, you knew Jim before I did. He used to tell me some of the things . . .'

Slowly she pushed her bikini pants over her hips, and stepped out of them. The top was about to follow onto the floor, and Priest looked at the black hair hanging down over her half-

79

exposed breasts and realized that the one emotion dominating all others at that moment was pity; in his mind she was still Jim's wife, and it was not for him to misuse her just because she was so very available, to take advantage of an old friendship and maybe break it in the process. But he wondered if she knew whose need was the greater, and there was a lump in his throat that wouldn't shift.

Deftly, he picked up one of the swimming towels and moved towards her, wrapping her nakedness in a flurry of damp stripes and hiding it from view.

'You're a very beautiful woman, Katie. A woman worth waiting for.'

She read the 'No' in his eyes, and trembled as she moved against him. The lips that sought his were salty.

'You'd have been doing us a favour Harry,' she said.

Chapter Five

The next morning, the same driver came at seven o'clock and took Priest to Wilson Airport, Nairobi's base for light aircraft. In Air Kenya's large hangar a variety of planes were being prepared for the day's work, and Johnny Gable waved when he saw Priest enter.

'How do you feel?' he called, and jumped down from the wing of a small Mooney.

'Not so bad,' Priest replied, and gestured, 'We're not going in that?'

'Hell, no,' said Johnny. 'I was just thinking that at one time that's all they'd let me fly.'

'And now you're on the heavy metal,' said Priest.

'Yeah. Like today. Cessna 172, with 52-gallon tanks, that one.' He laughed. 'What the hell got to you last night? You stay in Lavorini's for twenty minutes, eat half a canneloni, tell me nothing I don't know already, and piss off. Some reunion, Harry!'

Priest clapped him on the shoulder. 'I'm sorry, Johnny. It's these night flights, they screw me up.'

'You're getting old, son, getting old. Can't take it any more. Not like the old days.'

There was a pause and then Priest said 'Johnny, did you know Jim Abbott was dead?'

The other man dropped his bantering tone. 'Sure Harry, who doesn't? I was going to tell you last night, but I reckon you already knew. And in a car smash too. Kind of ordinary for Jim.' He looked up quizzically. 'Have you seen Katie?'

Priest looked at him 'Yes, I saw her.' He turned towards the Cessna. 'I'll put my stuff on board.'

An hour later they were fifty miles south of Nairobi, flying in bright early sunlight. Behind the small craft the Ngong hills were etched sharply by the morning shadows, black, green and brown. Priest was loading a roll of Tri-X into a black Nikon. When the sun was high he would be able to photograph at a 2,000th of a second to minimize the shake of the aircraft. He clipped a 135 mm lens into the mount and pressed the shutter release. With a whirr and a series of clicks, the motor-drive wound the film into position for the first shot. Johnny had a green map case open on his knees. In the top left-hand corner of the first section lay Nairobi, and about half-way down the red line that denoted the border.

'What's our exact heading?' Priest raised his voice above the drone of the motor.

Johnny pointed to the panel. 'About 230 degrees—almost south west to you!' He grinned. 'We're crossing the border now.'

Priest gazed out of the window. 'How do you know?'

Johnny banked the craft. 'See that white blob? Border marker.' He chuckled to himself. 'The Aussies had a bloke in trouble recently, he started shifting things around a bit so he could do a spot of private mining and still be in Kenya.'

Priest grunted, and Gable looked across the cabin and wondered what made the man tick. Harry Priest was friendly enough, the perfect gentleman, and whoever he really worked for always paid up, right on the line. But the man himself was a mystery. No emotion, no cracks in the plaster, he kept it all bottled up deep inside. And when Priest arrived, you could be sure that something unpleasant was going to happen. What would it be this time, more oaths and official secrets and night flying? Or perhaps they were putting Priest out to grass and it would just be a routine reconnaissance. Gable hoped so.

The plane was flying at 2,000 feet over one end of an enormous soda pan. It stretched away to their left, surrounded by bush-covered upland and high forests. Large areas of black stretched out on either side of the lake, and purple wisps of smoke rose into the air.

'The Masai.' Johnny jerked his thumb downwards. 'Burning off before the rains. That's Lake Natron.'

Priest asked 'Can you drive on it?'

'You can at the moment.'

To their right, always ahead of them, their tiny, frenzied shadow bounded over the earth like a hunted gazelle. The plane had been in the air for two hours when Johnny banked slightly and started to climb. They came up over a jagged range of hills and suddenly a huge depression lay before them.

'Remember this place? Makes you think, doesn't it?'

Ngorongoro crater, the tourist's Mecca, lay snugly below them, surrounded by a barrier of hills. On the lake in the middle Priest could just discern the pink scum that he knew were flamingoes, thousands of them, stepping daintily through the warm soda. White Volkswagens rolled like ant's eggs along brown string roads, carrying Americans and Germans and French to chase or photograph or merely ogle the animals.

Priest looked forward over the southern escarpment. He remembered it, all right, though over twenty years had passed. 'Twenty years,' he thought, and somehow the number seemed too large, because the memories were pristine as if they had happened yesterday. He had been ... twenty-five? Christ! The thought of the department employing him at the age of twenty-five, let alone sending him out to hunt someone down with a gun, was somehow incredible. Nearly a quarter of a century since he had met Jim Abbott, and now he was back and sooner or later almost bound to sleep with the delectable Mrs Abbott. Life sometimes played an unexpected hand. Now the Cessna was flying over rolling green hills devoid even of tourists, and to the right, hazy with distance, stretched the beginnings of the Serengeti.

At the western limit of Lake Eyasi they turned due west; almost immediately Priest pointed.

'There's the camp!'

Johnny throttled back but kept on the same course. Their air speed dropped, and Priest opened the window and raised the Nikon. The camp consisted of two lines of large, neatly-pitched tents, some twenty in number. At one end there were four square buildings with corrugated iron roofs. A large circular clearing lay between a small river and the preparations for an airstrip, and on one side of the clearing a pair of drab-green lorries were parked together. There was little evidence of life. Priest clicked busily with the camera.

'Where is everyone?' asked Johnny. 'Place looks deserted.'

He banked and pushed the nose down. The encampment slid towards them, tilted like a carelessly hung picture. Priest raised the camera again and brought it up to his eye. Then he froze.

'For Christ's sake, get us out of here!' In the thin moment that Gable took to react a yellow flickering started among the bushes behind the lorries. Three holes appeared magically in the leading edge of the port wing and the small craft rocked under the impact. Gable had been too long at the game to try for height and expose their belly. Instantly he went down into a dive towards the front of the trucks and spun the plane across the clearing; in seconds they no longer presented a target and he hauled back on the stick. The Cessna clawed its way over the treetops and then they were flying fast and low across the bush.

Priest grunted and raised his head. 'Nicely done. Are we still in one piece?'

Johnny relaxed slightly and wiped the sweat off his forehead. 'Just about,' he said, and gave a tense laugh. 'What the hell was all that?'

Priest shook his head. 'No friends of ours. Still, when they check the registration they'll find . . .'

'. . . it belongs to the Ministry of Natural Resources,' Johnny finished. 'Not very original, is it?'

A few minutes later they banked sharply to the right, and Priest packed the camera away. Suddenly he laughed. 'Before we go up to Fort Hall, try to find West Kilimanjaro,' he said. 'I think I know someone who might give us lunch.'

Johnny Gable licked his lips at the thought and pointed the plane towards a distant smudge on the horizon. 'Good idea,' he said. 'Even I can steer my way there.'

In the civilian sector of the Fort Hall military prison the thing that Flemming missed most was the sunshine. By standing on the bed and looking out of the small recessed window he could get a low-angle view of a parade ground, soldiers' legs, and the occasional vehicle. At the top of his field of vision was a thin ribbon of sky, tantalizingly blue, which stretched along the roof of the building opposite. In the distance, a tiny plane glinted briefly in the clear evening air. Flemming got down from the bed and looked at his watch. God knows, it had been an effort to hang on to it, all the prison staff seemed to care about in life were watches and transistor radios. He read the time and date off for the tenth time that day. 4 p.m., Wednesday the 13th of March. That added up to twenty-three days in this hole, eating posho and fatty stews. Christ, how much longer would it take these jokers to do something, anything, to tell him what the hell was happening? Flemming fought down a feeling of hysteria, and gripped the edge of the bed; there was nothing, but nothing, that he didn't know about this room. Its height, its length, its cubic capacity in feet, inches, centimetres. The cracks in the ceiling sometimes represented rivers and their tributaries, sometimes the Australian railway system. He lay back, wishing he could be home. One summer holiday at the age of eleven, he'd left Perth on the railway to Sydney to visit his uncle. The journey lasted eighty hours, and in those days you had to change five times because of all the different track gauges. The first train had been a big steam loco with quaint wrought-iron verandahs between the coaches where people could stand in the sunlight and talk. They wound up into the hills, through shady gum forests, and he'd felt pretty lonely with the carriages stretching away back down the track towards the guard's van and the sun setting over the trees. But the next day they got to Kalgoorlie, the gold town, and changed onto the 'Trans', a long, streamlined diesel where you couldn't even open the windows because of the air-conditioning. He remembered the country changing, until there was bright orange soil and saltbush as far as the eye could see, and little towns flashing by, Zanthus, Rawlinna, Haig. An old man looked down at him as he stood by the window, clouds of smoke belching from an old leather-bound pipe.

'Do you know what them plains out there is called, boy?'

Flemming had learned the name in school. 'Yes, sir,' he said. 'The Nullarbor Plains.'

The old man took another puff at the enormous pipe. 'Know what "Nullarbor" means, son?'

Flemming shook his head; the teacher hadn't gone into that, or if she had he hadn't been listening.

'Ha!' said the old man triumphantly. 'So you don't know? Why, it means "no trees", and it's a lattin word. Lattin's what the New Austrylians used to speak a long time ago, before they left Italy,' he added.

Flemming was impressed. It was a good name too, there wasn't a tree to be seen anywhere.

'Another thing,' said the old man. 'They ain't a bend in this track till we get to Ooldea, and that's a long way, over three hundred miles down the line.' He leaned over confidentially. 'In fact, it's the longest bit of straight rail anywhere in the world, yes it is, anywhere, even America.'

At last the train drew up at the little place called Ooldea. Chickens walked slowly in the heat, and there was a group of corrugated iron huts near the track.

'Why have we stopped?' Flemming asked the old man.

'Water, boy, water. That name there means "running water" in Abo.'

Flemming looked around. The land was parched and bare under a copper sky. 'I can't see any running water,' he objected.

'I know,' the old man said. 'Neither can I. It's all under the ground.' He hawked noisily. 'But sometimes it rains here, and then the desert blooms with flowers. They come up outa the ground in the middle of the night, more flowers'n you've ever seen. But it don't happen oftin, they ain't much rain.'

The train moved off, passing two black-skinned infants scratching in the dust. Above their heads, the blades of a wind-pump moved lethargically in the hot air. The old man watched the scene until it disappeared. 'They always was a hopeful lot, those Abos,' he muttered. 'Reckon you've got to be hopeful to live out here.'

Flemming brought his eyes slowly down from the ceiling. In the corridor outside there were footsteps coming nearer. His eyes watched the slot in the door where a face might appear to break the monotony. The small metal plate slid back, revealing a pair of eyes circled by black skin. Abruptly, the trap slid closed, and Flemming heard the keys jangling on their ring. The door opened and Joseph appeared, one of the day guards.

'You've got a visitor, mister.' Then to someone behind him, 'I will be outside the door, bwana, when you want to leave.'

A voice said 'Thank you, Askari,' and a man stepped past him into the room. His face bore the first flush of sunburn, and was deeply wrinkled around the eyes. He sat on the room's only chair and placed a small case carefully on the ground. He looked over at Flemming and started talking without preamble.

'Mr Flemming, you're in a lot of trouble, and the way things are over here it could take years to sort out. It's possible that I may be able to help.'

'A well educated pom,' thought Flemming, 'and he's just

arrived in Nairobi, and he wants to help.' He felt like screaming 'For Christ's sake, just get me out of here!' but instead he looked at the man steadily and replied:

'You want to help me? Why? Who the hell are you?'

The man was shuffling some papers that he'd extracted from the case. His voice was quiet when he looked up and replied: 'I'll come to your first questions in a minute Mr Flemming. And as to the third, my name's Priest.'

Two hours later Priest adjusted his tie and for the third time checked the result in the full length mirror of his room in the Norfolk. Not bad, he thought, for forty-four, and you have been through the mill a few times. It was 8 p.m., and he'd got back late from Fort Hall : Flemming had been an interesting character, to say the least. The man was bitter beyond belief, and at first Priest had thought that he might well be useless for the task in hand. The disappointment of his lost wealth had undermined the man's resilience and now, behind the tough façade, Priest suspected something was on the point of giving way. Flemming's first outburst had done nothing to dispel that opinion.

'Me? Get involved in a huli like that? You're out of your mind.' Abruptly he had jumped off the bed and stood over Priest. 'Listen, mate, just what is it you're trying to pull? First I'm put in this shit-hole for a couple of days pending some fuckin' inquiry, then the black bastards forget I'm here for three weeks, and now some half-arsed pom strides in cool as you like and invites me to go and get shot.' He slammed his right fist into his left palm, and the noise brought the guard hurrying back to the grill. Flemming turned towards the bed. 'I'll wait here, thanks all the same, you can find yourself another patsy.'

Priest waited for the guard to move away, then he said 'You disappoint me, Flemming. I came here expecting to meet some- one who could at least tot up the score for himself. But you? Not a chance. You're too wrapped up in self-pity. What do you think about when you're lying here and the sun's going down, or at least you think it is but you can't actually check because you haven't seen it for twenty-three days? Think about home, do you? The Swan river? Long way away, that is.' He paused to let the words sink in. 'Of course, if you want to look over your shoulder for the rest of your life, that's your business.

87

But there is a future, you know. What I'm saying is that I can help you start living it now. On the other hand, without certain . . . interest . . . in your case at a high level, these black bastards as you call them could easily forget about you indefinitely.'

Flemming sat heavily on the bed. 'Why don't you say what you mean, pom? If I don't play footsy, the "high-level interest" will make sure I stay down here with the mushrooms till bananas grow straight.'

Priest shrugged. 'I didn't say that. Naturally your high commission will be making all the right noises on your behalf. However . . .' He snapped the lock on the case and put it back on the floor. 'Then there's the reward, of course.'

Flemming looked up. 'What reward?'

'Four million shillings is the going rate for the gentleman we have in mind.'

The Australian did a quick mental calculation. 'A ten-way split and payment in funny money. Who's going to get rich on that?'

'Who mentioned a ten-way split?' Priest said lightly. 'Four at the most, assuming we all survive. And payment in dollars. Let me save you the trouble—$150,000.' His voice hardened. 'And now we're getting to know each other, you'd better start using my name—and it isn't half-arsed pom.'

Priest came back to the present and looked down at his bed which was covered in items of clothing.

His message to McLoughlin had included measurements and instructions to buy some equipment that would make him look like a tourist on safari. The younger man had used his imagination, and among the drab-green bush shirts and finely woven safari jackets was a huge, wide-brimmed hat circled by a band of real leopard skin. An attached note said: 'Hope some of the stuff fits—I'm told it's all the go. McLoughlin.' Priest tried the hat on with a wry smile; he'd look at the stuff in the morning and arrange for the tailor to come and outfit the whole trip. He was on the point of leaving when the phone rang.

'105. Priest here.'

It was McLoughlin. 'Oh, I'm glad I caught you, sir. I've been on to Pierre and he says that the Hartmanns were sent an invitation and phoned to say they'd be there.'

88

Priest frowned. 'What about Gould?'

He could almost hear McLoughlin shrug. 'We don't know, sir. He's not a very socially minded person. However, he's known the Steins on and off for years and there's no reason why he shouldn't show.'

Priest said, 'Right, I'll leave now, I have someone to pick up on the way. Oh, and Mac—thanks for the hat. Just the thing for a fancy dress ball.' He dropped the receiver onto the other man's chuckle. Picking up his jacket, he left the room and walked across the lawn towards the front of the hotel. It was a perfect night, cool and fresh, and groups of early diners were already moving into the hotel. Outside, on the Delamere terrace, young couples held hands across the heavy, rough-wood tables, part-shaded from the outside world by bougainvillea, banked like a distant audience under the soft lights. His car was waiting right there by the kerbside, and Priest was impressed by the way McLoughlin's efficient touch kept making itself felt. 'Keep it up,' he thought, 'and you too could end up literally anywhere.' His driver scrambled out as he approached.

'Jambo sana, bwana.'

'Jambo,' said Priest, and fished in his pocket. His hand came up with two twenty shilling notes, and he waved them in front of the man's face. 'Driver, you've been working too hard; I want you to go into town and enjoy yourself. Have a good time, okay, and be back here by eight in the morning in case I need you.'

The man said, 'Bwana, I have been told to stay with you all the time by Bwana McLoffin,' but his eyes watched the money.

Priest tucked the notes into the African's top pocket and snapped his fingers. 'Well, now I'm saying go and have a night in town. Where are the keys?'

'In the car, bwana,' but Priest was already in the driver's seat with the motor turning.

He looked up at the man, and decided to repeat the eight o'clock in the morning bit just in case. 'Sikiliza-rudi hapa kesho, saa mbili subui.' The rusty wheels of his memory had actually turned out an efficient sentence.

The driver's eyes widened slightly and he nodded vigorously. 'Ndio, bwana,' he said, and as the car pulled away, 'Asante sana.'

Priest turned off the Lower Kabete road and within three hundred yards saw the name 'Abbott' in white letters on a small post planted by the roadside. He turned into the drive and followed its foliage-covered path until the car passed briefly into the open before sliding under a large car port adjacent to the front of the house. Katie came out immediately, dressed in a long white gown, and Priest felt like a schoolboy on his first date as he got out of the car to greet her. A servant closed the heavy wooden door silently behind her, and they kissed. Above their heads, an old iron lantern glowed yellow amidst a cloud of moths and dudus. Priest steered her round to the far side of the car.

'Do you know why moths always fly in circles round a light?' Katie shook her head.

'Well, I'll tell you,' he said. 'In a minute.' Stooping, he moved a part of her dress away from the car door, and closed it. She watched as he walked round the front of the bonnet, the headlights casting his shadow grotesquely on the surrounding shrubbery; then he was sitting beside her, one arm round her shoulders.

'Well?' she demanded. 'Why do moths fly in circles round light bulbs?'

He turned to face her. 'Ah! Well, you see, it's actually because the muscles that control the wing nearest the bulb'—he pulled her towards him with his left arm to emphasize the point—'get slightly paralysed by the light. Thus the circles.' He kissed her lightly on the mouth and felt her breath fan his face. 'And the poor old moth just goes on like that until he can escape into total darkness. You see what I mean, don't you?'

She bit him softly on the ear. 'Yes, Harry, I see what you mean. But who's who in this little story?'

They sat like that for several seconds, and Priest slipped his hand into her dress and felt the warmth of her breast fill his palm. Her nipple stiffened against his skin.

'Harry?' she said after a while. 'You do want to go to this party, don't you?'

He let go of her then, and released the handbrake. 'The short answer to that is "no",' he said, 'but unfortunately it's not altogether a social occasion.'

Gould surveyed the crowded scene with mistrust. 'What in hell,' he asked himself again, 'am I doing here?' The ranch-style house was packed with people who spilled over on to the patio, the lawns and the barbecue area where an African was cooking

90

pepper steaks and kebabs. Under a fine net, fringed with minute lead weights, lay an impressive pile of food yet to be cooked, while along the walls of the parquet-floored living room long, cloth-covered tables stood up bravely under the weight of beef, suckling pig, eland, rows of avocados, salads and, specially brought from the islands, wafer-thin fingers of fried breadfruit. A separate table bore fruit, ranging from small bowls of cold, grey Seychellois coco-de-mer (to be covered in cream whipped with shredded coconut and a thick chocolate sauce) to tree tomatoes, portions of yellow jackfruit and chilled mountain paw-paw from the slopes of Kilimanjaro. Eddie Stein, hotelier by vocation, looked at his guests and saw Gould standing by himself gazing out into the darkness. 'Oy vey, but he's recovered well,' Stein thought. Six months ago he had made a visit to the house with George and Stella Hartmann, like tonight, but not a party, just to sit around the pool one evening and drink a few sundowners. It was the first time Stein had seen him for four years, and he'd never have believed it was the same man. The scar was still an angry red then and you couldn't help looking at it. Quite a thin line, Stein had thought, the line between life and the other thing that he didn't care to think about too often. Yes, six months ago you could count every rib that the man had, and his eyes were yellow with dark shadows ringing them in. But now, well, you had to marvel, he looked like a good insurance risk, even.

'Sam, hey Sam, what are you doing all on your own, hey?' Stein looked up at Gould. There were eight inches between them.

'Eddie, I'm sorry, it's a tremendous party, really it is. But you know me, I'm more at home in the bundu.'

'Have you talked to Ken Daley?' Stein demanded. 'He's here somewhere, and there's no one knows more about apes than he does. Did you read his book? Well, did you? I tell you, Sam—' He broke off, aware that he'd lost the big man's attention. 'Sam, hey Sam! What am I going to do with you? Where's George gone? Where's Stella?'

But Gould's eyes had glimpsed a face across the room. Something stirred in his mind, a picture, a memory. He struggled to concentrate while the chatter ebbed and flowed around him. Now she had moved into the light, smiling, laughing—she seemed to know everybody.

91

Where had he seen her? Or was it just a feeling? Rwanda? Burundi? The Congo? They were all fifteen years ago, buried, and the better for it. He looked down and saw Eddie watching him intently.

'You all right, Sam? Why don't you come outside and have some air? I know it's not the cup of tea for everyone in here.'

Gould stopped him. 'Eddie, who's that woman? The one in white?'

Stein stood on tiptoe, but he couldn't see a thing, so he stepped up on to the seat of an ornamental camel saddle, putting his hand on Gould's shoulder for support. 'You want an introduction, Sam—I'll fix it for you right now. That's my favourite lady in the town, and now she's been a widow for too long. Everybody loves her, nobody gets her. That's Katie. Katie Abbott. You stay here,' and without waiting for a reply he launched himself enthusiastically into the crowd.

Priest watched as Eddie Stein took Katie by the elbow and steered her through the packed room towards Gould. Picking up their refilled glasses he followed along behind, and then they were lost to sight behind a group of Italians. At last he emerged into the small clearing where they stood. The first thing he noticed was that after being introduced, Gould had forgotten to let go of her hand. They stood there looking at each other and it was several moments before Priest managed to make his presence felt.

'Harry!' said Katie. 'This is Mr Gould. Eddie just introduced us.' She turned from one man to the other. 'Mr Gould, Harry Priest.'

Gould released Katie's hand and turned to Priest. 'Please, people all call me Sam. Formality's not our strong point out here.'

'So it's that obvious that I'm not a local,' Priest thought. Somehow, the other man's casual assumption hurt his pride. They shook hands, and Priest seized his opportunity. 'I'm extremely fortunate to have met you here—you're actually one of the men that I came out to see.'

Gould raised an eyebrow quizzically. 'You from the parks syndicate?'

Priest shook his head. 'Not exactly.' He glanced round the

92

room. 'Look, are you against discussing business at social functions? Or could we find somewhere to talk?'

But he had already lost Gould's attention. A dark-haired man with his back to them was telling a nearby group about a hunting incident. Judging by the practised way the story was going it wasn't the first time he'd told it. Priest found himself listening.

'. . . so Buckley should have seen them, he crossed their tracks twice on the way in. Of course, he could never have known what was going to happen, I'm not saying that, but when you sit down and think about it . . .'

Priest realized that Gould had left his side and was standing just behind the talking man. Suddenly the man became aware that he had lost his audience and turned to find the reason. Gould took him by the arm in a friendly fashion; only Priest and Katie could see the strong, square tipped fingers clamped like steel spikes into the man's flesh.

Gould's voice was gentle, reasonable, as if he were talking to a child. 'Mr Corelli, I don't like to hear you talking about Karel Buckley that way. What you're saying is untrue. We all sympathize with you here, but it wasn't Buckley's fault, it was your own. What you have to do is face up to it. No one's blaming you. Just don't talk about Karel like that. You know what he'd do if he was here to defend himself, don't you?'

The man nodded and seemed to be on the point of saying something, then thought better of it. When the grip on his arm relaxed, he made quickly for the doors to the garden, massaging his bicep with his left hand.

Gould turned back to Priest. 'I'm sorry about that.'

Katie looked up at him. 'What was it all about?'

Gould shrugged and made a grimace of distaste. 'Well, briefly, that man Corelli runs a safari outfit. He arranged a safari for his brother, first time they'd met for fourteen years. His brother came from the Argentine. They were stalking elephant and got surprised by a buffalo. This chap—' he gestured towards the door '—got off two shots and dropped the beast at the last moment. They had to pull him out from under, shows you how close it was. When they got round to looking for his brother, they found him shot through the heart. Ricochet off the top of the horns. A chance in a million. Corelli's never forgiven himself.'

'And Buckley?' Priest urged. 'Where does he come into this?'

93

Gould sipped his drink. 'He doesn't. I've spoken to the Corelli watu and Karel was back with the wagon. But Corelli's taken to the bottle, and the story changes.'

'Where's Buckley now?' Katie asked.

Gould looked around him. 'Slung out,' he said. 'Found an African stealing from his house, so he strung him up by the feet. Meant to cut him down I suppose, but never got round to it. Some workmen found him the next day.' He finished his drink. 'You were saying? Before all this, I mean.'

'Yes,' said Priest, dragging his mind back to the matter in hand. 'Could we talk?'

The other man gestured with his arms. 'We are.'

'No,' Priest said. 'It'll have to be alone.'

Gould looked at Katie.

'Oh, I'll be all right,' she said. 'I'll pester Eddie.'

At the mention of his name the little man broke off the discussion he was having with another group of people and swung round. 'Who said Eddie?' he demanded.

Katie laughed. 'I was only saying that if Harry and Sam are going to discuss business, I'm going to need someone to protect me from the predators among your guests. They keep eyeing me up over the brims of their whisky glasses.'

Stein held out his arm. 'You know, it's about time that I had the good luck at one of my own parties. The first thing I do now is turn down the lights and arrange the slow music. Hey, I want to thank you gentlemen for having business to discuss.' He moved away, taking Katie with him.

The two men watched her retreating figure, and then Priest said 'Why don't we go outside? It's getting very hot in here.'

On the other side of the lawn there was an Italian cypress and they sat on a seat beneath it. From there, the house and the party seemed a stage upon which people were enacting the ritual of enjoyment. Gould sipped on a glass of passion-fruit juice, his face thoughtful.

'So,' he said at length. 'What's it all about?'

Priest was impressed by the power of the man. A few months ago he had been half-dead with a spear in his guts and now he looked as if nothing had happened. Suddenly, he was a little worried. Gould had tremendous self-assurance, the ability to cope when all the options were running out. And the effect he'd had on Katie made her seem like a schoolgirl staring at the PT instructor. The story he had prepared to enlist Gould's help now seemed inadequate. Unlike Flemming, the man had been born here, he was at home, and once again Priest would have to rely on his experience of people to try to feel the best way of approaching him.

'Well,' he started. 'I hope you're not in a great hurry. You see, it's quite a long story.'

It was after one when Katie saw the two men coming back into the light that ringed the house. They stopped on the verandah and exchanged a few last words before Gould turned and moved away. Briefly, his eyes caught hers over the heads of the late leavers, then he was gone, and Priest was standing beside her.

'Harry, you've been ages,' she said. 'I might just as well have come alone.'

He squeezed her hand. 'I'm sure you had a thoroughly entertaining time fighting off the hunting and flying fraternity,' he said. 'Anyway, I hate to say it, but I've been looking forward to the end of the evening since I arrived.'

'Harry! You mustn't say that.' She looked up at him questioningly. 'Tell me why?'

He looked down at her face, blue eyes, lips slightly parted. 'Patience,' he said. 'Harry Priest will reveal all in the car.'

She burst out laughing then, and took his arm. 'He'd better not! I have a perfectly good bed at home for that sort of thing!' She pulled him towards the far end of the room. 'Come on! Let's go and say thank you to Eddie.'

Driving home she said: 'Harry, you knew Sam Gould was going to be there didn't you?' He didn't reply, so she asked: 'What did you talk about with him out there on the lawn for two hours?'

'Things,' said Priest. 'A little business. Nothing important. Why?' He chuckled suddenly. 'You know, I think you've taken to him!'

She didn't answer for a moment, then: 'If I have, it's not what you think. I just feel that I've met him before, that's all. But I can't think where.'

Priest yawned and stretched. 'Probably déjà vu,' he said. 'You know, you see something a few seconds before you're actually confronted with it, and because of a short-circuit in the old think-box the memory seems to come from years back. Happens to me all the time.'

Katie leaned against him. 'Maybe you're right. But I felt that he felt the same way. We were almost . . . telepathic.'

Priest put his arm round her shoulder. It was best that she didn't think too deeply about a man that she might never see again. Although if anyone had an instinct for survival, it was Gould.

'Just tell me the truth,' he'd said, soon after Priest began to speak. 'Who you are, what you do, what you're really after. I'll know as soon as you start to leave bits out.'

He listened to Priest's well-rehearsed voice without interruption for twenty minutes. Then: 'Why do you assume that I want Omuria out?'

Priest kept surprise out of his voice. 'Your validity as a man seems to depend upon Africa. Uganda's where you were born, where you live now. Omuria's ruining your patch. It stands to reason.'

Gould was unimpressed. 'You've done this sort of thing before, Priest, it's all a matter of finding the right words for you. Nothing's that easy.' He put his glass down on the ground and leant forward. 'Should I care if some black with more nguvu than the rest starts thinning the population? Whoever you put in, it'll always be the same. I'm tolerated because I bribe the right people and I don't stand on the wrong toes. Whatever you do, you won't put the clock back ten years.'

Priest temporized. 'That may be true. But under Kalaba at least there was a show of democracy.'

Gould laughed rudely. 'The British floor me every time, Priest. Kalaba was fine until the fifty per cent nationalization bill. Then his name was trodden underfoot and Whitehall couldn't wait to see the skids put under him. "Who better than Omuria?" they said. Pro-British, no talk of nationalization, good ties with the near-East—after the coup they couldn't send roses quickly enough. And what happened? Instead of fifty per cent, he took the lot. Kwisha.'

Priest sighed. 'It's easy to be wise after the event, especially in politics. What you've got to remember is that whoever's in power there, whatever they do, however much mud is flung, there's not a developed country that doesn't go on rushing to invest in Africa. Britain, Japan, the US, China—there they are fighting to give, lend or sell. And you know the reasons.' There was silence and then Priest added, 'If this ever came off, you could be very well placed up there for some considerable time. Even peace of mind must be worth something.'

Gould stood up. 'While you go on thinking I equate everything to shillings and cents you'll never understand me. I'm not interested in money.'

'You used to be,' Priest told him, and regretted it immediately.

The two men eyed each other, then Gould said quietly, 'That was fifteen years ago, as you obviously know. Things change.' He sat down again, and the bench creaked under his weight. 'But you're right about one thing I suppose—getting rid of Omuria would be a move forward.'

Priest turned left onto the lower Kabete road.

'We're nearly there,' he said. 'Just a couple more minutes and we'll be snug in that bed you were talking about earlier on. Although I'm so tired that maybe . . .' He left the words unfinished, and the Rover swept on along the narrow road.

Over the years Priest had come to have a fair idea of what he did and didn't like about a woman's body. As a rule he preferred brunettes, the dark bushy triangle against the white of their skin excited him, and the more pronounced the mound on which that hair grew, the more ill-concealed the ultimate goal, the better he liked it. And he liked a woman with breasts, not like half the girls back home, with big arses and built like a boy from the waist up.

Slowly he sat on the edge of Katie's bed and leant forward to undo his shoe laces. He was very tired, and she was making, of all things, two mugs of cocoa, because he had said that milk at night helped him to sleep well. Consciously, he remembered the last time that he had made love, to a French girl that he'd found working in Oxford Street on a cosmetics counter. She had smelt divine, before, during and after, but he had somehow failed to pursue the matter. Little things about her annoyed him, like the way she took a comb and mirror to bed with her. Priest had never married. He had, at one stage, thought he might, but by then the demands of the job and his own ingrowing selfishness made the proposition untenable. He was the first to admit that as the years rolled by he was prepared to give less and less of himself; pretty soon the only woman eligible for the position of Mrs Priest would have to be a brainless idiot with her own views on nothing more controversial than the weather.

He took his shoes off and started to undo his shirt. The room was large, with an adjoining bathroom, and finished in unobtrusive French blues and greys. Priest heard a door close downstairs, and felt his stomach tighten at the thought of a beautiful woman walking up the stairs towards him carrying two mugs of cocoa. Suddenly, he felt nervous, like a younger man hoping to Christ he hadn't really been asked up to see the etchings. Nor was it a bad feeling: far too often in the past sex had been a fait accompli before it started, a mutual agreement between big boys and girls to blow the tubes through while they still worked.

Katie came in, silent in bare feet, and pushed the door to with her bottom. Priest sat on the edge of the bed and watched her as she placed the two mugs of cocoa on the bedside table. Then she came and stood in front of him, her long dress dragging on the floor without the extra height of her shoes. She turned and presented him with her back.

'Unzip me, Harry?'

Priest reached up and drew the zipper slowly down to the cleft between her buttocks. She watched his face in the dressing table mirror as he registered that she wore nothing underneath, and then turned to face him, letting the evening gown drop to the floor. Then she leaned forward and pulled his face in to her stomach.

For a brief moment Priest registered her breasts and the soft swell of her abdomen, the fact that she was everything he liked in a woman, then he buried his face in the warm fur between her legs while she leant over him and pulled his shirt off first one arm, then the other. She felt his tongue probing and hard, and tried to make him stand to take his trousers off, but he wouldn't, and she could feel her legs beginning to grow weak, and she closed her eyes and tried to say something coherent but nothing came out. Then he did stand, and picked her up with one arm round her shoulders and one thrust between her thighs and she felt herself dropped lightly in the middle of the bed. She reached forward and up and grasped him, tried to pull him

98

down, but he crouched over her and kissed her nipples, then her
lips, then stroked himself tantalizingly through her swollen flesh
till she thought she could hold out no longer.

'Please, Harry, stop, darling, wait,' the words came tumbling
out, indecipherable after months of disuse. Five minutes ago
she had been a rational woman carrying two mugs of cocoa, and
now she was incapable of doing anything except feeling, breathing, drowning in a broken dam of sensation.

Priest slid his knees back and let himself sink into her body.
She exhaled in a long shuddering sigh and immediately he felt
her loins pushing up towards him faster and faster, while her
head turned from side to side on the blue candlewick bedspread.
When she cried out, Priest could bear it no longer. Forcing his
hands under her backside he slid deeper and deeper into her flesh
while her hands urged him on, forcing him to greater heights,
gently squeezing his testicles while her inner muscles gripped him
on each stroke and her breath came brokenly in his ear. Priest
felt himself pass the point beyond which there would be no
turning back. Deep in his loins a mechanism had triggered. Now
what would follow was inevitable. He heard himself cry out
like a man in agony, 'Now! Katie, now,' and then, with the
final spasms of their bodies he felt the hardness of her pelvis
locked against him, and it was over.

Slowly he relaxed, and tried to take some of his weight off
her, but she pulled him back and nuzzled against him. When he
tried to speak, she laid a finger over his lips. For ten minutes
they lay like the dead, and then she said, 'If you like, we could
shower together, and drink the cocoa?' and her voice was warm,
and filled with the timbre of contentment.

Priest chuckled, and then suddenly he found himself laughing,
and she laughed too.

'I'm happy,' he said. 'Really. And it's all due to you.'

He lifted himself off her, and felt, as always, annoyance that
the aftermath to sex was so messy. As if reading his mind, she
said 'I don't like it when you go, either.' With a new found
intimacy he cupped her genitals in his hand, and felt the blood
still pulsing there. She looked between his legs and said 'He's
sleeping.' Priest got to his feet and walked into the bathroom.
'So would you be,' he said. 'Which is the light?' After a shower
and a mug of cold cocoa they went back to bed, and both agreed

that it would be to sleep. But the unseen light of dawn was already washing the outside of the curtains with early blues before Priest and Katie drifted into oblivion.

The next morning McLoughlin was ushered into a well-appointed office overlooking the international conference centre. 'Please sit down, sir,' the African receptionist told him. 'The minister won't be a moment.'

McLoughlin walked over to the panoramic windows and looked out over Nairobi's skyline. It was always changing, buildings going up everywhere, slowly but surely dragging the city's appearance into the twentieth century. The conference centre was dominated by a central tower, round in design like the Hilton, but taller and slimmer. It had been created floor by floor using wooden scaffolding, and most agreed it was the city's most impressive building.

A door swung open on the far side of the room, and a small, rotund man strode in, energetically mopping his brow with a large white handkerchief.

'Mr McLoughlin!' A huge smile whitened his face. 'Sit down, my dear chap! A small something before lunch?' He glanced at his watch. 'Whisky, perhaps?'

McLoughin sat in an easy chair, with the window behind him. To his right a grotesque carving twisted its way from floor to ceiling in a tortured amalgam of wooden limbs.

'Nothing for me thanks, minister.' He reached out to touch the carving. 'Impressive. You didn't have that the last time I was here.'

James Madega made a face. 'That! If you like it, you can have it. One of my wives acquired it on the coast. I told her, women have been divorced for less!' He laughed uproariously. 'Still, still, she meant well.' He mixed himself a generous horse's neck and sat down behind his desk. 'I shouldn't drink at all, you know. My gods forbid it, my doctors advise against it, but then, there's a little of the rebel in all of us.' He swallowed gratefully, and then put the glass down. 'Don't know which does the most harm, the brandy or the stuff I mix it with. Now: what brings you to the ministry?'

'Well,' McLoughlin started. 'There are two matters that I'd hoped to discuss today. They're rather more ... personal ... than official, if you see what I mean. Not the sort of thing we could have handled through channels.' He paused delicately, and watched Madega reach for his drink. 'The fact is that we've been trying to acquire property near Kilifi for some time now to use as a rest centre for staff, and also to have a place where our newcomers can acclimatize. Plus the odd commissioner's party of course.' He smiled. 'Kilifi's nice, isn't it? Watersports. Fishing. Diving. It would fit the bill perfectly. Then—by pure chance— we heard that you'd been trying to sell a place near the Mnarani Club and that you'd had ... difficulties ... with negotiations.'

The minister said nothing, but got up and poured himself another drink. McLoughlin pressed on. 'The property would be ideal for us at the price we believe you're asking. Naturally, we could arrange for payment to be made in the currency of your choice.'

The African sat down thoughtfully. 'Does it not occur to you, McLoughlin, that if this information has come to your ears it has probably reached others?'

McLoughlin cut in deftly. 'With respect, Minister, we spend a lot of time with our ears to the ground. It's extremely doubtful that anyone else knows of this matter. For our part, of course, the business could be arranged through an independent third party in the usual way.'

Madega finished his second drink and sat forward. 'I would certainly like to hear your proposition in more detail.' He frowned. 'Between you and I, well, it's extremely easy to have one's actions misinterpreted these days. Caution is paramount.' The frown turned back into a huge smile. 'I'm sure we can do business. Now,' he looked across at the Englishman shrewdly, 'there was another item, was there not?'

It was McLoughlin's turn to sit forward. 'Minister we need your assistance with a small problem,' he said earnestly. 'There's a prisoner at Fort Hall who we feel has been mistakenly accused. An Australian.'

Madega sat back in his chair and clasped his hands over his stomach. 'Ah!' he said. 'An Australian? Tell me about it.'

Two Chinese looked out at the Indian Ocean from the balcony of a white-painted beach-house. It was high tide, and a surf was pounding, down on the white sand beyond the coconut

101

grove. Along the water line, hundreds of pink crabs played chicken with the oncoming waves, and an evening breeze gusted damply across the straits from Zanzibar. They sat in easy chairs, clad only in swimming costumes, and tell-tale patches of burned red were beginning to show on the younger man's hairless skin. The elder man was tall and well built, with a hard, muscled body, and a weather-beaten skin. His subordinate was short and stocky, but already beginning to put on too much weight. He had just recited a verse in Mandarin, and sat with his hands clasped under his paunch like Buddha looking out over the waves. There was silence, then Tai-Ling snorted. 'What on earth brought that on?' Seng smiled. 'I wish I knew. It's called "Egrets". The sea, perhaps. Or the wind. It reminds me of home.'

Tai looked out to sea. There could be nothing in the world that reminded him less of home. Where he had grown to manhood the wind was a bitter lash that scarred the soul, and the nearest ocean was fifteen hundred miles to the south.

'Seng, you come from Foochow, which faces east onto a sea as big as this. When you recite, it's from Tu-Mu, who never went north of the Yangtse, and spent much of his time whoring in the brothels of Yang-chou. We talk in Mandarin, though the dialect of your family is Cantonese and of mine ... well, you wouldn't even recognize the name of my province. Our homes are as far from each other as London from Cairo, yours a sea-port, and mine a village beyond the mountains of Nan Shan. You know something of boats and lychees, I have spent half my life on horseback, and remember the almond blossom like a snow-fall on the steppes in spring. Yet in spite of all this, we are both Chinese.' He stopped, surprised at himself, groping for the point he had been trying to make. Seng was looking at him, surprised too.

'Probably thinks that no one else ever reads poetry,' Tai thought. Aloud he said 'Forgive me, my nationalism is showing. But still, that's part of the reason we're here.'

Seng leaned forward in his chair, until it overbalanced and tipped him on to his feet. 'Well, don't mind me. I'm going home to get the salt off. I'll see you later.'

Tai looked up. 'There is something you ought to know now that you're here permanently. Kalaba is arriving in Dar-es-

Salaam tonight. He's here on a pretext, because if there is going to be any trouble from the north, now is the time for it.'

Seng stopped by the door. 'Will Omuria really invade?'

Tai nodded. 'I think so. On paper he should do well, and now he has no real alternative; Uganda's internal state calls for a huge diversion away from his own inadequacies. For months he's blamed Kalaba for the chaos—now he has a chance to act. He believes in our disinterest, so let him come.' He rose to his feet in one lithe movement, and turned to face Seng. 'But we have to watch Kalaba. If he were to reach the right people up there, he could reinstate himself. And that's exactly what he'll try to do when he hears Omuria's crossed the border.' He smiled. 'In any case, you'll be at the conference in the palace tomorrow. In this part of the world we can often achieve a lot by doing very little.'

Seng grimaced. 'That much I have noticed. "In the country of the blind the one-eyed beggar may be king." ' He walked out through the door, calling over his shoulder, 'I'll be back at eight for the game.'

On the balcony, Tai looked forward to an evening of mah jong. Perhaps the ritual building of the great wall would do something to fill the emptiness he was beginning to feel, and not for the first time he wished the scented air would suddenly turn cold and clean. If he went on feeling as he did this evening it would affect his decisions and thus his performance. He must apply for a transfer, leave this place with its conniving, greedy, disloyal politicians, and stage a personal retreat. But first, the business of Uganda.

He stood with the breeze blowing lightly on his strong body and looked up the coast, but his mind was in the small town where he had grown up. Strange that there, too, trouble had always come from the north, over the plains and deserts whose extremes of climate bred the nomads of old and all the warring hordes of Mongolia. Tai walked into the house, wishing he were home. Paradise had palled.

22.00, Thursday, 14 March

William Kalaba sat in the front seat of a Land Rover as it sped through the night towards Dar-es-Salaam. The name of the city made him want to laugh: in straight translation it meant the 'Haven of Peace', but the Arab tongue was riddled with hidden meanings, and to the Muslim mind it could mean much more. A place, perhaps, where one could find inner tranquility, a peace of the spirit. Kalaba considered the whole misnomer to be in very poor taste. Of all the towns in Africa, Dar-es-Salaam was the one guaranteed not to supply peace of mind. At least Uganda's problems were basically tribal : down here the whole place was being invaded and no one seemed to realize it was happening.

William Kalaba was a product of the English system, tailor-made to take over when his country gained its independence. Unfortunately, the British had underestimated this quiet African, failing to see in him a real talent for government and a grim determination to unify Uganda and get the people working for a common cause. In this he faced a tremendous ethnic problem; Uganda was a small country, but full of minority groups who owed allegiance to no one but themselves. Thirty miles north of the lake were tribesmen who thought that Kampala was a type of gazelle. A Sudanese diplomat had once said to him : 'At least you got rid of the British after they developed the country. Here we haven't even got a road from Juba to Khartoum fit for a camel.' It was true that the British had invested money where there was profit to be made; Entebbe, the old administrative centre, was beautiful, and the tea and coffee country a joy to visit. But that represented a small percentage of the country's area, and the Africans who lived in those parts had been exposed to long contact with the colonials and their thinking did not necessarily represent that of the majority.

Kalaba was well aware that to the average Briton, particularly the colonials themselves, the independence of any black African state was a source of unending amusement; he had to admit that African politics were such an uncertain game that the players often faced and usually succumbed to the great temptation of salting away funds against a rainy day. And if the money was a backhander from an interested company, eager to enhance the attraction of its tender—well, did it harm the country? Kalaba knew that it did. Firstly, weak ministers would recommend on the size of the bribe and not the quality of the goods. Secondly, yet another concern filed in its computerized memory system the

104

fact that to do business in Africa all you had to do was offer more to the men signing the contract than the competition.

Kalaba had gone on a crusade to stop this, and quickly found that the one thing that would unify ministers of different tribes was the threat of a clean-up; they would unify against the man doing the cleaning. Kalaba found himself baulked, so he set about seeking a compromise. Gradually, by a series of amendments, he cut down the ways in which members of his government could be 'got at', and for a time things improved. The British started to treat him with a little genuine respect, and he had a man he could trust as his number two : Colonel Omuria. The Colonel, like Kalaba, came from the north of Uganda, though he had been through the British system at Sandhurst. The two men both came from minority tribes, Kalaba the Acholis, and Omuria a village on West Nile that had inter-bred with Arab traders from the north. Omuria, Kalaba had thought, was a good man to have in alliance, because he commanded complete loyalty from the army. And perhaps because of his Arab blood he avoided the stigma of tribalism.

The time had come when Kalaba felt himself strong enough to flex a few political muscles; one of those muscles was the implementation of a bill to nationalize all foreign owned interests on the basis of a 51% holding for the Ugandan government, and the squeal from the British had been heard all round Africa. Months later, during the Commonwealth Prime Ministers Conference in Singapore, a sealed communiqué had been handed to him just before he entered the conference chambers on the second day of the talks. Its contents were short and to the point : 'As you are no longer the leader and representative of the Ugandan people, will you kindly make your apologies and excuse yourself from the proceedings? The temporary Military Government under Colonel Omuria will convey its opinions upon the major issues by special envoy later today.' Kalaba was speechless. He turned to his ADC, and saw immediately from the man's face that he had known this was going to happen. Without wasting any time he sought out one of the aides to the British Prime Minister, and pressed for an immediate interview. The man had been polite, evasive. 'Perhaps this evening,' he had been told. 'Today's going to be very full.' Kalaba, not being blind, saw the pattern. As the news spread, he rapidly became

105

a source of embarrassment to everyone. Only with his friends from Tanzania did he get any joy, and a week later he was in Dar-es-Salaam, licking his wounds and wondering how best to get back into Uganda.

The Land Rover jolted off the road onto a rutted diversion. A snatch of mindless Swahili music touched the vehicle briefly as it passed a small African bar, recessed into the bush. The music here was terrible. And in Kenya too, for that matter. Up north, real musicians came in from the Congo, men with rhythm in their fingers and toes, men who'd learned to play at watotos in the shambas of their fathers. Kalaba's thoughts strayed to Entebbe : dew on the early morning grasses, and a view from his window over the blue waters of Africa's largest lake. But would he ever see the place again? Over the past few months the training had gone well, and morale was good among his officers. Intelligence from Uganda showed that support for Omuria was fading, that the man was holding the people in check by force of arms alone. But in spite of everything, Kalaba felt himself shackled. True, he had Chinese weapons and co-operation, and they had been everything he could have hoped for. There was just something wrong, something ... He tossed the thoughts around his tired mind as the Rover bumped back onto the main road. They closed on the vehicles in front, and behind them the rest of the convoy did the same. Now this trip to Dar. Ostensibly to talk about his progress, discuss his aims, to take a rest from the camp in the bush. Or was it to get him to the coast, as far from the border as possible? There was no way the Chinese could lose by inviting a direct confrontation. Having gained a good foothold in Africa it was obvious that they would want to extend their influence. It seemed sad that after Uhuru, and all the backslapping that followed independence, a new breed of colonials should find it so easy to buy their way in. There was another thing, too : leaving Eyasi suddenly meant he now had no idea what the British intended. Approaching them had been a bitter pill; he could only hope that the end would perhaps justify the means. Besides, if it came down to a straight choice, he would rather see British money and influence in Uganda than Chinese. At least when dealing with the British it was possible to draw on personal experience. But the Chinese ... ! Kalaba recalled an expression he'd read in an

106

American pin-up magazine. Tanzania was, without a doubt, a whole new Chinese ball game.

Outside Dodoma the procession came to a dusty halt, and re-fuelled from the four and a half gallon jerries the Rovers carried as standard. The men chatted and urinated and smoked Ten Cents by the roadside. There was still a long way to go.

09.30, Friday, 15 March

In a cloudless sky the sun was working up energy for the midday spree. Priest sat on the Delamere terrace and read the leader of the *East African Express,* while a waiter refilled his cup with black coffee. A tall figure slid into the seat opposite.

'Morning,' said McLoughlin. Priest said nothing, but passed the paper across.

The headlines were big : 'OMURIA RE-AFFIRMS 4,000,000 SHILLINGS FOR KALABA.' And underneath; 'In a radio broadcast to the people today, Colonel Omuria re-affirmed his offer of 4,000,000 shillings reward for the safe delivery to Uganda of ex-President William Kalaba, believed to be hiding somewhere in Central Tanzania. Omuria accused Kalaba of plotting to overthrow his regime, and of sending spies to infiltrate the country and subvert the minds of loyal Ugandans. Reports have come in that reprisals may already have been taken against the northerly Acholi tribe, of which Kalaba was a member. The Colonel promises the ex-President a fair military trial, but insists that if found guilty he must confess his crimes on television, so the world may see him in his true colours. In the south-west of Uganda troops continue to mass along the border, and a senior Tanzanian official said today that steps are being taken to safe-guard the security of the country.'

There was much more, largely repetition. McLoughlin folded the paper and put it down.

'The reason I came over early, sir, was to tell you that Kalaba's not in his camp any more. He's moving, or has been moved, to the capital.'

Priest studied his coffee. 'How can you be so sure?'

'Oh, we're sure all right. It came up the line this morning from Dar. If they have the same set-up down there as we have there'll be Asians in key posts in every ministry. It's the only way to keep an effective ear to the ground.'

107

Priest looked up. 'I thought all the Asian jobs had been Africanized? You mean they still use them?'

McLoughlin shrugged. 'The Africans are very tribal as you know, they never really learn to trust each other. Funnily enough, they tend to use Asians where the job involves money; they're very good at accounting.'

'Can you find out where the hell he's got to?'

'We already know that, sir : the old East Africa Rifle Barracks on the Bagamoya Road.' He gave a wry grin, 'And seeing that we built them, I've got someone on the hunt for photos and plans. I very much doubt whether anyone's changed or extended them at all; they've been virtually disused for years.'

Priest glanced at his watch, a heavy gold International that he'd had since his twenty-first birthday. On its scarred case every dent told a different story. It was the only permanent thing in his life, and the nearest he'd ever come to owning a good luck charm. 'Have some breakfast,' he told McLoughlin. 'What time's Soon coming? Eleven wasn't it?'

'Yes, eleven. All right, I will,' said McLoughlin, and beckoned a waiter. When the paw-paw came, he jabbed holes in it with his fork and filled them up with fresh lime. Scatterings of castor sugar covered the pink flesh like an early snowfall.

'Well,' started McLoughlin tentatively, 'How's it all going so far?'

Priest clicked his tongue in mock censure. 'I wondered how long it would be before your curiosity got the better of you. But since you made such a good job of the Kilifi "Better times for tired diplomats" deal I'll tell you : so far so good. The show is almost on the road.'

McLoughlin waited for him to go on, but Priest was silent, watching a group of pretty university students on the other side of the street. 'It's just that we don't get much of . . . this sort of thing . . . out here. Well, you know what I mean.'

'You ought to be grateful for a quiet life,' said Priest. 'God knows, I never planned to spend life chasing round the world like a bloody idiot. It just crept up behind me when I wasn't looking and there I was—lumbered. Now I haven't got enough imagination left to do anything else.' He looked at McLoughlin, and saw himself twenty years ago, eager to be tested under fire, to find out the ultimate truth about himself. Abruptly he got to his feet. 'Come on,' he said. 'Let's have a swim before our inscrutable friend arrives.'

McLoughlin followed him, complaining : 'I'll have to spectate I'm afraid—no swimming trunks.'

Chapter Six

16.00, Tuesday, 19 March

Two white microbuses drove steadily towards Arusha from the direction of Athi river. The Tanzanian customs at Namanga had been a formality and there had been nothing remarkable about the occupants or their transport. Big blue letters on the vehicle's sliding doors announced that Tamarind Safaris were based in Nairobi. It was hot and the engine covers at the rear of both Volkswagens were open; in the far distance, to the left of the road, the foothills of Kilimanjaro swelled out of the plains, but anything more that there might have been to see was obscured by a haze that hung uncertainly between earth and sky.

To Gould, travelling in the first vehicle, this was the main road away from Uganda. Eight or nine hours in a good car and he could be in the middle of Karamoja, surrounded by the bush, with the flat top of Kadam looming over his shoulder. What would the boys be doing now? Panga and Bunduki, Kitenge and the others? Pissed out of their minds on pombe, in Chepsicunya or Hatari probably. Waiting, perhaps, for another bwana to come and build a camp on the banks of Greek river.

The last five days had been spent in a sprawling property on the western shores of Lake Naivasha, some sixty miles north of Nairobi. He and Priest had spent most of the first morning checking through equipment. Then, in the afternoon of the same day, a tall man called McLoughlin had arrived with the Chinese, and the Australian, Flemming. Priest had given them a pep talk and explained the various facilities that existed for contacting the outside world, and from then on he had spent much of his time flying with the Australian.

Gould glanced across at Charlie Soon, leaning forward slightly

110

as he coaxed the VW up a gradient. The Chinese face was impassive; events had moved too quickly for him to grasp the full implications of what had happened; though whichever way he looked at it, it amounted to blackmail. That he should be sitting in his club one day, and involved with this bunch of shenzis the next, was very confusing. But Priest had been persuasive. 'An extremely straightforward matter,' he'd said. 'We don't anticipate trouble and there shouldn't be any. Two weeks out of your life and a nice little something in Switzerland. What could be better?'

Charlie wasn't convinced, and said so.

'Do you really want to go and live in the UK?' Priest asked. 'Because you'll have to. You've kept your British passport by choice—how long will it be before they serve you with a quit notice? And how much money do you think you'll ease through exchange control with your record? All right, so you've paid out heavily for a little bit of peace and quiet, but you know as well as I do there are agents watching the agents these days. You can't trust anyone any more, especially in a country like this.'

Charlie kept quiet.

'Come on,' Priest encouraged. 'Think about it. There'll be no swimming, no safari rallies and your relatives at the Bamboo doing a roaring trade after you've gone. They've taken out citizenship. Did you know that? No? Well, they have.' His voice softened. 'You know, I think you could still be in business when they're paddling back to Hong Kong if you play your cards right.'

The VW bounced over a pothole in the tarmac, and Charlie looked around him. Scenery that he'd seen so many times before now took on a vaguely sinister significance. Throughout the talk with Priest he had felt the chilly current of certain underlying implications. Could it be that the British Government weren't even convinced of his eligibility for one of their passports? If, by some devious administrative manoeuvre, he lost this document, and got a quit notice from the Kenyans, he'd wind up being stateless, and that would mean a return to Malaya on hands and knees, the last thing he wanted.

Maybe all this wasn't such a bad thing after all. Life had been dull since they stole his ivory; now, a couple of weeks and he could be a wealthy man. Perhaps he'd get a yacht, bigger than

111

Nlella's, and park the bloody thing right there in the water near the fishery steps.

In the second vehicle Priest too looked back on the last five days. He was used to bizarre situations, but the four of them made an unusual group. Their first meal together had been salad with thin fillets of black bass caught that morning in the lake. They had eaten and then Priest had given them a preliminary briefing; the Chinese had promptly helped himself to more food and carried on eating. But at last the strained atmosphere of the first days had been replaced by a grudging recognition that they all had certain talents and were all necessary to the job in hand. Priest's proposition to Soon and Flemming had been simple; for Flemming an immediate release and for Soon an updated set of documents and the promise of a renewed business permit. Plus, of course, the reward. They believed that upon delivery of Kalaba to Uganda the good Colonel would hand over the much publicized four million shillings, and as long as they believed it, then all well and good. And Flemming had at least proved he could fly an airplane. Of the three, Gould was the only one who knew the real objectives. It was possible that he saw it as a chance to start afresh, by returning to places left behind. Whichever way you looked at it, the man was out of his element in the confines of a town. And then there was his guarded interest in Katie. 'How long have you known her?' he had asked. 'Does she speak French?'

Flemming, driving the second microbus, slid another stick of gum between his teeth. Even after five days of comparative freedom he still found himself sweating at the thought of the cell at Fort Hall. The first day when McLoughlin had driven him down the escarpment towards Naivasha, Flemming had been unable to take his eyes off the landscape. Africa was full of views, each one more spectacular than the next—in time you got used to them. But that morning had been different. Flemming swore he'd never be blasé about a simple thing like looking at the scenery ever again. It had occurred to him that perhaps everyone ought to be walled in from time to time to make them realize how great it was simply to be alive and free.

The next day he had flown, and though he had to admit it felt good to be at the controls again, he still bore resentment at the way he'd been recruited. It was only when he looked around

112

that he remembered the prison and the resentment faded away. Sure, he would do what he had to do, and wind up with some bread into the bargain. Not that it could ever compensate for the treasure he had so nearly had.

Flemming's Ray-ban glasses had hidden a slight tic that momentarily distorted his features whenever he thought about the last six months, and then a cold rage would seethe through him, making his stomach freeze and knot with tension as if he'd drunk a gutful of liquid nitrogen. But the only sign of his turmoil had been a whitening of the knuckles that held the column and a barely concealed acidity in the ensuing conversation.

After levelling out over Lake Nakuru they'd headed south. It was good country to fly, with sign posts all over the place, mountains, volcanoes, lakes—not like parts of Western Australia where one salt pan looked much like a thousand others. He'd glanced over at Priest. 'Which jail did you bust the Chink out of?'

Priest had said nothing, but Flemming had persisted. 'So, what can he do that's special? Nuclear physicist is he?' He had ticked other possibilities off on his fingers. 'Karate expert? Makes lanterns?'

Then Priest had interrupted him. 'Sometimes you don't have to do anything special to be special.'

Flemming unwrapped a stick of gum and put it in his mouth. 'Very cryptic. I'll work on it.'

Now the Australian changed his grip on the wheel and watched Priest out of the corner of his eyes. They were entering Arusha and the day's drive was almost over. At five o'clock the four men parked the vehicles outside the New Arusha Hotel. The street vendors were just putting away their wares for the night, wrapping carvings and bowls in pieces of newspaper, and bundling them into dilapidated handcarts. Flemming dusted himself off, and watched them idly. Just occasionally, among the real Masai spears made locally out of car springs, and the genuine Makonde carvings stained black with ebony dye, there was something worth buying; but it was better to get souvenirs in the villages or by a river where the tribes were watering their cattle. And even in the remoter areas of the country, the natives retained a shrewdness that was inborn and seemed to know how much a spear would fetch in Arusha. To Flemming's mind, the noble

113

Masai was a myth: he saw them as the biggest thieves and most compulsive scroungers this side of the black stump. The other three passed him, and he fell into step behind them. At the door the four men ran the usual gamut of urchins, offering over the odds for Kenya money, and walked into the hotel.

13.20, Wednesday, 20 March

Priest nearly missed the small murram track marked by two name boards: Butler and Kaufmann. A mile down the road a left fork was posted again: R. Butler. The house was set in an oasis of luxuriant vegetation and the man who came to meet them was flanked by an Alsatian and a baby zebra that came up to his waist. Priest got out of the car and approached him, but the dog growled, and it seemed to Priest that even the zebra bared its teeth.

The man laughed. 'Don't mind them! They'll get used to you!'

Priest stuck out his hand. 'Bob Butler? I hope you weren't expecting us later?'

'Not a bit of it. As a matter of fact I completely lose track of time up here. Get absorbed in the studio, you know.'

Priest introduced everyone and the five men climbed the steps on to a spacious wooden verandah. Rattan seats were spread around haphazardly, and it was easy to imagine that on a clear day it would feel pretty good just to sit there and gaze through the trees and bushes at the view.

'Right!' said their host. 'What about a drink before lunch?'

A houseboy took their orders, and they sat down around a table made from an enormous piece of sea-polished wood that was using three of its wave-worn arms to support a heavy slab of glass, shaped like an artist's pallet. Only Priest and Flemming had asked for liquor. Gould seemed happy, as always, with fruit juice, and the other two were sharing a pot of tea. Butler put his cup down and asked:

'Have you heard the weather forecast?'

Priest shook his head. 'No. But for us the worse it is the better, within reason.'

'I hope you mean that,' Butler answered. 'You may get more than you bargained for. There's a big storm coming in from the north-east. Probably the beginning of Masika.'

114

He was interrupted by a clatter of hooves, and the zebra entered the room, hooves slipping and sliding on the smooth floor. Gould looked at the animal. Its stripes were still brown rather than black, and there were lots of them, close together and well-delineated. It came up to him and pushed its nose down towards the fruit juice.

'Three weeks old,' said Butler.

Gould stroked the animal's soft velvet muzzle. 'You're a long way from home fellah. How did you come to be in this neck of the woods?'

Butler poured himself another cup of tea. 'Yes, I expect you'd have to go a fair step from here to find another Grevy's. Last week I was doing a bit of filming up near Marsabit in Kenya and one of the game guards had that young chap in tow. Apparently they were out on patrol, and he'd got isolated from the herd. When he saw the Rover, he started trotting along behind. So, they led him back to camp. I know the warden up there and suggested he might let me have him, you know, a good subject for a bit of film, but really I'm afraid that it was just a case of not wanting to leave him behind.'

The baby endorsed all this by urinating loudly on the wooden floor.

'Edward!' Butler called to his houseboy, 'Kuja!' An old African appeared in the room, took in the scene, and went off to fetch a bucket and cloth. 'Happens all the time,' said Butler. 'Have to pay old Edward fifty cents a throw. He's making a fortune.'

The men laughed and started to relax.

'You were saying that you make films, Bob?' said Priest. 'Wildlife I take it, animals and the like?'

'Yes, but with a strong scientific flavour I'm afraid. You may have seen them. The "Last Safari"? "River of Dust"? "Living Pendulum"?'

Priest shook his head and glanced round the room.

' 'Fraid not,' said Gould. 'Not many outlets for film where I come from.'

'I've seen that one,' Flemming interrupted. 'It was on in the Intercontinental Hotel a few months back. The "Living Pendulum" was just the job, all about migration incentives.'

Butler was pleased. He turned to Charlie, draining the last

115

tea from the pot. 'Are you interested in wild-life at all, Mr Soon?'

Charlie looked around the table before replying. 'I was once,' he said. 'Elephants.'

Priest nearly choked, but Butler took the comment at face value.

'If you've nothing to do this evening, I've got some good footage on elephants.' He looked over at Priest. 'That's if you've got the time.'

Another servant came into the room. 'Chakula tayari, bwana.'

'Food at last,' said Butler. 'You must be starved.'

'Too flamin' right!' thought Flemming, and led the way into the other room.

'Does he live up here alone?' Flemming asked Priest. It was three-thirty in the afternoon, and from time to time a gust of wind shook the house. The men were seated round the table and Priest was laying out papers and maps.

'Some of the time, yes. But he travels quite a bit, as you heard. He had some sort of tie up with the administration in the old days, and now he's a dabbler in all sorts of things. This place is more than just a traveller's rest you know.' He turned his attention to the paperwork. 'Right, now we go through the whole thing for the last time. It should go smoothly with just an average amount of luck, but that's a commodity you can never rely on. So we're going to swing the odds by precision planning, divided into four stages. Number one: contact. Two: penetration. Remember, Kalaba thinks he's on his way to recapture the reins of power, so he'll be pleased as punch to go with you. Three: escape from the immediate vicinity. And lastly, the drive to the strip, back through the city to add a little confusion if they're on to us. Remember, we're concerned only with Kalaba. He's just got a few of his officers with him, the rest are billeted miles away on the Morongoro road.'

'Hang about,' Flemming interrupted. 'I know that if things go right we'll be in the clear, and it's a beaut plan. But you've always said we might have to shoot our way out, right?'

Priest nodded.

'Well,' Flemming scratched his chin. 'The last guns we saw

116

are up at the lake : we haven't got as much as a quokka-stopper between the four of us.'

Priest straightened slightly, and reached over to turn on the table lamp. Already it was almost dark outside, the sky visceral like fresh liver. 'Well,' he said, 'I did mention that this place wasn't a cheap hotel. After independence it was thought expeditious by various parties to keep a cache or two of arms in the country—just in case. You're sitting over one of those caches right now—there's enough fire-power in the cellar under this house to sink a battleship. But that's not what we have to do. So if you'll just concentrate for the next hour we're going to discuss this for the last time. Rest assured that nothing, and no one, is going to stop us.'

16.30, Friday, 22 March

Rain fell in torrents on the shanty town north of Kunduchi, and in the Bagamoya barracks William Kalaba felt his spirits ebbing, draining away like the water from the clouds. Rain pounded on rusting corrugated iron roofs and turned alleys into waterways. Occasionally, an African sprinted from one house to another like a demented hurdler, his feet lifting high out of the sea of mud, a scrap of polythene held over his head. In a doorway, near the main road, a woman sat on an upturned mafuti can and suckled her child from a goose-fleshed breast. On the road, infrequent lorries and cars crawled wetly through the deluge, headlights shining yellow in the dim, grey light.

Kalaba sat down by the blurred panes of the mess window; two days had passed since the meeting. There had been no Chinese present, but he was under no illusions as to where the directives came from in this part of the world.

Aimlessly he toyed with some bread left over from lunch and watched as a new detail of sentries set off to replace the men in the guardhouse. They were Green Guards, with headquarters over the water in Zanzibar. For all its apparent state of disuse, there would be no easy way to get out of here. Round the barracks' entrance, big piles of red earth and rolls of barbed wire said that as soon as the rain stopped the renovation and strengthening of the perimeter fence would continue. And not to keep anyone out : it was obviously expected that his stay here might go on for some considerable time. He glanced skywards,

117

but there seemed no end to the downpour; as the cook had been so happy to tell him, down here on the coast it could rain like this for weeks, with total disregard for established statistics. Something had to be done. But what? Kampala was one thousand miles away. Dejectedly, he turned away from the window and started to pace the room. The onset of evening made no difference at all to the pervading gloom.

07.00, Saturday, 23 March

Behind the Bagamoya barracks the ground rose slightly in a confusion of vegetation and this gradually thickened into the untended fringes of a banana plantation. Priest passed his binoculars back to Charlie Soon, while Gould poured out coffee from a flask and the Rover's windows steamed up even more. The vehicle and its three occupants were hidden among the rotting trunks of the old plantation; as the wind gusted through the huge leaves they flapped and cracked like unmanned sails.

The camp faced onto the main road, and the perimeter formed, with one exception, a large square. At the back of the compound a small-arms range was laid out parallel to the road, and it was the targets and butts at the end of the three hundred yard range that jutted out of the square, and caused an irregularity in the high wall and outer fences. A track passed close to the outside of the camp at this point which, after various convolutions, joined the main road nearer the city.

'Right!' said Priest. 'We'll make a back door in that wire tonight, down there by the range, and set a charge in the wall. Just in case we have to make a noise.' Gould passed him a plastic mug full of sweet, black coffee.

'The range must be disused or they'd never have built that wall at the end of it. The country out there was probably empty when they put this place together—or maybe the locals just learned to keep their heads down.' He sipped his coffee and sat back. 'Our big advantage is that Kalaba seems to have the freedom of the camp. More restricted than imprisoned.' He took another mouthful of coffee and turned to Charlie. 'That's where you come in. Have you got it clear?'

Charlie put the glasses on the seat beside him and nodded. 'I hope the things work.'

Gould handed him a coffee. 'Don't worry, they'll work just

118

fine. Gadgets like that were around when I was young, and that was fifteen years ago. They're pretty infallible.'

'That's right,' Priest cut in. 'Nothing but the best. Probably Japanese.' He pulled a photo out of his top pocket and held it up. 'Think you'll recognize him?'

'I feel I always knew him,' Charlie said.

Slowly Priest tore the photo and dropped the pieces out of the window. 'Then that's it. Midday for our first move, and tonight we adopt our rôle as tourists.' He passed his empty beaker to Gould, who dropped it into a bag beside the flask. 'Let's get back and see what sort of a job Flemming's done with the stencil set.' He slid the window shut, and started the motor. Slowly the Rover moved away, its back wheels burying pieces of Kalaba's picture in the soft earth.

12.30, Saturday, 23 March

The deluge continued as Charlie Soon turned an old van into the gateway of the Bagamoya Barracks, bringing it carefully to a standstill near the barrier. The sides of the van were inscribed 'Nam Fatt Catering', and through the window of the guard house he could see off-duty soldiers smoking and playing cards. Charlie waited, and a sentry appeared in the doorway, beckoning him to get out and come over : Africans hated rain and cold. Then he picked up his wallet from the passenger seat and extracted a slim, metal box from the glove compartment. Holding the box underneath the wallet, he climbed quickly out of the van, swinging the door closed behind him. As he hurried past the barrier post the fingers of his right hand relaxed their grip slightly and the wallet fell to the ground. He allowed himself another two steps before turning back to retrieve it. Bending down by the barrier, he had just enough time to clamp the white box to the white metal upright. With his body between the post and the sentry he felt the two magnets grip, then he straightened, wiped the wallet off, and turned, thoroughly soaked, to the guardhouse. The guards moved aside to allow him under cover : the little drama had taken fifteen seconds. Charlie addressed the African he had first seen.

'Salaam,' he began. 'Nataka kwenda jikoni na vitu hivi.' Then he looked from face to face, as if unsure who would give the necessary permission to unload stores at the cook-house.

119

A tall sergeant shouldered his way through the others and spoke to the corporal of the guard. 'Anataka nini?'

Before the corporal could reply, Charlie cut in. 'I have stores, bwana, for the kitchens. That is my van.'

The sergeant nodded. 'Where is your order?'

Charlie looked up at the African. 'Bwana, I have not sold here before. But if I can see the chef, I am sure we can all profit from today.'

The sergeant pondered, but the repeated use of bwana and the assumption that he knew English had pleased him. The thought of a rake off clinched matters. Dubiously he looked out at the decrepit van.

'Ayah, pita!'

The sentry went out into the rain and peered without interest through the back window, then he leaned on the counter-weight, and the pole lifted lethargically into the air. Charlie turned the key and the van started.

After driving down every road he could find to familiarize himself with the camp's layout, Charlie pulled up beside the kitchens. Inside, a dozen Africans busied themselves round steaming cauldrons of stew and small mountains of posho. Charlie asked for the chef, and was steered towards an elderly man with grey crinkly hair, carefully arranging a trolley load of food and implements.

'Mzee.'

The man looked round and appraised Charlie through time-worn eyes.

'Mzee, I have a food business in the town. They told me in Central Barracks this camp will soon be full again. So I have come to show you the things I have.'

The chef's eyes returned to the trolley. 'You have to come back later.'

'Mzee, I have made a special journey from the town. If you could give me just five minutes . . .' He spread his hands hopefully.

The African pulled a makeshift cover over the trolley and swung it round. 'When lunch is finished. Ngoja. Wait till then.'

He set the trolley in motion, and moved between the rows of stoves towards double doors at the far end of the cooking area.

Charlie hesitated : the man was in charge and yet he had

120

prepared a single trolley with his own hands. Then he moved back the way he had come, and out to the van. From the driver's seat he could see the chef and another man in white overalls pushing the trolley quickly through the rain. Twenty yards of tarmac separated the cook-house from the next building, and then the second man lowered his umbrella with some difficulty and helped lift the trolley up the four steps leading to the door. Charlie reached behind the seat for a towel and a light mac.

By the time he had dried himself off a little and put the mac on, the two Africans were on their way back to the kitchens. Charlie waited till they'd disappeared, then released the handbrake and let the van roll forward until it was nearer the other building. Taking a deep breath, he got out and walked briskly towards the steps.

Kalaba had just taken his first mouthful when the door opened at the far end of the room. His table was close to the window to get the benefit of what little light there was, and at first he could only see a vague shapeless form in the doorway. 'I'm sorry,' said a voice. 'I was looking for the toilets.' Kalaba was still trying to place the accent when he realized that the door had closed with the man still in the room, and moving quickly towards him. Then the intruder's face came into the light, and the African saw him put a hand to an inside pocket. In a surge of panic, he pushed his chair back from the table and tried clumsily to get to his feet. The man's hand came out of his pocket holding a book-shaped package which he slid quickly under a pile of newspapers. Then he was on his way back to the door.

As the latch clicked, Kalaba tried to relax. He realized his heart was beating madly and he couldn't swallow the mouthful of chewed food that still lay on his tongue. Carefully, he walked over to the newspapers and felt for the package. His first unreasoning instinct was to throw it out into the rain, tick or no tick. But if they'd wanted him dead it would have been a simple enough job with a pistol. Thoughtfully, he pocketed the small parcel and started chewing again. Then he walked quickly across the room and into his private toilet.

Just before 9 p.m. that night Priest opened the window of the Rover and stuck the tip of a small aerial out into the night.

121

Except for Gould, he was alone. After three minutes there was a series of crackles and then a voice, distorted but recognizably cautious.

'Hello.' Pause. 'Hello, is anyone there?'

Priest put his fingers to his lips and threw the world a kiss. Then he pressed the transmit button. 'Listen carefully for an important question.'

Gould leaned over and spoke slowly in Acholi: 'Who cured the great sickness?'

There was a moment's delay, then the voice came back, surprised. 'Dr Sielmann.'

Priest looked over at Gould. 'Well, it's him all right. So barring the unlikely possibility of his not being alone, we've made contact.' Again he pressed the transmit button. 'Correct. Now listen carefully to what I have to say . . .'

13.45, Sunday, 24 March

Once more Charlie coaxed the van through the sheets of water covering Bagamoya Road. The back of the van was piled high with sacks of rice, large bags of dried beans and bamboo shoots and among them, Gould, arranged so that he was almost invisible. Charlie turned left into the barracks' entrance, and Gould pulled a flap of cloth across his face. Charlie slid open the door and greeted the sentry. The man's face broke into a grin as he remembered the day before.

'Salaam,' he said. 'Ni jumapili lakini bado unashughulika.'

Near the cities, Africans generally had absorbed a liking for the weekend. That anyone, especially a white, should be out working on a Sunday like this was noteworthy.

'Askari—,' Charlie shook his head. 'Wanakula kama tembo kilasiku. Shauri yangu.'

The guard laughed. That soldiers ate like elephants, even on a Sunday, was a flattering allusion. He came quickly out into the rain and looked cursorily over Charlie's shoulder at the produce. 'Ayah, nenda.' The pole went up.

Gould moved to a more comfortable position and brought a Sterling machine pistol out onto his lap. 'Priest was right—a bit of rain and these clowns suspend everything.'

Charlie drove on for several minutes until he came to a small roundabout. Turning right, he headed towards a large, hangar-shaped building. Some soldiers in plastic ponchos splashed across the road in front of them and disappeared into the gloom. Charlie pulled into an alley between two buildings. Gould wriggled forward and slid into the passenger seat.

'Let's test the radios.'

The alley faced west towards the back of the camp. Gould pulled out his small transceiver and extended the aerial. His thumb whitened on the transmit button. 'Two calling one. Over.'

Priest's voice came back immediately. 'Receiving.'

Charlie thumbed his set. 'Three calling one.'

The reply crackled through both radios. Gould stowed his in a small satchel and slung it round his neck.

Charlie said 'You have nine minutes.'

Gould slid open the door and was gone.

At two precisely Charlie pulled up at a T-junction near the kitchens, and flashed his lights twice at the building opposite. Then he turned left and drove slowly towards the doors where he had parked the previous day. Before reaching them, he made the right turn necessary to bring the van alongside the steps leading to Kalaba's rooms. Right on time the African opened the door and came down the steps. Simultaneously, the double doors to the kitchen swung wide and two men in white stepped out, hurrying to raise umbrellas against the downpour. Then they saw Kalaba. For a second all motion was suspended, and Charlie watched Kalaba's momentary indecision register with the two Africans facing him. Then he wrenched the door open and called : 'Get in.'

Kalaba ran round the front of the van and climbed inside. Charlie pulled a silenced automatic from under the seat and slid smoothly out in to the rain. In one fluid movement he raised the gun, steadying his wrist with his left hand, and pulled the trigger. One of the Africans crumpled forwards like a broken snowman in his white uniform and fell across his umbrella. The other unfroze quickly and backed towards the kitchen doors. Lead chipped wood from the lintel above his head. He dropped his umbrella and disappeared inside. Charlie jumped in and moved the van away fast. Kalaba held onto his seat. 'He'll phone the gate.' Charlie grunted and accelerated. They slewed round two more corners, the wheels sending sheets of spray through the cold air. Ahead of them, buildings clustered more thickly as

123

they approached the central compound. Charlie brought the van in hard towards the wall on their right and braked firmly. 'What ... ?' Kalaba started, but then the door slid open and Gould squashed his way in. 'Mr Kalaba? Would you get in the back?' It was a command, and the African scrambled over among the jumbled sacks.

'They know he's gone,' Charlie said. 'Use the radio.'

Gould immediately undid the satchel and withdrew the radio, leaving the van door open. 'Two to one.'

Priest's voice came back. 'Receiving.'

'We'll need help at the gate. The others are set if you see us in trouble.'

He waited impatiently for the acknowledgement, and when it came put the radio down on the seat.

'Let's get going. I just hope he can see through those glasses of his.'

They rounded a corner, and the main gate was directly ahead of them, the guardhouse on the left. Kalaba got as low as he could, and Charlie kept the van in second gear. The distance lessened to sixty yards. Nothing moved. Gould's hands tightened round the Sterling. Suddenly guards spilled out into the road and blocked their path; Charlie could see a tall man shouting orders. Two more soldiers appeared carrying sub-machine guns. 'Come on,' Gould muttered. 'Come on.' As if in answer, there was a vivid orange detonation at the base of the barrier as Priest triggered the charge, and the pole lifted and swung round. The end of it caught the two soldiers furthest from the guardhouse and swept them into the opposite wall. But the same instant the chatter of automatic fire filled the air, and Gould realized they were never going to make it.

'Turn round, back to the range!' He slid the door open and, as the van veered to the right, emptied a magazine in the direction of the guardhouse. Hot cartridge cases spun round the cab, and the acrid smell of cordite travelled with them as the van picked up speed on the road leading to the far end of the camp. As they went into top, there were two explosions from the supply block, and then a deep, grumbling roar as two-hundred-and-fifty gallon fuel drums exploded. Dense black smoke tunnelled sky-wards, wrapped round an artery of livid flame, and pouring rain fled along monsoon drains, carrying on its back rivers of burning petroleum.

Gould looked ahead. 'Let's hope their wheels have gone up in the bang.'

The fleeing van reached the end of the tarmac and ran out on to the raised grassy bank of the firing point. Between the firing point and the butts lay an overgrown depression flooded in parts with pools of water.

Gould pointed to the left. 'Try along there.'

The van bumped along the edge of the depression, on what must have been a footpath, while armies of grass advanced upon the windscreen. They were only eighty yards from the end of the range when the front of the van dropped dramatically and they stalled. Gould found himself with his face against the windscreen, looking down at a tangled mass of flattened grass, and Kalaba slid head-first into the front seat. Gould levered the door up and back, and scrambled out.

'On foot! The van's had it!'

The other two followed his progress, and they climbed down through the foliage where the path had subsided and up the other side. Behind them, two bren-carriers had reached the firing point and spotted the van. The three moved as fast as possible, with the sound of engines getting louder in their ears. The grass was neck-high and sharp, and then the ground rose slightly as they approached the target area. Kalaba looked round, and as he did so a machine-gun started up from the far end of the range. They stumbled into the target gallery, a concrete slit between the mantlet and the stop butts where, in days past, British soldiers had stood in safety to raise and lower targets. Deafening volleys stabbed the air as bursts of fire passed overhead penetrating silently into the wet sand. The reports from the guns lagged badly, like a tired drumbeat struggling to catch up with the band, and ricochets from the wall sang angrily into the distance.

Charlie looked up and saw masonry jetting over the top of the butts like a flock of startled crows. He felt Gould's hands push him from behind, and heard his voice: 'Get going! For Christ's sake, move!!'

They scrambled out of the gallery, and round the curving base of the sand.

Outside the wall, Priest, watched the dust settle quickly, helped by the rain. The sound of firing grew louder, and carrying a Sterling, he ran down to the outer fence and pulled a section of the mesh aside; it had already been doctored. Between the fence and the breached wall coils of rusty barbed wire had also received the treatment.

A figure appeared at the hole, crouched, and came through. It was Soon. Kalaba followed, with Gould close behind.

Priest held the wire up as they crawled through. 'Soon, you'd better drive. Anyone hurt? Where's the opposition?'

Gould straightened and shook his head. 'We're all okay, and they're at the other end of the range. Let's get out of here.'

The Rover accelerated down the track, and Charlie leaned forward, peering through the windscreen. Priest wiped the inside of the glass with a piece of rag. God, was it really the middle of the afternoon? He turned to Kalaba. 'Not quite the way we planned it, but so far so good. How are you feeling?'

Kalaba managed to smile. 'Lucky to be alive. How did you know where I was?'

Priest wiped the glass again. 'We knew what barracks they put you in the day you arrived. It's an old British establishment.'

He pulled a bag out from the front compartment. 'Chocolate?'

Gould took a piece. 'We were lucky. Some of their trucks were in that hangar, and they won't be going far now.'

They bounced on to the main road without incident, and Charlie pulled out to overtake a crawling lorry. There was a sudden silence in the vehicle as each man re-lived the past hour.

Fifteen minutes later a yellow flicker of sheet lightning back-lit the clouds as they entered the city centre. The windows along the front of the Kilimanjaro hotel were lit, the tourists content to sit this one out. In the gardens, ornamental bottle palms bent low in the wind, and from time to time a branch or a trunk snapped and fell, causing havoc in the Canna beds beneath. Soon left Independence Avenue and headed towards the bus station. At the end of a side street they pulled into the kerb behind the two Tamarind Safaris Volkswagens.

Priest passed Gould a canvas bag. 'Put this in the back of number two, and bring the hold-all. I'd hate to get this far and go down with pneumonia.'

126

A few moments later Gould returned carrying a hold-all crammed with spare clothing and towels.

Kalaba looked around. One hundred yards away in the bus station groups of Africans were huddled, cold and dejected, under inadequate shelters, waiting for buses to carry them to Tanga, Iringa and Lindi. Drivers and conductors struggled to load mountains of sodden possessions onto the flat roofs of their ancient vehicles : wicker baskets full of chickens, blankets, vegetables and the occasional bicycle. Priest rotated the tuner on his receiver until he was listening to the police frequency. But there was nothing to be heard.

They drove on and as they rounded the corner and turned south the wind caught the vehicle side on, and rocked it alarmingly. Gould rubbed a towel through his hair.

'Do you reckon that plane's going to get off the ground?'

Priest didn't answer: it was anyone's guess. No one that wasn't desperate would go near a light aircraft on a day like this. Heavy rain, visibility variable from two hundred feet to nothing, wind gusting up to Christ knew what. Once again he withdrew the VHF set and tried the police frequency. This time a voice came in urgently, loud and clear: '... units, stand by all units. There has been a sabotage attempt at the Bagamoya barracks. Two askaris have been killed. We are joining the army to block all roads away from the area. All landing strips will come under immediate guard. Stand by for a description of the personnel and all unit assignments. I repeat, stand by all units, stand by ...'

'Where are we going?' said Kalaba.

Priest ignored him and turned to Gould. 'Better get your gun ready. Just in case we do run into trouble.'

It was twenty-five miles to the strip where Flemming was waiting, and so far they were on schedule. The route was pot-holed badly, and had been repaired with heaps of murram which were now washing away, staining the tarmac orange. A sign said 'Mkuranga 25'. That meant some twenty-three miles to the plane. Gould looked worried as he craned his neck and tried to see the sky.

'Don't worry,' said Priest. 'Christ, with a wind like this all he'll have to do is start the bloody motors and we'll be in the air.'

'And flying backwards,' said Gould, unconvinced. The Rover

made slow but steady progress. Besides the four men, it was carrying six jerries of petrol plus boxes of ammunition. Charlie chewed gum and said nothing. Gradually, what little traffic there had been on the road was left behind, and they picked up speed. It was 3.15.

Flemming looked at his watch : 3.20, and not a sign of anyone. The small airfield had two runways, one overgrown, the other hard and well drained. In the old days this had been the base of the South Coast Aero Club, but since Uhuru it had been maintained by Island Copra as a convenient staging post in the inspection of their plantations. All around the airstrip, palms bent before the wind and even a mile inland the soil was sandy, with chunks of needle-sharp coral lying bleached on the ground. Flemming was reading an old record book he'd found in the club-house. He wondered what had happened to the young men of the South Coast Aero Club. It must have been tough, getting the boot from a white man's paradise like this. He drank a little coffee from a flask and shivered; it was bloody cold. Through the window the outline of the Cessna could be seen nearby at the end of the runway, facing north into the wind. He'd re-checked the systems and there was nothing left to do. By the window the short stock and long barrel of a general purpose machine-gun reminded him that the whole bizarre setup was for real.

He looked out across the plantation, and suddenly his eyes narrowed. Lightning? No there it was again, headlights flicker-ing between the palms. He picked up the glasses, swung them towards the track and then his radio crackled into life. 'Three, three, we're coming in with company. Ran into a road-block. Do what you can.' The set stayed on, and Flemming could hear confused noises coming from inside the Rover. Yes, there were headlights. But how many for Christ's sake? Now the Rover was in the clearing and racing towards the club-house; seconds later another vehicle came out of the trees and then another. They splayed left and right, leaving a third truck, which had a machine gun mounted on its cab, to follow the Land Rover. Flemming tucked himself behind the gun. A belt of stripless 7.62 ammunition glinted dully in the grey light. The leaf was up and set at 200 metres. He opened the window further and changed

128

position, resting the gun on the broad, wooden sill. The barrel steadied on the truck, which was coming towards him obliquely. He flicked the safety catch and squeezed the trigger. The GPMG was not one of those guns where you could count the shots goodbye. Based on the German MG42, it discharged rounds at fifteen per second in a continuous crescendo. The belt jerked across the floor as Flemming concentrated. On the approaching truck one of the headlights went out, and suddenly it veered to the left and then to the right in a crazy zig-zag that exposed both its sides. Then the bullets found one of the tanks and the whole thing went up, throwing equipment and bodies high through the air and into the near-darkness beyond. Flemming ran the belt off, then dragged another one towards him, sweating. Outside, the Land Rover slipped to a halt.

Priest rushed in. 'Get that bloody plane loaded, leave the gun to me!'

Flemming ran out through the door and opened the side of the 402. Gould clambered in, carrying two Sterlings and a box of ammunition, and Kalaba followed with his case. Flemming climbed into the pilot's seat. First one motor, then the other, crackled into life. On the other side of the clearing another two trucks had emerged from the track.

Priest called to Soon 'Get that Rover round behind the building!' He left the gun and rushed to the door of the plane. Gould's face looked down at him in the half light. 'Tell Flemming to get this show in the air!' he yelled to him. 'You've got the power, you should make it.'

Gould's mouth started to frame some words, but Priest cut him off.

'NOW! We'll give this lot something to think about! Good luck!' There was a crackle of machine-gun fire from across the clearing. He dived towards the club-house, and heard Flemming powering the engines. Slowly at first, and then faster, the plane accelerated down the runway. Priest got behind the gun and started to pump bursts towards the trees. Now three guns were in action, all of them aiming for the fleeing plane. The noise seemed to go on for a long time, then the firing petered out only to start again with a brand new target: the club-house. He heard Soon telling him the plane had left the ground and called out 'Get the boxes in the Rover!' Together they ran to the other

129

end of the building and climbed through the window. Soon passed the gun to Priest who loaded it into the back of the car. Picking up a Sterling, he climbed into the front seat, and Soon started the motor.

'Where do we go?' he asked.

Priest pointed. 'Keep the club-house between us and them,' he said 'and head into the trees. There's another track out of here, but I doubt if we're the only ones who know about it.'

Flemming released the brakes and felt the plane move forward into the night, buffeted as gusts of wind threatened to lift the whole machine off the ground. He looked up as Gould slid into the right-hand seat. His hair was plastered flat on his head, and he glanced back to where Kalaba was struggling with a seat-belt. Flemming watched the needle on the speed indicator inching round, but already the plane was light and ready to lift. He began to ease back on the column when suddenly there was a sound like a thunderclap and the engine noise in the cabin doubled. Needles spun wildly, and the port motor coughed, then picked up again. Flashes of white shot ahead of them and were gone, lost in the trees. The plane slewed towards the left-hand edge of the runway and Flemming fought to keep it on the tarmac. Out of the corner of his eye he saw Gould shouting, but there was no sound except the roar of the motors and the wind. Where there had been a window, next to the seat in front of Kalaba, a gaping hole in the plexi-glass emphasized the frailty of the aircraft. The African sat hunched forward, leaning into the seat-belt and Gould was unable to tell if he was hurt or not. The end of the runway leapt towards them, backed by a beckoning wall of timber. Still Flemming waited, and then, when collision seemed inevitable, he moved both hands firmly towards his body and the plane hopped into the air. No sooner were they off the ground than the wind pounced. The plane climbed in a series of stomach-twisting lurches, each more vicious than the last. The undercarriage went up without trouble, and Flemming pointed briefly to a headset lying between the seats. Gould put it on and heard the Australian's voice in his ears.

'We're in the shit! There's the gyro in the wing they must have hit. And gas. Take a squint at the port gauge.'

Gould searched the panel for a dial that might mean petrol

130

shortage, and eventually found it. Even as he watched, the needle dropped slowly towards the left-hand edge of the scale. 'How far can we get?' He sensed Flemming's shrug.

'One thing's for sure, we can't go north. We'd use up all the juice and get nowhere. We've got to try to get up.' He looked at Gould. 'Christ man, don't ask me, I just dunno.'

Thick tendrils of cloud writhed damply around the plane. The altimeter read two thousand feet. Still they climbed. At six thousand feet the aircraft came into clear air between layers and the lurching stopped; Flemming adjusted the mixture, and they flew in relative calm. The port engine hiccoughed again but recovered immediately, and Gould looked back at the African, who smiled weakly and gave a thumbs up sign.

'Kalaba's okay.' he said.

Flemming nodded. 'South.' he said. 'It's the only way. This bloody kite's a no-hoper. I reckon we'll be going south whatever I do.'

Above their heads, towering columns of cumulo-nimbus reared into the sky, finally disappearing in a deep blue-purple haze. Gould jerked a thumb upwards.

'No chance of getting above that lot with oxygen?'

Flemming shook his head. 'You're thinking of Woomera, sport. This stuff can start as low as sixteen hundred and develop up to forty thousand. That's a lot of feet. And it's not so warm up there either, specially with half the bloody windows missing.'

Gould could feel the tension building up in the other man. He said nothing, and they flew on through gigantic chasms in the sky, deviating from their course only to avoid the monstrous, twisted roots of the clouds. Flemming pulled a map holder from beneath the seat and took a calculator from his breast pocket. Southern Tanzania was not a densely populated area; vast areas of nothing stretched down to the Ruvuma river and the border with Portuguese East.

After a little while Flemming said, 'We're heading down here, right? Slightly west of south. Enough fuel to reach Tunduru maybe, where there's an airport, or one of the small towns like Nachingwea where there's a strip. Trouble is, that's Tanzania, the place we're meant to be leaving. The option is to cross into Portuguese East, fix up the plane and think things out. Problem is there doesn't seem to be a town in range.'

131

Gould asked: 'What's our speed?'

Flemming looked down at the indicator. 'Airspeed's about two hundred knots,' he said, 'And a lot of that's wind. The port motor might not be with us for long.'

Gould scratched his head. 'Look, we've got to go virtually south, it's the only way to put miles between us and Dar, right?'

'Right. Unless you want a little safari inland towards that lot.' He gestured over Gould's shoulder to where a grim, vertical cloud face bleakly precluded escape to the west.

Gould said, 'If we come down in Tunduru or some other place, they'll be on to us like flies.'

Flemming thought for a second. 'I don't get you. It's a big slice of land. I mean . . .'

'For God's sake, don't you read the newspapers. Just because some monkey announces independence doesn't mean they'll stop fighting the bloody war down there. Guerrillas, chum. Nasty men with guns. Black and white Africa still meet at the Ruvuma river.' He snorted. 'If we're going to come down anywhere, let's make it Portuguese East. Okay, so if we're picked up it could take a lot of talking to get out again. But at least we'd be out of Tanzania.'

Flemming looked at the map.

'Nampula?' Gould suggested.

'Do me a favour.'

'It's not that far,' said Gould. He squinted at the map. 'Under five hundred or so from where we started. And we've got long-range tanks—'

'With holes in 'em,' Flemming spat out, 'and a fucking gale blowing up our arse.'

Gould persisted. 'Who knows? We could do it.'

Flemming looked about him, wishing he could be elsewhere. 'I'm here to tell you we can't make it. Remember me? The joker who gets left to land this bloody sieve in thick cloud on a mountain-side or something when we run out of gas.' He thumped himself on the chest. 'Suicide, mate. No chance. A wipe-out. Can't you see?—I'm the poor bastard who's got to sit here and do the impossible.'

There was silence. The time was 4.25, but although there was light above the clouds, it was unreal, like stage lighting for The Tempest. Deep organic yellows and plushed pinks threaded

132

through the clouds like tissue and slanting bars of cobalt held the sky at bay.

'Okay, sport,' Flemming said at length. 'Have it your way. Portuguese East.'

'Let's agree,' said Gould. 'It's no good your acting under duress.'

'No, no really, PEA, you convinced me.' He smiled thinly. 'I mean all those flamin' guerillas and things. Terrifyin'. But a small fatal crash, piece of piss, we could do it now, save ourselves all the anxiety.' He stopped suddenly and looked over at Gould. 'Sorry. We'll try it your way. I'm just a bit shickered, that's all.'

The air-speed held steady at just over one hundred and eighty knots, but many of the other instruments were inert, damaged by the gunfire, and radio communications were out of the question. Gould kept his headset on to keep out some of the noise. Ahead of them, an imposing grey cliff stretched from east to west, and the two men peered this way and that as it got nearer, looking for some break or flaw that would give them access. But there was none, and soon they were surrounded once more by swirling grey mists as they flew into the storm.

The severity of the turbulence took them completely by surprise. The plane fell out of the sky, only to be brought up, shuddering, by another current of fast-moving air. Kalaba was in a bad way, his body heaving as he tried to throw up a lunch that was already all over the floor. The compass swung wildly, and Gould held on to both sides of his seat and tried to think of something else. It was all the more terrifying because there was nothing to see, and it was easy to imagine that every plunge was taking them within feet of some boulder-studded hillside. Then, without warning, the port motor cut out completely. Flemming's hands were white on the controls, and a string of indistinguishable words carved their way through the headset into Gould's ears. Again the plane dropped violently, the noise built up to a crescendo. And then, brilliant sunlight flooded the cabin.

They had emerged from high up one side of a massive bulge in the cloud-face at a height of five thousand feet. Flemming grinned across the cabin.

'I think we just jumped the fence!'

Gould looked at his watch and made a swift mental calculation. He nodded slowly. 'Actually, that could be. We've probably gone far enough south. But how far inland are we?'

As if in answer, a hazy strip of silver on the starboard horizon drew their gaze. It seemed to grow as they looked, reaching as far as they could see from left to right. There was silence, and then Gould felt a hand tap him on the shoulder. He half turned, and heard Kalaba's shout: 'Nyasa.'

The name was one régime out of date, but the African was right. Gould looked at Flemming but his eyes were fixed on the clusters of dials.

'Murray. How much fuel have we got? Can't you feed both motors from the right-hand tanks?'

Flemming turned to Gould. 'No, it has to go to the port tanks first, and they're cabbage strainers. We should be just south of the border, but it's anyone's guess what happened to the track while we were caught up in that lot. We're flying into nowhere land. I say we cross the lake and work it north as far as we can, try to make Livingstonia or Deep Bay. That way at least we'll know what half-arsed country we're in.' Gould spread the map out and Kalaba looked over his shoulder. Instead of heading south it seemed that at the very best they'd veered south-west. Gould gazed out of the window, trying to discern the northern extremity of the lake. But the distance was blurred, giving nothing away.

'You're right,' he said suddenly. 'Cross the lake and head north. Malawi. I just hope we're as far south as I think we are, or we'll be back in Tanzania before we know what's happening.'

Flemming banked gently, and the world revolved. 'Or back in the shit we just left,' he muttered.

Now the lake was on their left, drawing slowly, obliquely nearer. Across the water the sun was opting out for another day.

One hour later, fishermen north of Nkhato bay watched idly as the tiny plane crawled northwards. It flew high, well above the ranges that culminated up-country in the ramparts of Mount Rungwe, still in bright sunlight, although down on the lake the shadow of the hills always brought evening prematurely. The fishermen were heading for home when the tiny buzzing noise from the engine of the distant plane ceased abruptly. But they had already forgotten it, and the talk was of other things.

The river was rain swollen and flowed fast and truculent along

134

its pitted course. Jagged rocks reached up for air through collars of white foam, or lurked, thwarted, just beneath the surface. Along its length, some deep flat stretches were good enough for hippo. The waters were one hundred yards wide, and flowed past sand beaches of surprising white. Out of the sand, duom palms grew everywhere, and the small, hard palm nuts littered the ground. The trees were alive with vervets and baboons.

The Cessna made its approach upstream, and came in fast and low. Wheels up, it touched the water in silence at seventy-five miles an hour, lifted and touched again. Then it was down for good, obliterating itself from view in a wave of froth and spray. Troops of grounded monkeys took to the trees and the plane ploughed on, hardly seeming to slow. Crocodiles disappeared like magic from a sandbar, and the fuselage gouged out a trench where moments before they had been lying. Describing a lazy arc, the plane left the main stream and headed neatly into a backwater. There was a tearing noise as one of the wings hit the roots of a baobab, and the craft slewed violently, coming to rest nose-down in a creek.

The outraged chattering of the monkeys went on for some time as they moved out of the area from treetop to treetop. Settled deeply in the brackish water of the creek the plane was almost invisible. Nothing moved. It was as if it had never existed.

Chapter Seven

19.00, Sunday, 24 March

Not far from the airstrip recently vacated by Flemming a man crouched watchfully beside the bole of a large tree, sheltering from the wind. He was dressed in drab, green denim and wore a cap of the same material, half peaked at the front. Above the peak a single red star was his only visible insignia. Not far away more men waited beneath other trees and low to the ground the pock-marked barrels of two machine-guns were angled for cross-fire. Somewhere the faint noise of an engine teased the air, but the wind took it away and brought it back distorted, without perspective. Chen cocked his head on one side, listening intently as he glanced at his watch. They must come this way, he reasoned, there was no other. But why so long? He looked around, half expecting the strange shapes of the bushes to come to life and charge him from behind. Three hundred yards down the track a small, coral bridge crossed what was normally a dry stream-bed. Now the water was angry, fast-moving, impossible to ford in a light vehicle. And the trap was set.

Despite his watchfulness, their audacity nearly took him by surprise. The Land Rover was only sixty yards away when its lights went on and the motor gunned noisily. Chen fired two shots in the air in quick succession, the sound of his Russian Kalashnikov pistol distinctive, loud to his heightened senses. All round the clearing head and spot-lights punched dazzling shafts of light towards the oncoming truck, and seconds later the guns started up, purposefully low, gouging twin trails through the sodden earth towards their mark. The Rover weaved and accelerated blindly. Its speed kept it momentarily unscathed, miraculously ahead of the bullets. In the middle of the clearing,

136

just as both guns were on the point of ceasing fire, each for fear of hitting the other, the bullets went home. The front of the vehicle crumpled, and great strips of rubber flew from the tyres. The motor and the firing stopped together and the front of the Rover dug its way into the earth. The back wheels lifted into the air, then dropped back. It was over.

Chen shouted orders, and his men rushed into the light to get the two men out of the wrecked cab. Within seconds Priest and Soon were standing, dazed but unharmed, while the Chinese stripped them of their possessions and collected weapons and ammunition from between the seats. Chen spoke briefly into a small microphone, then moved to his truck. Already the clearing had emptied of men, and the convoy was forming up ready for the drive to the harbour. Chen waited until the last lights were moving away through the trees, then he gestured to his driver and they pulled up briefly alongside the shattered Rover. Casually he tossed a small cylindrical object through its open door. They were nearly out of sight when the explosion lit up the trees behind them. It looked like summer lightning except that the shadows were in all the wrong places. Chen grimaced and wound up the window.

10.00, Monday, 25 March

In London, Mannering read once more through the Xeroxed file copies from the decoder. The report from McLoughlin in Nairobi had included a transcript of a newscast that was apparently to have been made by Radio Tanzania the previous night. But the information was never transmitted.

'AN ASSASSINATION ATTEMPT WAS MADE THIS AFTERNOON UPON THE LIFE OF EX-PRESIDENT WILLIAM KALABA, IN RESIDENCE NEAR DAR ES SALAAM. THE ATTACK WAS FOILED BY THE PROMPT ACTION OF SECURITY FORCES WHO CAPTURED THE MEN RESPONSIBLE IN A CHASE THAT ENDED NEAR MKURANGA, SOUTH OF THE CAPITAL. THE EX-PRESIDENT, BELIEVED TO HAVE BEEN IN DAR ES SALAAM RECOVERING FROM AN ILLNESS, HAS NOW GONE INTO HIDING UNTIL FURTHER ARRANGEMENTS HAVE BEEN MADE FOR HIS CON-TINUED SAFETY.'

Underneath, Nairobi's assessment of the facts:

X RELIABLE SOURCES TELL US PANIC IN GOV-
ERNMENT CIRCLES X INFORMATION GIVEN PRESS
LIAISON OFFICER FOR RELEASE NEVER REACHED
PRESS OUTLETS X TWO MEN CAPTURED NOW
TAKEN TO OLD SULTAN'S PALACE ZANZIBAR HQ
GREEN GUARDS X KALABA MISSING X PROBABILITY
PLANE AWAY WITH THREE X CONDITIONS IMPOS-
SIBLE VIRTUAL TYPHOON OVER WHOLE AREA X
NO REPORTS OF CRASH X AS OF 08.47 HRS GMT
MON 25/3 NBI DO(SL)HC.

And another sheet of paper datelined only twenty-minutes
later:

X LATEST REPORTS CONFIRM UNPROVOKED
STRIKES X UGANDAN PLANES BOMBARDED VILLAGE
OF NYAKANYASI WELL INSIDE TANZANIA WITH
ROCKET FIRE X THIRTY KILLED IN MARKET NO
RETALIATION POSSIBLE X EMERGENCY MEETING
OF HOUSE OF REPRESENTATIVES HERE X SOFTEN-
ING UP? X 09.07 HRS GMT MON 25/3 NBI DO(SL)HC.

Mannering tried to imagine what had happened, to reconstruct the events of yesterday. But there was nothing to go on.
They'd heard nothing from Priest since his rendezvous with
Butler at the depôt. What had gone wrong? The storm? But
with no apparent break likely in the monsoon, Priest had little
choice. Time was running out for them all. In Mbarara, Kampala and Tororo, anxious men were waiting for the signal to
move. And now the men upon whom that signal depended had
disappeared, two into the depths of a Chinese jail, and three
aboard an aircraft that could have crashed anywhere in several
million square miles of empty bush. Implications whirled round
inside his head like leaves in a gale. If ever there was a time
for Omuria to act it was now. He had the strength, the incentive
and the Chinese guarantee. But Dar-es-Salaam hadn't got
Kalaba, and didn't know where he was. No wonder there was a
bit of panic going on down there. Mannering tried to get his
thoughts into some sort of order. Assume Flemming and Kalaba
in the plane. Plus one other. Why hadn't they all gone? Trouble
on the strip? In which case, knowing Harry, he would have
stayed behind for the rearguard action. And the Chinese? A

vetoed newscast that would have told Omuria too much, leaving him to believe a lie, a lie with nothing to prove or disprove its substance.

On his desk the grey phone gave a single purr. Mannering shuffled his papers into a pile, and slid them into the slit mouth of a black hide document case. Then he answered the phone. 'Yes, sir, I'll be right up.'

10.00, Monday, 25 March
Zanzibar lay fugitive in the surrounding seas. Much had changed since the days of the Sultans when every decade would see a Speke, Burton or Livingstone set out to explore the unknown continent, to march a thousand miles over grassland and swamp until racked with fever, bludgeoned by heat, they could plant a gaudy fluttering square of cloth and claim that every mile and all horizons were Victoria's. After independence the island joined with Tanganyika to form a united republic which eventually adopted the name of Tanzania.

In a room of the old Sultan's Palace, a stone's throw from streets once worn smooth by the bare feet of the slave trade, a meeting was in progress. The room was high off the ground in the west wing of the building. Narrow angular slits in the outer wall of the corridor revealed a view over the minarets of the town and, on any ordinary day, the straits. The doors to the room were of massive yet intricate design, carved and cunningly inlaid with ivory and silver. Now they swung silently open and six men walked quickly past the guards. The meeting was at an end.

Inside the room Tai-Ling gestured to the Arab servant. 'Funga milango.' The doors closed, and he eased himself into his high-backed chair and turned to Seng. 'Well?'

'Well what? You got your own way.'

'I usually do. But how many of them agreed with me?'

Seng considered. Then he said, 'None of them, I would think. But then it's not politic to disagree with you.'

Tai started to reply, but broke off. Perhaps Seng was right, and he was becoming difficult. His mind sought the familiar sources of irritation, no horses, humidity, Africans ... but he said : 'Look at it my way. First, what do we want to know? Who they are? Where they come from? Who sent them?' He

139

snapped his fingers. 'We know these things without crude ques-
tioning. In these days ... a talk on the radio, a look in the
files ... and it's done.

'The point is that we didn't guard him adequately, no, worse,
we didn't guard him at all. A child could have spirited him
away. We have only ourselves to blame.' He looked at Seng. 'Oh,
they could give us some dates, some times, but these matters
are purely academic. The sad facts are that the aircraft could
never have got near Uganda last night. The storm alone would
have made such a flight almost impossible, and to settle the
matter our guns hit it before takeoff. Inspection of the runway
showed large quantities of petrol floating round on the rain.
Our two prisoners are as much in the dark about Kalaba's
whereabouts as we are.'

There was a heavy silence and then Tai said suddenly, 'What
was the name of the security captain who caught them?'

'Chen.'

'Yes, Chen. He did well. Arrange a meeting. I have an idea
for our two captives.'

He stretched, his heavy shoulders threatening to break the
seams of his tunic. 'It's not easy when officially we don't exist.
Still, Omuria's on the move. If we can continue to escalate
affairs there'll be war, and two losers at the end of it, looking for
a loan.' He got up. 'Well, I have to go to the mainland, you
have a rendezvous with our two prisoners.'

Side by side the two men left the room. Tai's distorted voice
came back down the corridor followed by hollow laughter: 'And
don't forget Seng, orientals are expected to be inscrutable. No
point in destroying a belief like that.'

Behind them, green in a world of white, the guards relaxed.

10.00, Monday, 25 March

Charlie Soon sat unmoving on a narrow bench, a thick and
ancient plank of wood spanning one end of the cell, wedged
into the damp mortar to provide the only furniture. A full ten
feet away, Priest leant with his back to the opposite wall and
tried to forget that he was cold. The only evidence of technology
was a fifteen-watt bulb, countersunk into the stone-work behind
a piece of dirty perspex. Despite its chill, the air smelt bad; the
place was poorly ventilated, and both men had been forced to

defecate in one of the corners. Soon had initiated proceedings without a word, just as Priest was wondering how to broach the subject himself. He looked away as Soon squatted in the corner, and when he finished, manoeuvered himself awkwardly into a similar position : without a doubt it was by far the most repugnant thing he had had to do in years.

Priest's mind was tired, his thoughts going this way and that, round and round, with no conclusions reached. How many hours had they been here? It must be morning outside, wherever that was. He flexed his knee and ankle, swollen from the crash and wondered if being pushed up against a wall expecting God knows what, and then just being photographed, was a prelude to some unthinkable mental torture . . . but they must know by now, who he was, if their organization was all it was cracked up to be. Priest tried to concentrate on their predicament, but all he could think of were the gardens in Singapore that Haw Paw had built for his grandson, where a section of lifelike plaster miniatures enacted the tortures of Chinese overlords. The work was so good that as one walked and looked, the agony of the disembowelled business rival, beheaded thief and horribly mutilated adulterer became quite real, and one could imagine how it might have been all those years ago in China.

Harry Priest, lover of comforts, looked across three yards of dank cell at Charlie Soon. The Chinese was still unmoving, eyes closed, feet crossed. In a trance Priest thought, floating around in some strange Oriental vacuum.

'Charlie.' His voice came out broken, silent from disuse, so he coughed and tried it again. 'Soon, you awake?'

Charlie kept his eyes closed : there was nothing to look at. 'Sure I'm awake.'

'How are you feeling?'

'I don't like it here.'

'You and me too,' thought Priest. Aloud he said, 'What dialect were the soldiers using?'

'Cantonese,' said Charlie. 'All Cantonese.'

Then he opened his eyes and cocked his head on one side. 'What's up?'

'They're coming.'

Somewhere footsteps rang faintly on a stone floor. Priest turned his eyes to the door. The steps got nearer, built up to a crescendo.

141

Then they stopped. Keys in the locks, the door swinging open.

'Chu lai!'

Priest looked at Charlie.

'He said come out.'

'Okay, let's do what he says. The man with the gun is always right.'

Gingerly, the two men stooped through the open door and into the darkness. They found themselves in a long, low ceilinged corridor. Priest felt a gun in his back.

'Tsao!'

They started walking, picking up speed slightly as their eyes got to grips with the dark, and the stone floor smoothed out. Priest sensed rather than saw another guard standing at the side of the corridor, and felt him fall into step behind them. In no time at all they were level with a series of narrow grills, all set just below the ceiling, some seven feet off the ground. Fresh air wafted over them, and Priest breathed deeply. For all its greyness the daylight seemed blindingly bright. At the other end of the passage there was a sharp left turn, and steps rose steeply to the threshold of a walled courtyard. They crossed it, and were pushed into a narrow anteroom. More soldiers stood to attention around the walls, and as the little procession halted, two of these stepped forward and gripped the heavy handles of large, arch-shaped doors. Priest and Soon found themselves in a cool high-ceilinged room with a long, roughwood table and some chairs. They looked around them. To their rear the doors were closed, and two guards had taken up positions on either side of them.

'Might as well sit down.'

Charlie nodded and they sat, backs to the guards. Almost immediately a door opened at the other end of the room, and a heavily built Chinese entered, followed by another uniformed guard. They approached the table, the guard looking like the popular conception of Genghis Khan, dark-skinned and tough, with black hair and black eyes. The officer was younger, not so fit, with the fleshy face of a successful merchant; he inclined his head in greeting and sat. Priest and Soon made no response, but watched and waited. The Chinese studied them carefully, taking his time. Then his gaze locked onto Priest's and he spoke.

'Well. There is little time for games. We know who you are and you have demonstrated what it was that brought you here.

The rest will follow when you have been with us for a day or two.' The eyes never wavered. 'It will do no harm to tell you that the plane was badly hit before takeoff. There was petrol everywhere on the runway. They have crashed.' He waited for a reaction, but there was none. Purposefully he continued.

'Before I would have said "Where was it going?" and prompted you for a quick answer. Now that can wait while we fill in some of the other gaps.' He turned to Charlie and addressed him in Chinese.

Charlie shook his head.

Seng smiled faintly. 'An attitude to be expected in one who had adopted so perfectly the habits of the west.' He waited again as if for a reply, but none came.

'I wonder, Mr Soon, if you really know who you're working for? What have they told you, your precious imperialist friends?'

He broke into rapid Chinese and went on for several minutes. Charlie's face remained immobile but his eyes dropped to the table. It occurred to Priest quite suddenly that he was the odd man out. Everyone else was Chinese and they could quite openly put Charlie on the payroll and he would know nothing about it. The thought went round his mind several times before he discarded it. At length the high-pitched sing-song voice stopped momentarily and then reverted to English.

'You could at least tell your people the truth, Mr Priest—trust is an integral part of efficiency. In any case, you will both remain here until we can no longer make use of you. A captain of security will be visiting you from time to time, to ask a question or two, that is all. I trust that you will help him to do his job efficiently.'

He placed a piece of paper on the table in front of him, smoothed it out and looked up at the two prisoners. 'Don't do anything stupid while you are here; it would not be easy to escape from the building, and if you did, Zanzibar itself is a fortress. Remember, we don't wish to inflict any more discomfort on you than is necessary. Now this will help convince you that events are moving too fast to be changed.'

He pushed it across the table and Priest glanced involuntarily at the first words: 'An unprovoked aerial bombardment was made today on the village of . . .' He looked up. The Chinese was on his feet.

143

'From the BBC,' said Seng. 'World Service.' He turned and made for the door; behind their back Priest and Soon heard the approaching footsteps of the guards.

20.00, Sunday, 24 March

The night was warm and dry, but Sam Gould shivered as he worked. Some of the cold he knew he could put down to his frequent immersions in the creek, but the rest was reaction to the crash. It was important to keep busy, to work his way through it. Everything was soaked, but he had gone back into the plane and removed what gear there was that might prove useful. A pile lay between the tortured roots of the baobab that had nearly been the death of them all: two guns, some maps, the first-aid kit, plus an ex-President and one would-be geologist. Flemming lay unconscious with his head on a box of ammunition wrapped in a bush jacket. Gould had slipped his feet and legs into a polythene seat cover from the plane in an attempt to keep him a little warmer. Kalaba had a leg that was already twice its normal size and he kept grunting with the pain.

Gould worked deftly at a task he had performed many times before. With his knife, he carved a shallow groove in a sun-bleached log. Where the main trunk tapered into smaller branches he cut out a straight piece some ten inches long, an inch in diameter. Then he collected a handful of dead moss and bark fibre from around the tree and grass and twigs for kindling. Lastly, he rounded the end of the straight stick to match the concave of the groove. A vibrant whirring sound mingled with the quiet sucking of the creek as he slid his palms backwards and forwards, rotating the wood fast between his hands, always keeping the end in firm contact with the groove. Shortly a wisp of smoke came from the point of friction, and the smell of charcoal. Quickly, he thrust the hot end into the midst of the fibre and blew gently. At first nothing happened. He cursed, because the system only worked infallibly with dried elephant dung and nothing else was half so good. But then, from nowhere, a flicker of yellow, a wisp of grey. He fed on some leaves and dry grass, and soon the flame was alive, the need for delicacy gone.

With the fire burning he was able to sit and warm himself, and try to work out their position. Whichever way he looked at it, things were not good. They had guns, which was something.

144

But food was only one of their problems : Kalaba couldn't move and Flemming was out cold. The warmth from the flames relaxed him, and steam came up from his trousers. He decided to strip and lay the clothes round the fire, they'd dry a lot quicker like that. When that was done, he pushed more wood on to the blaze and felt his skin lose its tackiness as it dried.

'Sam.' The voice broke him out of his reverie, and he padded round the fire towards it. Kalaba's eyes flickered open, and he smiled weakly as Gould passed by. Flemming was awake and seemed calm.

'Thank God for that. You feeling all right?'

'We all make it?'

'Yes, we did. Don't ask me how, though—Kalaba's leg has been bent all the wrong ways, and you'll have to take it easy yourself with a head like that.'

Flemming said 'At least we're on the ground. Let me get at that fire, I'm bloody frozen.' He went to sit up, but started to retch violently.

Gould pushed him firmly back. 'I'll drag you round just now, but for Christ's sake don't try to move yourself.'

Flemming's face had gone a blue-white colour. 'Yeah,' he managed. 'Maybe you're right. You don't think the crash fucked up something inside?'

'Murray, you'll be fine . . . a good sleep and a few pints of that lager you keep talking about, and you'll remember it as one of your better landings.' Hoping he was right, Gould lifted him under the shoulders and dragged him to within five feet of the fire. He turned to the African. 'Maybe a little nearer for you too, eh?'

Kalaba nodded, and bit his lip as Gould manoeuvred him into position.

'What happened?' said Flemming. 'I don't remember much, just those crocs and then the tree. And what time is it?'

Gould had the lid off the first-aid kit, and was poking around inside. He glanced at his wrist. 'It's packed up.'

'8.25,' said Kalaba.

Gould was arranging the medicines and squinting at the small print. The pile of mexiform, daraprim and calomine grew until at last he came up with a yellow tube and some elasticated bandages. 'Not much to be done for you, Aussie—I'll put some

145

of this on the cut, and for the rest, just get plenty of kip.' He smoothed antibiotic cream over a gash on Flemming's forehead and covered it loosely with a plaster. 'Takes people different ways, concussion. Common thing is getting angry and insisting that you're OK when you're not.'

Flemming grunted. 'Didn't know you were a medic.'

'I'm not. But I've seen a lot of people recovering from things, and you get to know the patterns.' He knelt by Kalaba, and started to roll up his left trouser leg. But the flesh was too swollen, so he cut into the material high up on the thigh with a knife, and started to slit.

Kalaba watched him. 'Careful what you cut off with that knife.'

'Don't worry, cowboy,' Flemming broke in. 'You'll live to ride again.'

Kalaba grunted. 'I wonder.'

Something in the man's voice pricked Gould's skin. He heard himself asking quietly 'What do you mean by that?'

Kalaba looked down at his knee. The joint was enormous, skin taut and black, glistening in the firelight. 'I would have thought that was pretty obvious. Speaking as a man who had hoped to be in Uganda by now.'

Gould struggled to control his temper, at the same time wondering why he should be in danger of losing it. What the man said was quite true. The plan was a cock-up. It was just that criticism was the last thing he needed from some jumped-up black politico after all they'd been through on his account.

Gould probed the knee none too gently. 'Can you bend it at all with the trousers gone?'

Kalaba tried, and winched it through a painful twenty degrees. He could sense the other man's anger, and wished he'd kept his thoughts to himself. But it was too late.

'I don't like it any more than you do,' Gould told him. 'I appreciate the fact that as operations go, this one is running on three flat tyres. But we didn't organize the weather, nor, for that matter, your political demise.'

Kalaba knew that someone would go too far if he didn't stop it. But he couldn't bring himself to shut up entirely. 'I'm grateful for your help,' he told Gould. 'I'm sure you're both motivated by the highest ideals.'

146

Gould breathed deeply. Then he slipped a hand under the African's foot and told him : 'I'm going to push a little, just keep it locked in that position.'

The black face tightened in readiness for a blinding shaft of pain. But none came. Gould swabbed the whole area down with spirit, laid on some lint, and bound the entire joint firmly in one of the bandages. 'Nothing broken,' he pronounced. 'But it could be a few days before you're giving Keino a hard time. We'll cut a pair of crutches in the morning.' He put the medicines back in the first-aid box and turned to stoke up the fire. 'Are either of you hungry?'

Flemming and Kalaba shook their heads in unison.

'That's good, because there's damn all to eat. Still . . .' a canteen landed on the ground between the two men, 'Water's plentiful anyway. Should be OK, that river's flowing like hell.' He stretched, wondering at the lack of insects so close to water, and then lay down on the other side of the fire; both the Sterling and his knife were close at hand. There was quiet, and then Flemming said :

'Thanks for getting me out, Sam.'

Gould muttered something, embarrassed, and Kalaba answered for him.

'Thank you for bringing us down, Mr Flemming.'

Above their heads moonlight filtered through the branches of the baobab, and the night birds went about their business. On the ground, each with his own thoughts, the three men slept.

At six o'clock next morning Gould was awake. He stirred the embers of the fire and added wood. Soon it had picked up again and was taking the edge off the morning chill.

Flemming sat up and yawned. 'Christ, I'm stiff.' He made to get to his feet, when suddenly his eyes dilated in disbelief and he froze on the spot. 'Sam! Behind you! !'

Gould heard a low growl, and turned to see a lion walking towards him, fur wet from the river. His mind registered instantly that it was only young, perhaps just over a year old, but even so it would weigh as much as a man. Cautiously, he reached for the Sterling, but there was something strange about this cat. It seemed at ease, unhurried. Nor was it displaying any attack signals, the head-down belly-to-the-ground, tail-twitching

147

slink that would precede, sometimes by almost no time at all, a crouching run, gut-melting roar and final leap to kill. Then, some twenty yards behind the young lion, he saw a sight that was unbelievable. First into view through the foliage was a huge black-maned lion, also moving purposefully in their direction. It was followed by a young lioness with a single cub just behind her. And last of all, in faded green, an ancient Mauser slung over his shoulder, came an old man. By this time Flemming and Kalaba were on their feet, ills forgotten. Gould stood his ground while the young lion reached him, sniffed enquiringly round his boots. Then it was up on its back legs, front paws on his shoulders, wiping a large expanse of tongue over his face. He was forced to lean forwards to avoid over-balancing back onto the fire, and they were locked together in this fashion when the old man arrived. He stopped, and the big lion promptly lay down. The lioness and cub wandered round the fire towards Flemming and Kalaba, who didn't move a muscle. The old man's face was brown and lined, with a silver moustache and clipped, goatee beard. His eyes took in the three men, the guns, the first-aid kit and then he turned to where the rear half of the plane stuck lopsidedly out of the creek. Gould disengaged himself as best he could from the leonine embrace, and the old man turned back to him.

'É a primeira vez que cá vem?'

'English,' Gould managed, 'We speak English.'

'Sim,' said the man. 'Inglès. It was just a small joke: I asked if this was your first visit.' He jerked a thumb at the guns. 'Are you soldiers?'

Gould shook his head. 'No, we were on our way from Blantyre to hunt up-country, and the motors cut out. Lucky to get down alive.'

The old man looked disbelievingly at the machine guns. 'Yes, I can see. Where is the place that you hunt? Maybe I help you.'

Gould was silent, and Kalaba broke in. 'Karonga, inland from Karonga. You know it?'

The old man said nothing, but dragged a worn leather-bound meerschaum out of his pocket and started to fill it with tobacco.

Gould broke the silence. 'Well, I've never seen a stranger sight than you and your friends here bearing down on us. But now you've arrived, my name's Sam, Sam Gould, that sorry-looking

148

joker over there is Murray, he's Australian, and our African friend is called Bill.' He stuck out a hand, and, after a hesitation, the man took it.

'I am call' Almeida,' he said. 'Laurens Almeida.'

A small chorus of greetings went back and forth across the fire. The big lion yawned hugely. Almeida lit his pipe.

'I have a camp, it is eight kilometres from here. You are welcome to come with me until you can—fix up something. Now I am going to Kipen, a colina where the lions stay. After, we can go to the camp.'

Gould looked at Flemming and then Kalaba. 'Can you make it if we help you?'

'Sure, I don't want to stay here.'

'OK, let's cut the crutches and you should be a lot better off.' He told Almeida : 'We'd be really happy to go with you. Just give us a minute or two to get our things together.'

The man nodded, and Gould picked up his heavy hunting knife and set off along the water. The only wood remotely suitable was thick bamboo and he chopped away at the base of two fifteen foot stalks till they fell out of the clump. The ends trailing through the undergrowth attracted the cub, who stalked them intently, occasionally pouncing with high-pitched growls. Kalaba stood up straight for Gould to measure him up and mark the canes.

'Going to have to wrap something round the top and then put a seat cover over it, tight.'

'He can use his spare boot on one,' said Flemming. 'Wrap the cover round the wood and jam the boot down over.'

Almeida watched quietly from behind a cloud of pipe-smoke, surrounded by lions. At length they were ready to move off, Kalaba making a last trial circuit of the fire pursued at a safe distance by the suspicious cub. The big lion got to his feet with apparent regret, and followed Almeida into the foliage. The other cats did likewise; behind them came Flemming and the ungainly figure of Kalaba. Gould brought up the rear.

Their path led from the river and soon they left the lushness behind and found themselves in thorn country, green enough because of the rain, but obviously subjected to long periods of drought. Outcrops of sculptured orange stone reared above the trees and dry luggers filled with bright sand bore the tracks and

149

droppings of elephant, rhino and giraffe. After one and a half hours they reached the gently sloping face of a large kopje and started to climb. By ten they had scaled a ridge of bare orange rock and could see the river winding through the scrub below them. Suddenly Almeida called a halt. But the lions turned in to a gulley and reappeared after a few minutes climbing towards a promontory that jutted out over the country beneath.

'It's their favourite place,' Almeida said. His eyes narrowed in the sunlight. 'Cats like to see around them.'

At eleven, Kalaba was struggling. Gould called out 'How far to camp?'

Almeida didn't look round. 'It is near. Sometimes I go along the river and come back this way. Âmbar loves the water and chases macacos.'

Almeida led the way down through a narrow defile and stopped at the bottom. It was the strangest camp that Gould had ever seen and in one of the best locations. To him the word camp had never meant permanency. A camp was tents, or at the best, makuti huts that the termites ate all the time you were there and finished off after you'd gone. But not this one. Flemming slapped the dust off his trousers and said it looked like Australia, but for Gould it was a scene stolen straight from the American West. There was a bungalow with an old Rover parked outside, lean-tos covering benches and tools, and a high, mesh enclosure that was presumably lion-proof. Strung from a wire, beyond the reach of man or beast, wafer-thin slices of biltong dried in the wind. They started in, and Gould smelt meat cooking over a fire; it reminded him that they hadn't eaten, and a gnawing pain started in his gut. They were still thirty yards from the door when a figure came out into the sunlight, dressed in a T-shirt and faded beige dungarees. Long black hair cascaded round her shoulders as she ran up and embraced Almeida.

'Pai, sao onze e vinte! Tu estás atrasado!'

The old man looked at her lovingly, and the other three did the same, feeling their weariness drop away. Almeida half turned, but offered no introductions.

'Senhors, let us go in. My daughter tells me I am late, but still she will serve us with some food.'

The roof of the house spilled out over a wooden verandah, and

150

inside the large living room it was cool and dim. Grainy, black and white blow-ups on the walls depicted exclusively the girl, the lions, or both. Almeida pointed to a screen in the corner of the room.

'The bathroom is there if you care to wash. And the toilet is outside, along to the right. Just holes in the ground, I'm afraid. When you are finished, we can have a beer.'

For the next ten minutes the men came and went from bathroom to toilet, and the smell of cooked meat got stronger. Eventually, they congregated outside on the verandah and Almeida motioned them into chairs. The girl arrived with four beers and set them on the table. There was a hiss as Flemming pulled the ring on his.

'Ice cold, hey! Well, here's one that won't be seen again!'

The beer flowed chill and frothy, and for a moment no one said anything. Then Almeida motioned to the girl.

'Senhors, my daughter Suzanna. Filha, these men crashed in their plane on the Rukuru. They are lucky to be alive.'

She looked from one to the other around the table and smiled. Flemming felt his face begin to flush.

'Senhors, welcome to our house. Not many pass this way, but those that do can expec' to be well fed.'

Flemming swept his beer into the air, spilling some down his shirt. 'I'll drink to that!'

The girl laughed. 'Are you so hungry?'

Gould rocked back in his chair. 'I apologize for my wild colonial friend. He's just realizing how good it feels to be alive.'

'Me a wild colonial? That's very good!' Flemming grinned, and made a grab at Gould's beer. 'If you're not drinking Sam, I'll have your beer.'

The girl said, 'I'm sorry, do you not like beer?' but Gould's arm snaked over the table like lightning and retrieved the can.

'I may not be much of a drinker, but I'd hate to see Murray get more than his share.' He took a mouthful. 'Where did you learn to speak English so well?'

The girl looked at her father.

'My wife,' he said. 'She came from England. From a town called York.'

Gould waited for him to go on, but instead he changed the subject.

'Why did you not shoot my lion, Senhor, this morning by the river?'

Gould shrugged. 'I don't shoot everything that moves. Besides, I could see that it was only young.'

Almeida considered this. 'Mos' people do not stop to think when they see a big cat. And when he jumped on you, still you did not move.'

'Look, Mr Almeida, I've lived my life with animals. If they threaten me I feel it here.' He tapped the back of his neck. 'If I trust anything at all it must be the few instincts that we humans have left.'

The old man sipped from his glass and wiped his beard with a handkerchief. 'No matter. If you are an animal man, that is why you did not panic. I, too, trust my instincts when I bring you here; you tell me you are hunters, but I think that you are not.' He turned to Suzanna: 'Filha, bring food.'

Source of the tantalizing smell proved to be a variety of meats done kebab style over a charcoal fire. Kalaba sniffed appreciatively.

'It certainly smells better than ng'ombe watatu.'

'What language is that?' asked Almeida.

Kalaba glanced across the table and swallowed a mouthful of meat. 'Swahili. It just means three cows, a brand of corned beef in Tanzania. Sometimes I visit my cousin in Iringa, and the words are easy to pick up.' He laughed. 'Do you know, some tinned meat is so bad there that once he got a can and there was a whole finger inside? He told me that, and I can believe it.'

'White or black?' Flemming asked, eyeing the girl.

'White or black what?'

'The finger, man, the finger. White, and there's a good chance of finding the joker who owns it.'

Kalaba shook his head regretfully. 'My cousin never told me that. But I'll write and find out.'

Gould felt slightly dizzy and concluded that it must be the unaccustomed beer on an empty stomach; he decided that the feeling was not totally unpleasant. Flemming watched the girl's even white teeth pulling meat off a skewer.

Almeida addressed them all: 'One of you can sleep in the main house, and later I will put beds for two in the small *casa*; but for the moment you can relax on the verandah—now you

152

have food inside, sleep is the bes' medicine. I have to go along the river to find some meat for the lions.'

Gould said, 'I'd like to come with you if I may.'

The old man inclined his head. 'As you wish. But your friends are hurt : they should rest.'

He stood up, and Flemming leant over to give Kalaba a hand. 'I reckon he's right, Sam. I'm pretty shickered, and Bill here's got to rest his leg.' The girl stood close to him as she cleared the table, and he breathed in to catch the scent of her.

Almeida agreed. 'Good. Then we go. I may also pick up two of my men from the village. Suzanna, you better come with us.'

The others looked on as Gould held the Rover door open for the girl and then climbed in after her. When they were out of sight Flemming shook his head and slapped Kalaba on the back. 'Mzuri kabisa, eh, baba? A diamond in the dust, and nothing between me and her except a suspicious dad, four flamin' lions and Mr Sam Gould.'

The African turned, and started slowly into the house. 'If that's the way you're thinking, mister, it's time for a bit of beauty sleep. You've been looking tired lately.'

Flemming trailed along behind him, working his way through the chairs. 'It's the responsibility I can't stand. Takes a lot out of a bloke, being an ace pilot.'

He followed Kalaba's derisive shout of laughter into the house.

The Rover was old but game, and jogged along through the bush until they came to a broad expanse of sand with a trickle of water flowing along it. Almeida shifted the gears, and they crawled over without difficulty.

'When the sand is hot and dry, then, sometimes, it is not so easy.'

They reached the other side and bumped up onto dry ground. The girl clutched at Gould's knee for balance as they leant first to the left, then to the right, and she smiled up at him in apology. Close to, her face was dominated by slanting hazel eyes, flecked with green. It was difficult not to stare, for she was perhaps the most bizarre element yet in an extremely surreal set-up. Her hands, one gripping the seat between her legs, the other lightly on his knee, were brown, fingers long, slim and ringless. Gould smiled back. Almeida slowed the vehicle.

153

'Can you shoot, Senhor?'

'I used to, some time ago.'

The old man nodded. 'Ahead there is a clearing. To the left is some thick stuff going to the river. Sometimes I am lucky and find waterbuck there. Soon, when the rains finish, more game will come. But at the moment water is plentiful and they have no need.'

He pulled off to the right, by the foot of a small hill, and got out, taking the Mauser from behind the seat. Gould helped the girl, and the three of them started to clamber through the rocks. Soon they could see an area of bright green grassland stretching down to a loop in the river. Dense thickets separated the water from the grass. Almeida lifted his binoculars, but they were hardly necessary. Immediately to their front three grey-brown blobs grazed at the side of the track. The glasses enlarged two does and a fair-sized buck. Gould looked over at the old man and wondered what the hell was the point of it all, living out here in the middle of nowhere with a pride of cats that he had to feed by the gun, and a daughter who should be enjoying life somewhere civilized with other people of her own age. Only thank God that he'd wandered along when he had. It was the one good break that'd come their way since the whole abortive affair began. And tonight would come the big discussion, the attempt to thrash something productive out of the shambles. Perhaps somewhere, eight or nine hundred miles to the north, hopeful people were still waiting, hour by hour, believing them alive. Almeida was moving back down the way they'd come.

He called up: 'I think it easier to go back, then round.'

Gould looked at the buck. 250 yards. No wind. A wartime rifle. 'If it's the buck you want, let me try from here.'

The old man turned and smiled. 'Forgive me Senhor, it is not that I doubt you, only my rifle is perhaps not to what you are used.'

Gould said, 'If I miss, you get sole rights to salvage the plane.'

They faced each other for a moment, then Almeida unslung the rifle. 'And if you hit?'

'Then it's a good day for lions, because you won't find me or the others eating waterbuck.' He leant forward against a rock, adjusted the sling, and brought the gun tight against his shoulder. A round snicked into the breech, too loudly for comfort. The girl

154

sat watching quietly, and out on the green the buck raised its head. Gould inched the barrel up onto target, steadied and squeezed the trigger. Before the sound of the report was over the three animals were in the air and sprinting towards the bush. But only the two does made it : the buck's instant evasive action had been only a reflex.

Almeida lowered the glasses and accepted the gun back again. 'It's a good day.'

Gould wiped his palms on the seat of his jeans and started back to the pick-up. 'And you can have the plane as well if you want. With a little bit of ingenuity those seats'd add a lot of class to your toilet.'

15.00, Monday, 25 March

Max Ebert of CBS Television News stepped out of the Skylane, stretched and looked around. A tall young man came from the front of the aircraft, the pilot, wiping his palms on a piece of rag.

'Well, we made it.'

'Yeah.' Ebert's voice lacked all trace of enthusiasm. He looked around to where Jim Schreiber, the cameraman, was lowering a heavy silver case onto the ground. Behind him stood Mojo Peters, who handled sound. Ebert helped them down with the gear, and glanced at his watch. Three pm—eight hours since the telephone had disrupted a deep sleep in the Cairo Hilton. Ebert had been chasing trouble spots for fifteen years, and in all that time he had never known epidemics, wars or famines to start at a reasonable time of day. There'd been two flights available to Nairobi, a PAA 707 at eight and a TWA Jet Clipper an hour later. They'd flown TWA—Ebert couldn't imagine the catastrophe that would induce him or his crew to fly Pan-Arab. And by one they were in the Cessna, eating sandwiches, and flying almost due west across Lake Victoria, to Nyakanyasi.

An open Datsun pulled up beside them in a cloud of dust and a European climbed awkwardly out of the cab. His face was lined and streaked with blood, and a rough bandage swelled his left knee. He gestured to the cases.

'Thank Christ ! Those supplies from Dar ?'

Ebert took a pace forward. ' 'Fraid not, they're full of cameras.

155

We're a news team, CBS, come down from Cairo to cover the bombing.'

The other man spat in the dust and wiped the back of his hand across his mouth. 'Fucking great! A TV company gets people here from the other side of nowhere, and the bloody government can't even send pills to cure the pox.'

Ebert shrugged apologetically.

'Look, fella, we just go where it says on the ticket.'

'I'm sorry, I'm sorry, as you can imagine, it's been a bad day.' He offered a large, dirty hand, which Ebert shook. 'My name's Barrett—if you put your gear in the back I suppose the least I can do is run you into town.'

They drove straight to the market place, an area of beaten earth, where Barrett stopped the car and got out. 'They came in low just before seven this morning. Two of them.' He pointed north. 'One run and they were gone. Can't have lasted more than thirty seconds at the outside. Forty-three dead, and a whole lot more wishing they were.' He spat again, the futile gesture somehow emphasizing the monstrous futility of the morning's events. 'They must have been back at Entebbe in time for breakfast. And then the rest of the morning to stick golliwog transfers along the sides of their cockpits.' He turned and got into the car. 'I've got to go. If you like I'll send the taxi round from the Shell station to get you mobile. He'll tell you where the hospital is and a hotel of sorts in case you decide to stick around.'

Ebert said, 'Thanks, Mr Barrett, that'd be fine. Tell me though, maybe we'd like to talk to you later, what exactly is it you do out here?'

Barrett leaned his foot on the accelerator and eased forward. 'You're the man with an instinct for these things Mr Ebert—you tell me exactly what it is that anyone does out here.' With that, he let the clutch all the way out and was gone.

After two and a half hours probing Ebert had enough footage. He returned to the market in the evening for the last setup. Schreiber framed him by one of the rocket craters. The camera pulled slowly back from the hole, and Ebert's face came into shot as he started his wind-up.

'It took just a moment here this morning for forty-nine civilians to die and a further seventy to sustain crippling injuries. Colonel Omuria, leader of the military junta that dictates policy in Uganda has stated today that he will spare no effort—and I quote—"to persecute and demoralize the populations of those countries that harbour enemies of the state".' Schreiber zoomed in to a tight head as Ebert went on : 'If this is the case, it seems certain that without external military intervention there is little the Tanzanian government can do to prevent invasion from the north. This is Max Ebert in Nyakanyasi, Tanzania, for CBS News.' It would make a good little piece and they'd be first on the air. In TV's inverted terms bad news was good news, and the worst news was the best.

Chapter Eight

16.00, Monday, 25 March

Gould, the old man and his daughter were sitting by the river fishing. The bank dropped away steeply, eroded by the recent floods, but now the water was down and a sandbar could be seen just beneath the surface. The tackle was simple, a two inch hook on the end of a length of nylon line. Offal from the buck was bait.

Almeida teased his line up and down. 'You don't ask many questions, Senhor.'

Gould shrugged. It was peaceful by the river, and the Rover stood just behind them, full of butchered meat. Suzanna, knees drawn up to her chin, watched a family of hippo break surface upstream; their snorts came down faintly on the breeze.

'As I have said, Senhor, we meet few people here. But I have all that I wan' from life. When you and your friends are gone, to do the things that you must, we will still be here. Who knows? Perhaps we shall hear of you one day on the radio.'

Gould said 'You have a radio? In the camp? I didn't see it.'

The girl said, 'Only to listen. The transmitter got broken and we never go anywhere that could repair it.'

Almeida jerked his line hard, and the ugly, whiskered head of a catfish came out of the water in a flurry. He hauled it in, a good twenty pounds, and chopped it hard on its large forehead with a panga. The mouth was big enough to take a man's fist.

'You know,' said Gould, 'the tribes up north use waterbuck to catch crocodile. They set a stake in the bank with a piece of palm rope leading into the water—the meat goes on some of the nastiest homemade hooks you're ever likely to see. The croc makes up his mind and comes in hard. That's his first mistake.

158

He takes the spiked meat and backs off fast, twisting like always. That's his second. They finish 'em off with spears.'

Almeida finished extracting his hook and pushed the fish away from him. 'I, too, worked for a game department, a long time ago.'

Gould looked round sharply. 'I never said I worked for anyone.'

'No, but I think that you did. You sound too much like me, disillusioned. We are people who hoped to change things for the better and failed.' He passed his line to Suzanna and drew out his pipe.

Gould looked at Almeida and at the hippos in the dimming light. It was a trick of the memory, of course, déjà vu, but it seemed at that moment he had been here before. Only the girl didn't belong. She was part of a different past, a girl called Katherine standing with her mother on the platform at Bafwabili, waiting for a train that wouldn't come to take them to the airport at Kamina and safety. Always there were rivers, the Nile of his boyhood, the thick waters of the Congo; in another man's history the Zambesi, Limpopo, Rukuru. Draining the uplands of Africa, draining the tears of those who still lived there, but no longer belonged. Almeida and his daughter were on their feet and Gould walked with them in silence along the bank. Only when the engine started with a clatter did his mind come back to the present. Confused, he opened a window and braced his feet on the floor. But they were all in other places, other times, and no one said a thing.

Evening, Monday, 25 March

'We've got to try it,' said Priest. 'And God knows if we'll get another chance.'

Charlie Soon listened to the footsteps getting nearer. 'It will not be easy to escape from Zanzibar.' He shuffled his feet on the damp floor. 'Even for agents of the British government.'

Priest sighed. 'It was for your own protection. We didn't know what the set-up was down here. If you'd been taken on your own they would have shot you full of dope and found out it was an independent job with a nice, simple motive—profit. Much healthier than working for a government.'

159

Charlie grunted. 'My motive has always been a nice simple profit. No money, no incentive.'

Priest moved to the corner of the cell. 'Money might be off the menu, but we'll come through with the other goods. Now, will you get ready? I've got all the incentive I need right now to get out of here, and cash doesn't even come into it.'

Charlie made some strange motions in the air with his hands, and moved towards the door. The footsteps halted outside the cell.

Priest crouched in the corner, his hands on his stomach, and began rocking gently to and fro. The keys clanked in the lock. Charlie positioned himself against a side wall.

'Come out!'

They felt a gust of cold air, and Charlie called out something in Chinese. There was a brief discussion in the corridor and then a guard came in, and another. They stood on both sides of the door. A captain entered last and pushed past them, stooping towards Priest. He was about a yard distant when Priest reached up and grabbed him by the tunic. The razor-sharp splinter of perspex from the light cover pricked the man's throat. A trickle of blood rolled downwards.

'Tell them to drop the guns.' Even as he spoke there was a grunt and a clatter. Before either guard had a chance to move Soon hit them both in the face with a small flurry of punches that landed with a sound like running feet. Priest pushed hard and the captain straightened. Soon's arm whipped down to chop the exposed side of his neck, and withdrew. The captain dropped. Priest looked around. The captain was breathing, saliva gurgling in his throat, but the two guards lay crumpled with their faces battered and awash with blood. They seemed very dead. Priest looked from Charlie to the bodies and back again.

Charlie nodded, a small almost imperceptible movement of his head.

Priest exhaled softly. 'Jee-sus!' Any doubts that might have crossed his mind about Charlie vanished instantly.

The Chinese turned away.

'Come on,' Priest told him, swallowing his revulsion. 'Let's get changed.' He collected the guns together, picked up a torch, and palmed the keys. Soon stripped the captain and donned his

160

clothes; they weren't a good fit. Priest shook his head, and tucked some hundred shilling bills into his pocket.

'You'll do. Here, take this.' He passed over a machine pistol and glanced down at the guards and the captain, ridiculous in his underwear.

'Let's go.' Quietly they slipped out into the corridor, locking the cell behind them. Priest put the spare weapons down and for a moment they stood and listened, alert for the slightest noise. But there was none. Together they worked their way along the dank wall, not even chancing to use the torch. The courtyard was dark and empty, and no light showed in the palace buildings. The whole place seemed deserted.

Priest whispered, 'I don't like it. Where the hell is everyone?'

Charlie said nothing. They passed through an archway and entered an alley, narrow between high walls. This came to an abrupt end at a heavy wooden gate; they inched it open and peered through. In front of them stretched a parade ground of indeterminate size. Faded white lines showed where tennis courts might once have been. Clouds of insects crowded round blue-white lights high above them, and to one side trucks were drawn up neatly in front of a low-slung barrack building.

'This way.' They headed away from the trucks and found themselves once more in the shadows of the palace. The wall gave way to a tall fence of taughtly stretched wire which sang in the wind. The moon appeared half-heartedly through a bank of cloud, and they could see a road on the other side of the fence. But there was no way through it. After a few more paces Priest stopped and pointed.

'The guardhouse.' Ahead of them the road swung into the camp through high reinforced gates. Two soldiers were on duty, and lights blazed from the windows of a small accommodation block. Further up the road, uniform bungalows were spaced at intervals, square like dice. The fugitives scrambled down into a monsoon drain and clambered along its terraces towards the toylike houses. Beside each one was a green toy jeep. After ten minutes they reached the back of the first house, and silently edged their way towards the jeep. It was parked just outside a pale circle cast by one of the street lights; Priest gazed in disbelief at a single key hanging from the ignition. He got in between the front and back seats, hunching up as small as he could.

161

'Free-wheel down the hill before you start her up.' Charlie put the gun on the passenger seat and released the brakes. They moved forward soundlessly, except for the slight crunching of gravel under the tyres. Slowly the bungalows receded as they picked up speed. Charlie turned on the ignition, put the box in third, and let out the clutch. They slowed, then the motor fired, and they were on their way. A short, right-hand bend, and ahead lay the guard-house and the gates.

'Maybe we should have cards.'

Priest's voice was muffled. 'If there's trouble put your foot down.'

It was too late now, they were stopping. One of the sentries moved to the gate, the other called out something in a sing-song voice. Charlie laughed and replied. The gates opened. They were moving. Priest tensed for the shouts, a sudden burst of fire. But nothing.

'Christ, we've made it! What did he say, what did he ask you?'

Soon accelerated along outside the fence, and passed the wall that hid the palace gardens. 'He just told me I'd better put my lights on, or the police would get me in the town.'

Priest gave a terse laugh but sobered quickly. 'It's not over yet. Remember what they told us, even if you get out of the palace, Zanzibar is its own fortress. Now we need a boat.'

Noisily, the jeep sped along the ever narrowing streets of the old town.

In the cell they had so recently left Chen knelt distastefully by one of the dead guards and took a small radio from the man's equipment. His head felt as if it were on fire, and he moved it slowly, with great care. It was ironic that his involvement in the plans to ensure that the two men escaped in an authentic fashion had ended in his falling for the oldest trick, but the final result would be the same. He pressed the transmit button and called, but there was no reply. Perhaps the thing had been damaged in the fight; not that it had lasted very long, some ten seconds had been enough for the Chinaman to lay them all out. More likely the walls . . . how thick were they? He cast around by the door with the tiny set, but there was nothing. He began to feel cold and worried. How long would it take them to realize

162

where he was? Half an hour, maybe, by which time ... His eyes looked around for a machine pistol, and flickered to the door, but it would take a bomb to shift it. As a last resort he stuck his head close to the grill and started to shout. But the ancient masonry absorbed the noise and threw it back at him. The captor was the captive. There was nothing to do but wait.

The harbour lay still as a snap-shot, shaded with the darker tones of blue, green and grey. All the sounds were distant : a yelping dog, slamming door, the invisible diesels of a passing coaster. Loose roofing on two large godowns clattered in the wind, and scattered boxes bore the trade marks of the clove industry. Of nightwatchmen, sailors, drunks, there was no sign; the jetties were deserted. Priest peered into the shadows, sensing danger but seeing none. Perhaps he was being over-sensitive. Docks the world over quietened down during the night, and there was hardly enough work here for a shift operation. Along the harbour wall, iron rings rusted above empty berths, and the paint of long-forgotten names faded on grey stone bollards.

Charlie Soon nudged his arm and pointed. Nosing towards the jetty was a powerful launch, with a small wheelhouse and a large cockpit aft. The water churned as it sidled against the wall, and a man carrying a rope stepped onto an iron ladder and started up it. There were three of them altogether, of indistinguishable nationality. Their voices carried as they flipped two tyres over the side and tied up fore and aft; then they climbed ashore and headed along the wharf, disappearing into the narrow streets that led away from the waterfront.

Priest turned to Charlie. 'There's something bloody funny going on. Empty palace, those jeeps with full tanks and keys ... and now, in a deserted dockyard, the friends of the hunted arrive with high-speed transport. Makes you wonder what's been happening in the world while we've been under lock and key.'

'We'd better get moving anyway,' said Charlie. 'You may be right. But it don't make any difference. We still got to go.'

Briskly they walked out of the shadow's anonymity towards the boat. Nothing else stirred. Their feet made deafening noises on the silent wharf. Somewhere behind them a voice called out and Priest felt a familiar tingling between the shoulder blades.

But the shout was not for them. The wind tugged at their clothing and it started to rain.

'Can you handle this thing?' They had reached the boat. Charlie nodded, and climbed down the ladder. Priest passed him the machine pistol and went to unfasten the ropes before following. Gently, he pushed them off from the weed-covered stonework of the harbour wall, and pulled the tyres inboard. The bows swung round towards the sea. Charlie had removed a wooden board beneath the control panel.

'Shine the torch here.' Priest did so, and Charlie squatted down, unwrapping an oily length of rag from around a bunch of tools. The ignition was a simple two-way switch. He shorted out two of the pins with a screwdriver and a red light glowed briefly on the panel. Working quickly, he cut a four inch section out of one of the wires and rejoined the ends. Then he twisted the short piece across the two terminals. This time the red light went on glowing.

'Maybe we go now.' There was a blue flash as he held the screwdriver across the juice wire, the engine caught and the exhaust burbled into the night. He stood up and eased the throttle forward, the wheel turned. Black water slid past them in a confusion of broken reflections. Charlie pushed the throttles open and steered towards the gap in the harbour wall. Priest clawed his way up out of the cabin.

'We want to hold this course outside for a minute, and then steer 175°. They've even got an Admiralty chart on board. It's the best part of forty-five miles to Dar.'

Charlie was getting the feel of the helm. 'We can probably make twenty-five knots in this thing. Why don't we just go straight over?'

Priest looked at the tank gauge. Under half full. But ample for where they were going. 'Because there's nothing there. The main road is way inland, and we'd never make it to Kenya on what we've got.' He shifted his grip. 'I don't get it. If they're following, where the hell are they? I just have this feeling . . .' A sheet of water came through the night towards them and slapped against the windscreen.

Charlie throttled back. 'We'll get a big sea when we leave the island.'

The land was dropping away fast off the port beam, and the

hull powered into the rising waves with a noise like thunder. Priest braced himself, holding on to a grab rail.

'You know what I think? I think we escaped too soon. It was all meant to happen later with a cast of thousands . . . monitored of course, from a discreet distance.' He looked behind them where their wake disappeared, foaming, into the blackness. 'We might, we just might, have lost contact.'

'And in Dar?' asked Charlie. 'What happens there?'

But Priest had ducked down into the cabin and was poring over the chart.

Chen strode fuming through his office door in 'A' block clad in a bathrobe of black brocade. Across his back red dragons writhed in mortal combat. He had been incarcerated for thirty-five minutes, and it was now twelve past eight.

'Kae dae hai ping doah?'

His ADC relaxed from a position of attention. 'No one realized, sir, I mean we weren't expecting them then and nothing was ready.'

Chen sat down heavily. 'What happened at the gate?'

'They went straight through. Then the guardhouse rang me and I sent men over to the cell.'

'And the boat?'

'They took it anyway. Luw's men brought it round and our squad was still on its way. They had the luck of the devil. *Tanga* saw them go out and radioed in. Of course, I told them to follow, but the sea's rough and they've lost time.'

Chen drummed his fingers on the desk. 'If they lose contact they'll be on the next ship home. As soon as there's some idea where they're heading contact the po loy on the mainland and ring me. I'll be in my room changing.' At the door he turned. 'You realize they must be aware we organized the escape? Which means they know we're close behind them. And why. They're going to be very careful.'

He left abruptly. The ADC breathed out slowly and lit a Sportsman. Then he reached for the phone.

It was nine-thirty when they saw the lights of the city to starboard. The rain had stopped but occasional flashes of sheet lightning showed greenly through the heavy clouds. Priest

165

counted to himself, eyes fixed on an intermittent light dead ahead.

'That's the one! Three blinks every twenty. The main channel leaves that light to starboard and follows a series of constant greens. We want to go on past the town, try to find an old wharf or something.'

Charlie said: 'Fishing vessel ahead.'

They were coming up fast behind an old MFV, showing one white light on her mizzenmast. Charlie moved the wheel to give her a wide berth, but Priest stopped him.

'Get in alongside! If we take their boat we can send this thing off on its own as a decoy. Fishermen should know where to land around here without being seen.'

The vessels closed fast and two Africans came on deck shouting and waving. Charlie throttled back and steered a parallel course some fifteen feet off. At seven knots the sleek launch rolled badly. Priest brandished the gun and the Africans stopped shouting.

'Tell 'em Charlie.'

'Tunavjia mtumbwi weni—tutupie kamba. Suria!'

The launch edged nearer and Priest waved the gun again. One man ducked into the wheelhouse and the MFV lost impetus and slowed. The other cast a loose coil of rope at Priest. He made a couple of quick turns round a cleat and then pushed the tyres outboard. There was a grinding bump as the two craft touched. Priest, standing on the foredeck waited for the next swell and jumped over to the other vessel. The Africans stared dumbly at the machine pistol and with a gesture he moved them round behind the wheelhouse.

'Charlie! Lash the wheel amidships, yes, that's it. Now get a line from the stern locker, put a loop round the throttle and pass the end through the fairlead in the bow.' He waited while Soon put a bowline over the throttle and crawled carefully forward with the line. Then he called:

'OK, pass me that and hop aboard.'

Soon had one leg on the heaving deck of the MFV when Priest saw the Africans tense. Without hesitation, he squeezed the trigger and bullets sprayed the air. There was a crash as the windows of the wheelhouse disintegrated. Then silence. The acrid smell of cordite was gone in a second. The fishermen froze on

166

the spot. Then slowly they relaxed, retreating in unison to the stern. Soon resumed his climb aboard.

'OK Charlie, ease us ahead, slow as you like. Get her heading straight out.' When the two boats were both facing due east he moved forward and thrust the gun into the wheelhouse.

'Watch 'em.' He bent forward and quickly undid the rope. The swell was catching them broadside and there was a shuddering crunch as they parted for the last time. Priest pulled hard on the throttle rope and the launch leapt forward snatching it out of his hands. They watched the craft pick up speed in a lazy arc until eventually it straightened out and disappeared to the southeast. The MFV got under way and Priest took the gun.

'Time we had a talk with our two friends about a landing place.'

It was after ten o'clock when the commander of the *Tanga* realized that his quarry was heading in the direction of Australia. He put on speed, and ten minutes later the launch came into sight sending up clouds of spray as it crashed awkwardly through the waves. Searchlights revealed the empty cockpit and roped-off wheel. The commander despatched a radio message, feeling glad that someone else was going to have to leap aboard the bucking boat. At moments like this he was happy to delegate.

Chen placed the receiver back on its rest and looked at his ADC. 'They've lost them. Lao tien yeuh! Don't ask me how.'

The ADC said 'I don't understand—*Tanga* is well equipped, and in any case the launch has an emitter.'

Chen got up and moved over to a wall map of the coast. 'Get me Po loy.' He drew an imaginary line round the city of Dar-es-Salaam with his finger. 'I don't mean they've lost the boat. I mean the men are no longer on the boat. It was rounding the headland, apparently going south of the city. Only it never turned, just kept on out to sea.'

'Fortress for you, sir.'

Chen picked up the phone. If only he had more intelligent men and less so-called African Security Units there'd be a much bigger chance of success. 'Priority One. I want road-blocks on all routes out of the city and descriptions of any cars stolen circulated immediately, especially cross-country vehicles.

167

And get men out to the airport, full alert, check every plane. You know what we're looking for. Make sure you find them.'

Chen gave the phone back and poured himself a small measure of rice wine. Heads would roll when this got out. And he was under no illusions : the first would be his.

The MFV nosed slowly through a narrow slick of water leading off the main channel. On one side the high wooden walls of an old warehouse reared against the sky; on the other sewage splattered down from an unseen duct set in the stonework. They were about ten yards into the channel when the boat touched, first to port then starboard. Charlie cut the motor, and there was quiet except for the hollow splashing of the muck in the water. The two men dragged the Africans, gagged and bound, into the wheelhouse and laid them on the floor. On deck it was impossible to see far, and the building cut out what little light there was from the sky. Charlie got his fingers under one of the planks on the warehouse wall, and pulled. It creaked outwards, leaving a rectangular slit of total darkness. Priest joined him, and soon there was a hole big enough to climb through. Their torch revealed thousands of barrels, and rats' eyes reflected its beam in a shifting pattern of red and yellow. Priest eased his way through the gap, and Soon followed. They moved slowly, working their way between mountains of ancient casks, sinking deep in the glutinous mud carpeting the floor. They headed away from the water and gradually the slime underfoot grew less. When they had nearly reached the side wall of the building Priest slipped and fell. He grabbed at a barrel as he went down and suddenly a whole stack started to collapse. For twenty seconds the air was full of falling wood, and then there was silence. Charlie got up from where he had been crouching and groped his way forward. The torch had gone out. He called to Priest. 'You all right?' He could hear the other man struggling to his feet some yards ahead, but could see nothing.

'My arm,' Priest told him. 'I think it may be broken.'

The torch came on and Charlie could see him gingerly flexing the fingers of his left hand. There was a grunt of pain, and then he said 'It seems to work after a fashion, let's get out of here.'

Within a minute their path led to a small wooden door, set in the bottom corner of two much larger doors. Priest pushed

168

against it firmly. A padlock clanked to the ground outside, and one of the hinges came out of the woodwork in a shower of fine dust. The door fell open and they stepped into a small yard overgrown with weed and grass, and beyond it a mud track led away past the remnants of storage sheds. Charlie took the torch and switched it off, and Priest held the gun under his good arm, wrapping it as best he could in his damp denim top. After the warehouse, the night was warm. The track led to a hole in a link fence and on to a disused railway. Priest tossed a mental coin, and they turned right, moving briskly over the unevenly spaced sleepers. Around the first curve was a small road crossing the line, and the sound of a car. They broke into a trot, stopping in the shadows just short of the road to watch the vehicle approach. It came towards them slowly, an ancient Peugeot with only one headlight, and the two men ran out into its path waving their arms. The car slowed as if to stop, but then the driver thought better of it and revved the motor noisily. The gears crunched as he tried to change down, but the engine backfired once and stalled. Priest ran to the car door and pulled it open. The Peugeot came to a standstill, and the driver scrambled out, arms high in the air.

'Please! You are wanting my car, then take it, but don't shoot! Please don't shoot!' Priest found himself confronted with a middle aged Sikh, his turban bright above the dark, bearded face.

'Don't worry,' Priest told him. 'We mean you no harm. Just drive us to the bus station in town, and you can go home.' He passed the gun to Soon who got into the back of the car and held it across his knees. Shaking, the Indian got back into the driver's seat and fumbled with the ignition keys. Priest slammed his door and they pulled laboriously away.

'How far to the big bus station?'

Soon watched the driver's face, strained and nervous in the rear-view mirror.

'Four miles. Not far at all. We can be there quickly.'

'Take small roads, we don't want to be seen.' Priest looked ahead as the car ground its way along the uneven road. Forgotten warehouses crowded together in the night, and the route was crossed and re-crossed by the rusting rails of disused sidings. Priest said: 'We can use this man, in the VW.' He turned to

169

the Sikh. 'Listen. We have to get out of Tanzania quickly. That means getting to the airport.'

The man nodded mutely as they turned on to a small suburban road. Cheerless windows patterned the bleak walls of identical corrugated pre-fabs, row upon row, without hope of change.

Priest went on : 'We have a vehicle in the town. A good one, new, not like this. All you have to do is drive us to the airport. That's all. Then you can keep the car.'

'You are the men they are looking for.'

'What men?' said Priest. 'What are you talking about?'

The Sikh's throat worked for a second, then his voice came. 'The city was full of troops. All waiting for something to happen. Yesterday.'

'And today?' Priest urged. 'What about today?'

But the man just moved his head wordlessly from side to side, as if recent events were too much to take in. Abruptly, they came into a narrow street of sufficient rank to merit dull lamps at irregular intervals. Dirty signs announced the Hotel Africa and the Mulango Niteclub. The Peugeot's cycloptic light flickered wanly on pairs of girls walking hand in hand along the street. Painted faces gave the car bright, commercial smiles of black and crimson before fading into the night like spectres. The Sikh pointed.

'The bus station is at the ending of this road.'

They were only one hundred and fifty yards from the turning when a vehicle pulled into the street, blocking it completely. Six or seven soldiers got out and took up positions in the shadows.

'Pull in,' said Priest. 'Here on the left.'

They hit the kerb outside the open door of the Kampala Club and stopped. A black curtain muffled the sounds of music from inside and tatty photos proclaimed the presence of Meli from Arabia—Non Stop Floor Show and Dancing! Incurious eyes watched the car from a payslit above the pictures.

Priest turned to Charlie. 'The vans are parked round to the left. But there was an alley by the one Sam used, and that's the van we want.'

Soon said 'If we make a left here, then a right, we'll come to them.'

Priest looked at the Sikh. 'Charlie, you'll have to go it alone. We need our driver and it's too much of a risk taking him up

170

there. He's only got to shout at the wrong time and it's all over. I'll keep him here where there's plenty of noise. Try to get the bus round the back and up this street. You should still be worth a bit of respect in that uniform.'

'Okay—but I'd better leave the gun here.' He climbed out of the Peugeot and disappeared. Priest opened his door.

'Right, we're going to see the dancing. And don't forget, one stupid move and you'll get hurt.' He moved to get out but the Sikh touched him on the arm. Priest looked into the dark eyes. 'My name is Devji Singh. Last year government took my business. Now I rent it from them. They think my house too good for me, now I live where you would not place your pig.' Priest's attention wandered and his eyes slid to the end of the street. But the soldiers hadn't moved. Following his gaze, Singh gestured towards the army unit. 'I am not a stupid man. All these soldiers, searching ... and bombing in the north.' He stopped, fumbling for words. 'Good or bad, you must be ... important. One day we will all be told to go, like Uganda. Perhaps, if I am helping you now, you will remember my name when that day comes?'

Music from the club percolated thickly through the black drape.

Priest dragged his mind back to what the man was saying. 'Singh, if we ever get out of this place I'll make sure your name goes on the right list. You have my word that I can do it.'

Together they left the car and crossed the pavement to the club.

Inside, the air was heavy with smoke and the smell of alcohol. White sailors shuffled with their whores on a tiny beer-soaked floor. The band was brass and drums only, a combo that had already left the threshold of pain far behind, and on benches in the recesses of the room girls from twelve to forty sat, waiting for the soft touch. Priest and Singh pulled a table round and sat with their backs to the wall, a couple of yards from the curtain. A man appeared to their left, a small towel tucked into his waistband.

'What you drinking, Jack?'

'Nothing,' said Priest. 'Maybe later.'

The African leant over the table, forearms running with sweat. 'Everyone drinks in here.'

171

Priest looked up into his face, fat lips, black eyes with yellow whites. 'We don't,' he said.

The waiter stayed there for about five seconds, then his gaze dropped. Muttering, he straightened and moved off.

An African girl, wearing a long Asian-hair wig, stopped at the table. She wore a shiny green dress and high heels. Smiling, she worked the dress up over her thighs revealing minute white panties, brilliant against her skin. In a second she bent at the knees and lowered herself onto Priest's lap. Then she leaned back and slipped an arm round his neck. He could feel the muscles in her buttocks twitching provocatively against his loins, and perversely felt himself start to react. Annoyed, he lifted her roughly and parked her, protesting, on a near-by chair.

There was a tinny screech as the band played a fanfare, and a mauve light lit the dance floor. The bandleader gave a spiel in broken English, and then the drummer broke into a clever syncopated rhythm on a set of tuned bongos. And on came Meli, in naked time to the drums. Priest caught his breath and the chatter in the smoke-filled room died away. The girl was perfect, even in an African way, beautiful. Her head was shaved, her nude body glistened with oil. High, full breasts moved to a rhythm of their own with an elasticity that revealed she had yet to bear young.

She might not have come from anywhere near Arabia, but she twisted and writhed, bent and spread with a controlled abandon that had the room spellbound. Now she had a beer can in one hand, shaking it suggestively up and down. She hooked a finger through the ring and eased it open. Froth under pressure hosed up her belly, over her breasts. With one hand she smoothed it in to her skin, and teased the blackness of her nipples until they stood erect with fine white beer spray frothing around them. A man in the front row started out of his chair, but his friends held him back. Soon the drummer went into a limbo, and the girl slithered over the floor like a serpent, legs wide, under a stick resting on two beer bottles. The drum beat slowed as first one breast, then the other, cleared the stick by a hairsbreadth. The audience started to applaud but the girl rose effortlessly and picked up one of the bottles. Without preamble she licked its neck and inserted it between her legs. The drummer's hands were a blur as she leapt into the air. When she landed the neck of the

172

bottle had disappeared. Legs wide, she crouched on the floor and little by little absorbed the bottle with her body. Ripples of muscle flowed over her abdomen and she kept gasping with pain, whether real or part of the act it was impossible to say. Then she threw back her head and went into a crab. The rhythm slowed, her body opened, the bottle slid from her flesh and clanked to the floor. The lights went out.

There was a pandemonium of shouts in various languages. Priest found himself clapping with the rest, wanting more. Then he felt a gust of air as the curtain moved and Soon's voice cut through the uproar.

'You can come now.'

Priest and Singh moved through the curtains. Behind them, the band struck up with a parody of Colonel Bogey.

The Tamarind Volkswagen was ticking over in the street outside, facing the way they'd come.

Priest said, 'Singh, you're driving,' and he climbed in through the big sliding door. Charlie appeared with the machine pistol from the Peugeot and got in.

'You're getting to love that thing,' Priest grinned. 'Have any trouble?'

They pulled away and Charlie watched the dingy streets passing to the left and right. 'Africans all over the place, but they don't know what they're looking for,' he said. 'Trouble comes if we meet Chinese.'

Priest thought for a moment. 'Depends how far ahead of the action we are. We haven't wasted much time, perhaps they're still chasing the boat.'

'What will happen at the airport?'

Priest smiled and wished he knew. 'Let's see what's there when we arrive.'

Singh drove out of the city through a latticework of tiny streets. The airport was eight miles away, and normally the journey took under twenty minutes. Once they pulled out into a street where an African patrol stood grouped around a truck. But the soldiers barely spared them a glance; in East Africa theirs was the most innocuous sight possible : white safari bus, native driver, whites on their way to hotel, airport or club. The same combination occurred a thousand times a day. Priest and Soon had pulled two black holdalls and an attaché case

173

from a locked compartment under the seats behind them. The holdalls contained spare clothes and lightweight waterproofs, folded and vacuumed in minute polythene packs. In the attaché case were duplicate documents, miniature glasses, currency notes, and two small transceiver sets. Priest undid the zip of his denim top.

'I'm going to smarten up a bit just in case we have to make a public appearance. Maybe you'd better stay with the Chinese gear for a bit longer.' He chuckled. 'If we get stopped, I'm your prisoner and we're going to Peking. Here, take one of these, you might get locked in the toilet.'

Soon tucked the little radio into the top pocket of his tunic and straightened the cap on his head. The VW turned onto the airport road; there was no sign of a roadblock. Distant orange lights marked the terminal building. As they drew nearer, light aircraft came into sight parked neatly along the perimeter fence and then two big jets, floating in individual pools of light, surrounded by petrol bowsers and maintenance crews.

Priest reached for the glasses. 'Pull in here will you, Singh? Make like you're checking the tyres.'

They stopped, and Singh got out. Two other microbuses and a taxi passed by. Priest opened the window and focused on the jets. The first was an East African Airways VC10. As he watched a tractor pulled the steps away. The second plane was partly hidden by the first, but there was no mistaking the insignia on the high tailplane.

'British Caledonian 707,' Priest muttered. 'Christ, I don't believe it.' He dropped the glasses into the case. 'OK, drive on slowly. Let me tell you what's going to happen.' He reached back into the case, wincing as he moved his left arm and came up with a biro and paper. 'That 707's a cargo plane, I can see them loading pallets. That means they'll have a loadmaster organizing things inside the plane. You've got to bullshit your way through the air freight gate and take this piece of paper to that man. Tell him to give it to the captain, immediately.'

He folded the paper which bore a single line of figures and passed it forward. Singh reached back and took it. They were half-way to the lights when the road started to veer away from the perimeter fence. There were no other vehicles in sight. Whatever was happening elsewhere in the cause of national security,

174

it wasn't happening here. Priest reached up and wound a handle set in the roof. A section slid back leaving a big square hole, used by tourists for game viewing.

'Pull right in to the fence. We'll be by that blockhouse, can you see it?'

Sixty yards inside the airfield on the edge of the tarmac there was a small brick construction. It was barely visible, picked out of the night by the faint overthrow of the spotlights illuminating the jets. The wire scraped the side of the VW abrasively, and Soon, still carrying the gun, disappeared through the top. His weight bent the roof and there was a percussive sound as he leapt and the metal popped back into place.

Priest tapped Singh on the shoulder. 'Good luck. If you can't get in drive straight back this way and we'll see you. Don't stop. If that happens, we'll have to make contact ourselves.' The roof bent again. Then he was gone, and the microbus pulled back onto the road and headed down into the lights.

Priest and Soon crouched in the grass watching the two planes and the terminal buildings. The jets on the VC10 rose to a crescendo and dropped again. Slowly the nose swung round till it was pointing straight at them, like the predatory beak of an angry condor. Priest watched the plane move out. When he looked round again, the unassuming shape of a white microbus was moving slowly along the various embarkation points. Then it turned towards the 707, and Priest watched the sidelights progressing in the darkness. It stopped half in the light, and Singh appeared. He walked quickly towards the plane, and started to climb the steps that normally led to first class. A man in uniform appeared to stop him. Singh waved the paper. They both climbed towards the cabin. The hydraulic table that lifted crates was backing off, and over the loading bay's square black mouth a huge door gullwinged down, ready for takeoff. One by one the engines worked themselves into a fury. Minutes passed. Singh came down the steps carrying a parcel. He got the VW started and began to move, describing a large circle which would eventually have him heading back towards the terminal. The sidelights came obliquely towards the blockhouse, while out on the main runway the VC10 lifted, leaving waves of noise behind it which rolled in every direction. As the plane rose, the VW turned away. A parcel dropped to the ground. Then it acceler-

175

ated inaudibly, and the tail lights receded. The two men ran forward and tore at the paper. Inside were two pairs of white overalls marked British Caledonian in big blue letters. Seconds later they were approaching the plane from the runway side, keeping it between them and the terminal. They walked behind the nose wheel and out beside the steps. The tractors were pulling away, and the noise was frightening; no one even tried to say a word. A white-shirted crew member met them at the top of the steps, and they ducked left through the bulkhead door and on to the flightdeck. There was barely room to stand. Dials covered the walls and part of the ceiling. Three men turned as they entered and Priest saw a revolver trained on his stomach. He handed a set of documents across the cabin to the captain, and Charlie parked the machine pistol on the floor as a gesture of goodwill. The man flicked through the papers, glancing up to check the photos. He seemed satisfied, and the other two men relaxed.

'Welcome aboard Africargo. I'm Captain Pryor, the man with the gun is Captain Bill Seymour on conversion from VCs, and there's our engineer, Jim Duncan. No hosties on this run I'm afraid.' Pryor stuck out his hand and Priest shook it. 'You don't know how lucky you are. We've been grounded in Lusaka for three days with a bloody cherry picker stuck up alongside our back end. Your number came in on the end of our new flight instructions. We're Nairobi—London now—take your pick.'

Priest looked over at Charlie. 'Nairobi sounds great.'

'You'll find two seats just outside the door, strap yourselves in. I've been flying since the war but this is the first time I've had a number up from Intelligence.'

Priest turned to go, but Charlie stopped him. 'We better move quick.'

The four men followed his glance. Streaming down the perimeter road in to the orange light of the terminal was a convoy of military vehicles. Even as they watched, some peeled off on the road to the freight gate. Pryor shouted to the man behind Soon: 'Are those steps away? Then let's get the hell out of here.'

Priest had never realized a big jet was so manoeuvrable. On normal flights they banked gently, taxied slowly, descended evenly. Between the passenger and the void outside lay a thick layer of comforting insulation, the in-flight magazines, sweet-smelling hostesses and deep reassuring voice of the captain. Now, suddenly, there was none of that. They sat on foldaway seats looking back down the dimly lit interior of a fuselage half-full with crates. One small window in the personnel door showed the port wing and a revolving pattern of lights and yellow lines. On the flightdeck the radio crackled into life.

'Air Traffic Control calling Africargo BC217. Your clearance for takeoff is withdrawn. Return immediately to your stand. Repeat . . .' Then the engines drowned out the voice and someone slammed the bulkhead door. The craft shuddered, then leapt forward. Outside the oval window Priest watched frail necklaces of moisture wind-chased across the perspex, and beyond them the glow-worm headlights of trucks racing over the grass. The vehicles came nearer and nearer, approaching at an alarming speed. The fastest were already over the inner slipway and on a collision course but they looked incapable of inflicting harm. The nose angled, and after just twenty-four seconds the 707 swept into the sky, as lively as a falcon in the cool night air. Priest closed his eyes and began a prayer to the great god Boeing. They climbed steeply on and up, and as the nose wheel folded home a slight vibration ran through his body.

Behind and below the airport lights flickered into obscurity, and the trucks that were so real and dangerous drove home to toytown.

Chapter Nine

Dusk, Monday, 25 March
The sun had already set over Almeida's canyon. Downwind of the house two Africans were building a big open fire, and from somewhere out of sight came the puttering of the generator.

Flemming and Gould sat on a log and watched the silhouette of a lion leave the shadows, and make towards the house. It climbed onto the verandah, tail twitching, and lay down, effectively blocking the doorway.

Flemming shivered. 'This place gives me the creeps.'

Gould swatted a mosquito, invisible on his leg. 'You mean the lions give you the creeps.'

'You got it first time.'

'They shouldn't hurt you if you just follow a few basic rules. Try not to make any sudden movements, and don't approach them from behind, or if you do make plenty of noise about it. Avoid crouching down or diminishing your size when they're around—'

Flemming interrupted him. 'OK, OK, I think I've got the picture. Don't do anything, right? Where the hell's the percentage in that? Before you know it, the flamin' cats are running things. The only reason they don't eat the lot of us is because he wipes out half the game round here to feed them.'

Gould shook his head. 'The reason they don't eat us, Murray, is more probably because we smell bad.'

Flemming scowled in the darkness. 'Speak for yourself mate. What the hell are you saying—*we* smell bad to *them*?'

'I just mean carnivors nearly always prey on herbivors. Look what happens when the lionesses in a pride make a kill. Big daddy comes straight in for the first helping, and ten to one he'll open the gut and suck the insides like spaghetti. That's the way cats get their green stuff. They can't digest it if they eat it raw, so they take it when it's already broken down.'

Flemming said: 'Spare me the lecture, for Christ's sake. You sound as though you think this is healthy, lions everywhere, that girl drying out in the bloody wilderness, and the old guy ... I'm telling you it's weird.'

'He told me a bit of his life story this afternoon. He's been around. It's best not to judge people too quickly out here.' There was silence for a bit and then Gould said, 'Anyhow, that's not what I wanted to talk about.'

Flemming waited for him to go on.

'I don't really know how to put this, in fact I can't quite work out how I got involved in the first place. But it's all gone wrong now, so it doesn't matter anyway.'

Flemming turned to face him. The fire had caught well, and reddish light accentuated the colour of his skin.

'Priest got you out of jail to help on this trip. He told you we'd be flying up to Manugila for a secret meeting with Omuria; that he represented British and American business interests that couldn't afford to risk a war in the border country; that we were going to take Omuria up on his offer of four million shillings for Kalaba alive.'

Flemming's voice was tight and expressionless. 'Right. That's what he told me.'

Gould leaned forward. 'Murray, we're really taking Kalaba up north to lead a revolution. We're working for the British government. Omuria's a maniac. He's got to be stopped.'

A tic started over Flemming's eye. He asked quietly, 'What about the money?'

Gould shrugged. 'I'm sure there'll be pay for the job. But not four million. As you would say, no way.'

The Australian's face went white in the firelight. 'Do you mean we've risked our lives for fuckin' nothing? Nothing? Is that what you're saying?'

'There's more to life than cash, Murray. Thousands of men are dying up there for one man's megalomania. Heaven knows, I'm no lover of Africans, call 'em what you like, niggers, munts, coons—they're idle, deceitful, lazy—you name it and they've got it. But that's my country up there, that's where they first

179

wound me up and set me going. If I belong anywhere at all it's there. And I want to see that bastard Omuria fed to the silverbacks.'

Flemming spat violently onto the ground. 'Don't give me a heap of sentimental shit about Uganda, I don't want to know. Four million between us meant nearly two hundred thousand dollars to me. Enough to risk my life for. A little while back I was the richest man in the word. You don't believe me?' He clenched his fists. 'I never thought anyone would. For just a month I was King Solomon and General Motors all rolled into one. But I lost it all because I got used. It's not going to happen again.'

The two men sat there in angry silence.

At length Gould spoke. 'I've already talked to Almeida about us getting out of here. We don't have a lot of time, we leave before first light. You'd better make your mind up whether you're coming along or going off on your own. In the meantime, the girl's gone to a lot of trouble to get dinner together. I don't reckon there's much of a social life out here so don't spoil the evening for her, or I'll break your bloody neck.'

He stood up to go but Flemming got to his feet and blocked his path.

'Who the fuck do you think you're talking to, Mr flamin' Gould? You'll break my neck? You poor bastard, I'll take you to pieces first and still have enough left to do a better job on the girl than you could.' His finger jabbed convulsively into Gould's chest. 'You're old enough to be her dad.'

Gould swung his arm up and caught Flemming's wrist. Slowly he forced the other's arm down. 'Murray, you're not well. Maybe that knock on the head did do some damage. Why don't you take the advice of an old man and grab half an hour's shuteye?'

He dropped Flemming's wrist and moved towards the house. Behind him the Australian hunched, rage-frozen, by the log, still as a carving in the flickering light.

Gould ground his chair back from the table and shifted his position. He was full. Everyone seemed to have enjoyed the meal, even Flemming, and now it was over Almeida handed round some thin cigarillos from a tin. Suzanna pushed through the

180

leaves of the indoor jungle carrying coffee on a tray. She had dressed for the occasion in a white lawn blouse that was thin enough to look pink, and a long green skirt. Gould knew women that spent a lot of time preparing themselves without achieving a fraction of this girl's simple elegance; it was all a matter of raw material.

When everyone had coffee, Almeida addressed the table. 'Sam has told me something of your business.' He looked at Kalaba. 'It is remarkable. I thought that I would die without being surprised again in my life, but it is not so. Tomorrow in the morning I will drive you north to Lura. There you can phone for another aeroplane. The country is remote, there is little risk of being seen.' He raised his glass and drank the last mouthful of wine. 'I wish you all "boa viagem" in the days to come.'

Kalaba smiled. 'I thank you, Mzee. If all goes well maybe we'll meet again.'

The old man shrugged. 'Time goes quickly and people forget. But I will listen for news.'

From somewhere outside in the darkness came a strangled roar, followed by a series of staccato coughs at four second intervals. The young male on the verandah, Ãmbar, stirred slightly and raised his head. The coughing bark went on, broadcasting its message of dominance to Africa. Abruptly, the young lion got up and disappeared into the darkness. Kalaba looked at Almeida enquiringly. The old man sucked at his meerschaum.

'Have you not heard a lion roar, Senhor? He tells everyone that this place is his. You should see the effort that he puts into it. Every sound like that he makes with all the muscles in his body. And I have lain in bed and counted one hundred and fifty of them before I fell asleep.'

Suzanna laughed. 'Tell them about Ãmbar, Pai!'

'Ãmbar? He tries but cannot. You saw him leave just now? He goes away and practises to roar!'

Suzanna added, 'But he's not old enough and it sounds like someone dying!'

Gould asked, 'What are all the lions called, Laurens?'

'The big one is called Um (he pronounced it "oong")—it's our word for "one" because he was the first. The female has a Portuguese name, Natalia, and the young male is called Ãmbar for his colour. The cub is Nyada, where she was found.'

Flemming said, 'Is it true what they say about lions mating, Mr Almeida?'

The old man smiled. 'You tell me what they say, and I'll tell you if it's true.'

Flemming flushed slightly and looked at the girl. 'They say the male shows great stamina. That's why the testes are prized by some tribes as an aphrodisiac.'

Almeida wasn't at all put out. 'Lions can mate twice an hour every hour for three days, Mr Flemming, and lose thirty-five kilos of their weight. But whatever gives them their strength they don't leave it in their testes when they die.' He put both hands on the table. 'Shall we sit outside and take some brandy?'

Between the two bungalows was a stunted tree covered with curved thorns. It appeared to be in bloom, hundreds of white flowers catching the firelight. Gould said : 'It's not often you see a White Horse tree with that much blossom.'

Suzanna laughed delightedly, but Almeida was serious when he replied. 'It's thirsty work, looking after a tree like that.'

Gould got to his feet and walked over to the nearest branch. He came back and tossed one of the 'flowers' onto the table—a miniature plastic horse from the top of a whisky bottle. Everyone laughed, and Almeida said 'Four years is a lot of whisky.'

'Up north we call those thorn trees "ngoja kidogo",' Kalaba put in. 'It's Swahili for "wait a little". Whoever thought up that name must have got well and truly caught up in one.'

Almeida shook his head. 'The South Africans have the same words—"wachte-een-beche" they call them. "Wait a bit".'

Flemming got to his feet. 'If you'll excuse me I'm going to turn in. It's been a long day.' He looked down at Suzanna. 'Thanks for the tucker—' he tapped his stomach, '—just the job.' He walked off the verandah and a string of 'goodnights' trailed after him.

Puzzled, Suzanna turned to Gould. 'What is tucker? It means food, no?'

'That's Australian slang for food, yes. When they really get going it's a job to understand one word in ten.'

Kalaba and Almeida got to their feet together. Kalaba wincing when he put his weight on his leg. 'See you in the morning. We're off at five o'clock, right?'

Almeida pushed his chair up against the wall of the house.

'That's to get you to the nearest telephone by the time they open at seven-thirty. The game department is nearer, but it's not in the same direction, and they may be out in the bush.'

'OK,' said Kalaba. 'Five am it is. And Miss—I'll remember you and your cooking for a long time. If ever you're up north ...'

He left the sentence unfinished, and the girl's face flushed with pleasure. Almeida bent and kissed her.

'Why don't you ask Sam if he'd like some more coffee?'

Suzanna looked questioningly across the table. Gould raised his hand in protest, but somehow ended up saying 'Well, maybe just a little. Good coffee.' He looked up. 'Night Laurens. And thanks for everything.'

When the girl brought the coffee she moved her place and sat beside him. 'Are you married, Sam?'

He shook his head. 'No. Nearly, once, but—no.'

'What happened?'

'Oh, you know, the wrong time, wrong place.'

'The wrong woman?'

He laughed. 'Maybe that, too.'

He turned his head, and found that her face was so close he could see his reflection in her eyes. He heard himself thinking 'Flemming's right, she's almost young enough to be your daughter,' and he slid his chair back, the noise helping to cover his sudden discomfort.

'What about you?' he said. 'It's not the most heavily-popu-lated neck of the woods.'

The girl laughed softly. 'Neck of the woods,' she repeated. 'I haven't heard that for a long time.' Then, 'Life here is good. We have the lions to keep us company, and lots to fill the time. Papa has no idea of time. He came to Africa to see what it was like for a few months and stayed for forty years. He could never return to the cities.'

'Your father is like me,' Gould told her. 'I'd be lost if they ever kicked me out.' He stirred his coffee thoughtfully. 'You know, the white remnants of what was British East Africa make a fairly sorry picture. All hanging on with their finger nails, getting more and more bitter and waiting to be Africanized.'

The girl's eyes seemed to be getting bigger as the night

183

darkened. Gould allowed his mind to wander to the circumstances that had brought him here. Almeida's canyon.

'Time seems to go so quickly,' she was saying. 'Four years we have been here. I feel it's running out for me.'

Gould almost reached out to stroke the masses of black hair that hung round her face, but the moment passed. 'For you there's all the time in the world, Suzanna. It's when you get to my age that you begin to notice how quickly it's getting used up.'

Reluctantly, he looked at his watch and stood up. 'I hate to say it, but it's time I hit the sack. And you should as well. Tomorrow's going to be a long day.' He walked her inside the house, across the wooden flooring and through the hanging curtain of threaded bamboo that led to their bedrooms. Outside her door he stopped and faced her, trying to analyse his lack of initiative. What was wrong with him? Was he tied by a code of behaviour that forbade the seduction of the benefactor's daughter under the benefactor's roof? Or had long periods of abstinence numbed his appetite, leaving him indifferent and cold? Clumsily, he put his hand on her shoulder and said, ' 'Night, Suzanna. Maybe see you in the morning.'

She reached up and squeezed his arm once, hard. 'Goodnight, Sam. It's made a big change having you all here.' She dropped her arm and turned away; the door closed quietly behind her. Gould stood undecided in the passage for several minutes before he padded back towards the verandah and outside to shut down the generator. The night was warm and starry. On his wrist, tiny marks faded where her nails had gripped his skin.

As he recrossed the room a few minutes later the girl came back through the screen, dressed in a pair of boy's pyjamas.

'You're still up,' he said superfluously, and stood to one side.

'Salty food and too much to drink.' She smiled. 'It's made me thirsty.'

Much later, when Gould tried to reconstruct the moment in his mind, he blamed the pyjamas. His arm went out like a pole, and the girl walked straight into it. The next moment she was in his arms. Minutes later, he half-led, half-carried her into his room, slid out of his clothes, and pulled her with him under the sheet. Her toes slid down his legs and she began to tremble violently. He gentled her as he would a captured animal, and gradually the movements slowed and finally ceased altogether.

184

His hand slid under her arm and the pyjama jacket opened. Her breasts pressed against him, firm and pointed in the darkness. It occurred to him that without the wine she would probably never have been here at all. They lay in the same position for what seemed to be a long time, her head resting on his arm while he stroked her back with his free hand, then he moved the hand down over her stomach and let his fingers stray into the fur between her legs. To his surprise she pulled his hand away, and tried to burrow her face deeper into his chest. Gould withdrew his hand, and put it back where it had been before; he felt both cheated and relieved. The girl was lonely, naïve, probably a catholic and almost certainly a virgin. It was a miracle she was in bed with him. If he used her now, cajoled and coaxed till he broke her down he'd carry the guilt of it when he left in the morning. This way and, well, life was a strange animal. They might even meet again sometime.

He pulled her towards him, and gradually her breathing deepened. Gould felt pins and needles start in his bicep, but he just lay there motionless gazing at the ceiling. Sleep came slowly down upon him like a long-lost friend; a friend from long ago with dreams for sale . . .

They had very little time, that much was clear. The convoy limped through the rain forest, a shattered force. Many had died, Schwartz and Decker, Collins and the huge negro, Kulmo. There'd be no more card tricks from Lafitte either—a burst of gunfire had taken his head from his shoulders. The trucks slithered and slipped on the damp leaf floor of the track as if they, too, were wounded, or just stunned from having driven into so violent an ambush. It was twenty kilometres to Somba. So near. But the oppressive tunnel through the trees showed no sign of widening. At Likato everyone had died. The village was as silent as the graves that no one ever found time to dig, for women, goats, sheep, children and chickens, all cut down indiscriminately in the drive for Luluabourg.

Bafwabili was different, on the railway. Like figures in an old colonial painting, a group of people had been standing on the platform. They seemed to be made of wax, waiting there for the train with their bags and their pathetic dignity.

'Le train n'existe pas,' he told them. 'It's not coming, there is no train.' They looked at him, stunned, hopeless, lost, and he acted against his better judgement. 'Vous voulez, montez dans les camions.' So they'd thanked him, and got into the trucks, eight people and a girl of sixteen or seventeen. It was Boyd who'd done it, not even one of the Africans. He went to help the girl up, but somehow pulled her dress over her hips as he lifted her into the air. The men roared and clapped while her legs kicked out, and Boyd grinned hugely and started pulling the long cream underskirt down from her waist. The father had tried to intervene, but collapsed when a boot caught him on the kneecap.

He could remember calling out, but when the girl's backside came into view like a pale fruit slung over Boyd's shoulder he took aim and fired. The bullets stitched a row of holes along the front of the station. Boyd dropped the girl. There was complete silence as she straightened her clothes and looked up. Her eyes were dry, and she walked over to the lead lorry. 'Puis-je . . . ?' He'd helped her up, and her parents into the back. Two minutes they were on the move again.

There'd been seven trucks then, now there were three. The girl was with him still, her face stiff with fright and grief. He caught the driver's eye across the cab and touched her hand.

'Comment vous appelez-vouz?' he tried in accented French.

'Katherine,' she replied. 'Je m'appelle Katherine.'

He gripped her hand tighter and tighter, but still she was slipping away and the cab seemed to swim around him. In a second it was gone . . .

Gould woke to a distant shout, and the fading of a motor. Then there was a quick knocking on the door and Almeida came in. He held a torch, and the beam revealed Gould propped up on one elbow and the tousled hair of his daughter spread all over the pillow. The torch flicked out.

'Senhor. The Australian has taken my jeep and gone.'

Gould swung his legs out of bed and sat up.

Suzanna said, 'Pai, venha ca, por favor, é escute—' but Almeida cut her short.

'Kalaba—he too has gone.'

01.30, Tuesday, 26 March

Flemming drove northwards through the night. The track

186

was good, and he smiled to himself and followed its twists and turns. On the front seat the corners of a map twitched in the wind, but it was held secure by the weight of a Sterling. In the back, Kalaba lay barely conscious and helpless, hands and feet tied with rope. It was over seven hundred miles as the crow flies to the Kagera river, but Flemming was confident he could make it. Just before dinner he'd offered to get the jeep ready for the morning trip, and Almeida had accepted gladly. He'd forgotten nothing, a full tank, five jerries, spare wheel, hot patches, tools, a Sterling, ammunition, plus a packet of Reactivan to keep him going when his mind had other ideas. Thirty-odd gallons—it should be enough for five hundred miles, and there'd be plenty of chances to get more.

After an hour and a half the track made a long curving loop to the left and joined a small road. Flemming turned left and built the speed up to forty-five miles an hour. It was about as much as the old bus could handle. So far so good. By dawn he'd be two hundred miles up country, a tiny needle in an impossibly sized haystack. The Rover bounced over a pothole and the lights flared briefly at the sky. Beneath the plaster on his forehead, eyes of unnatural blue stared brightly down the murram road.

02.30, Tuesday, 26 March

The two men started walking at two-thirty. It was cold but they soon warmed up. Almeida covered the ground steadily at a pace that never varied, and Gould followed behind him carrying a small haversack and a rifle. They went some way along the track, and turned off into the bush. The game post at Nyada was thirty miles distant, and short of making a long detour to stay on the track there was nothing for it but to head across country. They walked in silence, following animal trails and flat ridges of rock, working their way west. By half past five they'd covered ten miles, and Almeida called a halt. They sat and watched the first flush of blue, then pink, enter the eastern sky and drank coffee from a flask.

Gould broke the silence. 'Laurens, I know it looked bad, but if you'd just let me try to explain . . .'

But it was no good, and the old man wouldn't listen. 'Let us do what we set out to do. Talking is for when one has time.'

They moved off again with the early rays of sunlight warming their backs, and found themselves in an area of open savannah; giraffe browsed by a clump of acacia and a family of ostrich kept well out of harm's way, but Gould was actually looking at one of the birds when it happened. The group consisted of a redneck, one female and six chicks. Suddenly there was a streak of black and the muffled sound of an impact, like a broomhandle beating a carpet. Feathers floated to the ground, and the ostrich milled around in absolute confusion looking for the lost chick. Not once did they look to the dawn sky, where a Marshall eagle held the young bird securely taloned, and had already won the fight for altitude. The speed of the attack had been incredible. As if conscious of their awkwardness by comparison, Almeida lengthened his stride.

At six-twenty they came back onto the road seventeen miles from Nyada. They walked for another hour, and then an African gave them a lift on the back of a tractor. They reached the village just after eight.

The Department of Wild Life and Fisheries was a low building on the outskirts of the community, with a corrugated iron roof that glinted in the sun. From its highest point a radio mast rose lopsidedly into the air. Almeida went straight in and confronted a tall, bespectacled African who was rubber-stamping behind a desk.

He asked in English, 'Is the radio working?'

The man looked up and then beamed broadly. 'Eeh! Mr Al-meed! So you have come to see us again? How is the things in your camp?'

The two men shook hands and Almeida replied, 'Everything is fine there, but my friend here has had a breakdown with his car, and he wants to telephone Nairobi for help.'

'Nairobi!' He shook his head. 'You must wait for Sergeant Nkuma to come here, you know him I think. But Nairobi is far.'

Almeida wiped his brow with a handkerchief. The roofing turned the place into an oven, and yet in many parts of Africa families with a corrugated iron roof had arrived socially in a big way.

'You know that once, from this same place, I spoke with my friends over the sea in Portugal.' He stretched his arms to demon-

188

strate the distances involved. 'That is far like Nairobi many times.'

The African's face brightened at the news. 'Then it is so. But we have never spoked with Nairobi here.'

They went outside and Almeida said, 'The boy is simple in the head, but he means well. We will wait till the sergeant comes.'

In the shade, on a scrap of lawn, an old woman was hemming a piece of cloth. Gould watched her at it, fingers nimble despite her age. Her only tool was a bucket, smeared around the rim on the inside with honey. The bottom of the bucket was a crawling mass of siafu, large safari ants with big pincers. When the ants reached the honey they went no further, and the old woman picked them out one at a time between finger and thumb. Then, with the other hand, she slipped the fold of cloth between the ant's jaws. When it bit, she nipped the insect's body off with her nails, leaving a single organic stitch in the material. If the method was laborious and time consuming, what did it matter?

Almeida sighed. 'So many days to do what a machine would do in a second.'

Gould said, 'There must be a machine round here.'

'Oh, there is, in the general store, worked with your feet. But it would cost her money to use it, and there's no rush.'

At nine o'clock, Sergeant Nkuma appeared and greeted Almeida. The call was duly placed to Nairobi and the two men sat down in the shade to wait. At ten o'clock the clerk brought them a cup of tea. Once more Gould tried to raise the subject of the girl.

'Laurens, I've got to say this.' He took a deep breath. 'Your daughter's a lovely girl, but maybe she's a bit lonely and has too much time to think about things. Last night, well, it wasn't quite what you imagine.'

Almeida looked at him over the top of his teacup but said nothing. Gould's voice was defensive.

'Whatever physical and mental state she was in before last night, she's still the same way. I just happened to be in the wrong place at the wrong time, that's all.'

The old man finished his tea. 'Don't think I am so shocked because I found you in bed with her. I'm not so old I can't

189

remember how it was when I was young. Rather I am sad, because what you say is true, old men are selfish and I have kept her with me when perhaps . . .' His voice trailed off into nothing.

Gould scratched a pattern in the dust with his toe. 'I just don't want you to get the wrong idea.' He chuckled suddenly, 'Do you know the joke about the gorilla?'

Almeida raised his eyebrows at the change of subject. 'No, I have never heard any jokes about gorillas.'

'Well,' said Gould, 'There was a man talking to his friend and he said "I've got an unusual pet at home." His friend said "Oh, yes? What is it?" So the man said "It's a seven hundred pound gorilla." "A seven hundred pound gorilla?" said his friend. "Where does he sleep?" "Oh," said the man, "Anywhere he likes." '

Almeida's eyes twinkled a little and he said, 'You're the gorilla, I suppose.'

Gould shook his head, his face serious. 'I have some things in common with you Laurens, and at the moment one in particular.' He hesitated. 'I don't think either of us is too happy about the future.'

Almeida shrugged. 'I don't worry for myself. I have everything I need out there, and enough to last until I die. But the girl . . . she's my worry.'

At eleven-thirty the clerk came bursting through the door. 'Come quickly! We are talking to Nairobi!'

The wheels of the 402 touched earth in Nyada at four-thirty and taxied to the end of the strip. Priest got out, followed by Charlie Soon and the pilot, Johnny Gable. Gould met them and introduced Almeida. Priest produced maps from his holdall and the five men squatted on the grass. Almeida got up almost immediately.

'Gentlemen, there's nothing I can do, and my daughter waits for me in the camp.'

He shook hands with them all in turn and Priest said, 'Two things before you go, Mr Almeida—your Land Rover—were the papers in it? And is there anything that would help us to pick it out from the air?'

Almeida shook his head. 'No. Nothing. Except the lion plat-form.'

'What?' Priest started, but Gould said 'I'll tell you about that in a minute.'

The old man tugged at his beard. 'And the papers . . .' He frowned. 'Yes, they were in the front.' He turned away, and Gould went with him.

'Don't hold it against me, Laurens.'

The old man stopped, sighed and finally tapped him on the shoulder. 'I'll only hold it against you if you don't come back, and then you will never know anyway. Adeus, e boa sorte!'

He moved off and Gould went back to the group. But he felt a lump rise in his throat and heard himself calling out. 'What-ever happens I'll come back to tell her about it. One way or the other.'

Priest moved the map impatiently and leaned forward. 'Right. Let's get our minds round the facts. He left here at 1.30 this morning to drive to Uganda. It must be a good eight or nine hundred miles by road, what do you say, Johnny?'

Gable thought for a second. 'More,' he said at length. 'More like a thousand, and that's only to the border.'

Priest said, 'He's out of his mind. If the car's as old as Sam says it is he'll be lucky to make it to Mbeya.'

Gould found himself defending Flemming. 'I want to make one thing quite clear. If he is out of his mind it's because of the crash. People have been in hospital for days after smaller knocks on the head than he got.'

Priest looked at him. 'We're not casting stones, Sam, but facts are facts. There'll be time enough to sort out the reasons if we can only catch up with him. He must be getting pretty tired round about now.'

'Not necessarily,' Gable put in.

'What do you mean?' Priest asked. 'It's been about sixteen hours already.'

Gable fished in his pocket and pulled out a packet of tablets. 'Bennies, or something like them. Most pilots out here keep them handy.'

Soon said, 'But Flemming's from Australia.'

There was a silence.

191

'OK,' Priest began. 'Let's start at the top. Which way would he go?'

Gable pointed to the map. 'There's only one logical way he could go, but it would mean crossing into Zambia at Chitipa and then back into Tanzania at Tundumu. Look here.' His finger traced a path up towards Mbeya in Tanzania, and then along the eastern side of Lake Tanganyika through Sumbawanga and Mpanda. Further north, the road skirted the Burundi border and made a good line for Bukoba.

Priest said, 'If he gets there he's home and dry. He could have crossed both these border posts by first light this morning. He's got a passport and documents for the vehicle. As long as no one looked in the back.'

Gould laughed, a mirthless sound. 'At that time in the morning he'd have had a job to wake anyone up. Chances are he was through before they realized it.'

'No barriers?' said Priest.

'Oh yes, plenty of those,' Gould told him. 'With five hundred miles of nothing immediately to the left and right.'

'So much depends on the state of that road,' Gable added. 'It's the stretch from Namanyere to Mpanda that's tricky. You start off with high country and before you're through it drops a few thousand feet into a valley full of swamp. If it's too wet, that's where he'll get stuck. The whole area drains into Lake Rukwa.'

Priest started to fold up the map. 'We've got to move fast. First, Mzuzu for fuel: then get ahead of him and search backwards. It's our only chance.'

'So it's got to be Ujiji?' said Gable, stretching.

The others got to their feet.

'Right,' said Priest. 'Ujiji. All the best colonials wind up there.'

17.00, Tuesday, 26 March

Two hundred and twenty miles north of the border Flemming pulled in before starting the last fifty miles to Mpanda. Progress had been slow since he left Sumbawanga, the road degenerating, its surface covered with rocks and craters. Once, during the heat of midday, he had closed his eyes for a second too long and

192

nearly plunged off the road into a ravine. Shaken, he'd stopped the car until his heart beat normally again.

The country here was incredible, huge buttresses of rock reaching out of the greenery above him, but he was in no mood to appreciate beauty. He walked to the back of the Rover and peered inside the canvas tarpaulin. Kalaba's body was bent in a Z where he had been trying to brace himself against the movements of the truck. A strip of rubber inner tube was strapped round his face as a gag, and the yellow of dried vomit caked his chin and throat. Flemming leant forward with a knife and Kalaba started but his eyes were steady on Flemming's face. He placed the point just below the African's ear and sliced upwards. The rubber parted, and Flemming pulled it away. Then he did the same with the rope binding the man's feet, and pulled him out onto the ground. Kalaba coughed and rolled over, his wounded leg still bent in the same position.

'If you want a piss, now's your chance.'

Flemming lit a cigarette and inhaled deeply. The smoke made his head sing slightly, and he went back round to the cab to get some water and a couple of pills. When he came back, Kalaba was half kneeling by a rock at the side of the road trying to urinate. Painfully, he finished and started to crawl back to the Rover, his whole body on fire as the blood started to circulate again.

Flemming pulled him to his feet. 'Come on, come on, don't hang about. Here, have some water.'

The man drank greedily, and after a couple of seconds Flemming snatched the canteen away.

'Take it easy, you'll just bring it all up again. Now get in the back.'

Kalaba looked at the Australian, the tall lithe body and the bright, tired eyes. How could he overcome the man with his hands bound?

'What do you want, Flemming?'

The Australian got him by the shoulder and turned him round. 'You in the back of the truck,' he said. 'Move!'

Kalaba felt his temper surge out of control. Clumsily he kicked backwards at the man behind him, and felt his boot crunch against bone. Flemming shrieked and swore, but by the time

193

Kalaba turned he was at the front of the Rover and reaching in for a gun.

'You fuckin' stupid black bastard! I'll shoot your ass off! I'll bloody well kill you!'

Kalaba watched as the man limped towards him and stared madly into his face. A lock of blonde hair fell over Flemming's forehead, and the African closed his eyes. A real fear entered him: there was no reasoning with the insane.

As if interpreting the man's thoughts Flemming turned aside and pushed the gun into his shorts. His voice, when he spoke, was on the way back to normal. 'Don't force me to hurt you. Get in the back.'

With Kalaba securely bound, the Rover started off again, winding down out of the hills till the rocky track gave way to earth. The grass increased in height until it was taller than the cab, and Flemming found himself slapping as tsetse flies homed in on his scent. The engine began to labour and the heat in the cab built up. Soon he was forced to use the four wheel drive and then low box. The Land Rover laboured on through a world of vivid green, its wheels releasing a sickly stench of wood-rot and fetid vegetation. It flattened grass and small bushes but the ground got no drier, and after fifteen minutes Flemming could see a brown strip of water to his left. Inexorably, the track curved round to meet it and stopped.

Flemming pulled up and got out. Insects landed thickly on his skin, but he scarcely noticed them. Between him and the other side lay twenty feet of the murkiest water he had ever seen. Black cotton soil crumbled away from the banks, and spirals of thick white froth revolved lethargically downstream like effluent from a brewery. It was dinosaur country; there was no way he could see the Rover making the crossing short of evolving wings. But return was out of the question, so he deflated the tyres until the walls bulged slightly and wearily got back in the cab.

At first the nose went straight down into the water and for a moment it seemed that the Rover would stay there, balanced precariously in the mire. But then it lifted, and the machine moved forward, making a sort of bow-wave in the creek. Flemming kept his foot steady on the accelerator, wishing he had a diesel with no electrics and an exhaust pipe sticking ten feet in the air. The front wheels reached the other side and started to lift, but it was hopeless, the black mud provided no grip at all, and the soft roots were broken and churned by the tyres. Flemming smelt the bitterness of burning clutch, and let the revs die away to fast tickover. Once more he opened the door, climbed round to the bonnet, and jumped down onto the ground. Slipping and stumbling, limbs awkward with fatigue, he started to uncoil a thin cable wound round pegs on the Rover's front bumper. When it was all on the ground he looked up the slope for a suitable tree, and started towards it. The vehicle had a capstan winch linked to the front of its crankshaft, but it was a lot easier to operate with two people. Flemming passed the cable round a tree, and leaned there for a moment with his eyes closed. A sudden feeling of nausea and vertigo flooded him and he opened them again; then the sickness passed, leaving him cold and weak.

In the Rover, Kalaba dropped his head as Flemming came back down the slope. His bruised face was alive with hatred, and behind his back he sawed the ropes feebly to and fro across the metal of the seat. It was still six hundred miles to Uganda.

07.30, Wednesday, 27 March

Flemming arrived in Mpanda feeling feverish and ill. His face was pale under the tan, and uncontrollable waves of shivering shook his body. The night had been long; by midnight he'd found that the trail improved, and after ten miles he shifted back into two wheel drive. Kalaba had refused all food, weak and semi-comatose after thirty hours in the back. Suddenly frightened that he might die, Flemming loosened his bonds and made a pillow of spare clothes.

Just outside the town on the road to Kasulu they stopped for petrol. It took a little time to fill the tank and the four jerries that Flemming had in the front with him. The African attendant chewed mirundi twigs while he pumped, and petrol fumes shimmered above the filler. Between the canvas cover and the metal back of the cab was a thin slit. Something moved, and the attendant stopped chewing and leaned towards the gap. He got a quick, distorted view of Kalaba's gagged face and closed eyes and then felt Flemming's hand on his shoulders.

'That's enough! Close it and put it in the front!'

The man did so, clamping the top of the jerry can, and lifting

195

it into the cab. Flemming paid him with a mixture of Kenyan and Tanzanian notes. Then he started up, and bumped out onto the road.

The African stood for a moment with the money in his hand before moving; then, stuffing it into the pocket of his tattered shorts, he turned and began to run back down the road into town.

06.00, Wednesday, 27 March

Priest and Gould spent the night watching the road north to Kibondo from the front of a Land Cruiser belonging to United Touring. But there had been little traffic except the occasional bus, crammed to capacity, making the long run from Kigoma to Bukoba. At dawn, stiff and cold, they pulled out on to the road and turned south. Priest had brought two short-wave radios from Nairobi, and they were well armed. Johnny Gable had reluctantly relinquished the 402 in favour of a 185, a highwing with a low stalling-speed and good visibility. At eight o'clock, together with Charlie, he'd fly straight to the swamps that lay south of Mpanda, a trip of one hundred and eighty miles, and then follow the road up towards Kasulu. One worry in particular nagged at Priest's mind : supposing Flemming had already gone? Could he have driven six hundred and seventy miles in an old Rover by eight the previous night? It worked out at an average of thirty seven miles per hour, assuming the car had never stopped moving. Every hour off the road meant, at least to start with, roughly another two-and-a-half miles per hour to be added to the average speed. And Sam said that fifty was about flat out. It had to be impossible. Unless, of course, he had hijacked another Rover or Toyota ... tired, he tossed the figures around inside his head. Last night there'd been nothing from Nairobi or Dar, and the news consisted variously of skirmishes in the north and exhortations from the government to the people to 'stay calm and not to panic'.

After the Malagarisi river, Gould pulled up as agreed, at eight, and they waited for the plane to come in on the radio.

At seven-thirty Gable and Soon walked past the low-lying buildings fringing the airfield, and on towards the hangar. Unlike the others, they'd passed a comfortable night in an hotel after arranging aircraft hire the night before. A few small machines were parked nose-in towards the hangar wall, but the field was dominated by a Tanzanian Army Hastings, of indeterminate age, that hadn't been there the night before. Gable looked the plane over with professional interest, and shook his head as they walked past it. 'Beats me how they keep it in the air. She's a real grandma.'

Their Cessna was on the other side of the hangar. Gable and Soon turned the corner of the main building and walked out towards it. Neither of them heard a sound until they reached the wingtip, and then there was a slight scuffling noise behind them. Charlie spun round to see two men, one of them looking at him along the barrel of a lightweight rifle. The other man, Captain Chen, smiled humourlessly.

Gable said 'Who the hell are these characters?'

'Chinese,' Charlie told him needlessly. 'From Zanzibar.'

Chen spoke to his subordinate, who moved closer to Gable and Soon, relieving them of their pistols. This accomplished, they motioned Gable up to the door of the aircraft, keeping him well covered, and while he was unlocking it, Chen spoke to Charlie in Chinese. When the door swung open, Gable called out, 'What's he plan to do now?' but the question was rhetorical. In silence the four men boarded the plane, and minutes later they were in the air.

By eight-twenty Priest was convinced that something had gone wrong, but he couldn't see what. Gould was more patient.

'Maybe they've had engine trouble, it happens.'

Priest grimaced. 'There was nothing wrong with the plane or the radio last night. They were meant to be in the air and on the air twenty minutes ago.'

Gould leaned forward and turned the ignition key. The four-litre motor took time to catch.

'Let's drive, we can't achieve very much sitting here. Try opening the hatch, it may help to clear our heads.'

Priest nodded, and they moved away fast. Soon they were cruising at sixty and the dusty road fled backwards under the tyres.

Inside the Cessna, Gable headed slowly south, keeping the road

197

off the port wing. There was a strong wind from the south-east, and the country unrolled gradually, harshly-lit in the morning light.

Chen sat in the back behind Charlie Soon, and harangued him with a monologue in Cantonese, while his subordinate held a pistol near the back of Gable's head. The aircraft droned on. When Chen stopped talking Gable asked Charlie : 'Do you mind keeping me in touch with what's going on? What the heck would he have done if no one spoke his lingo?'

'Used English, maybe,' Charlie said. 'Who knows what he speaks.'

Gable accepted the warning, and looked out at the huge landscape. A long soda pan stretched away to the east, and the road veered towards it. And on the road . . . Gable leant forward and looked again. No doubt about it, a Land Rover. He sat back, but Chen must have seen him looking down, and in seconds he'd spotted the vehicle too, and was focusing a pair of binoculars on it. Then he started speaking, but Gable anticipated the order, and banked left to cross the road. At the same time he pulled his microphone towards him on its extending lead and depressed the send button. 'What does he want me to do now?'

'Stop him,' Soon replied.

'I see.' Gable gave it a moment's thought. 'How does he suggest I do it?'

'He says go down low,' Charlie told him, 'and fly straight towards him till he decides to stop.'

Gable kept the mike in his hand. 'Try to force him out onto the soda, is that it? Well, I'll see what I can do to oblige.'

He brought the plane round in a sweeping turn well ahead of the Rover. The wind was almost head-on, and slowly the Cessna sank and lost speed as he increased the flap, keeping the power on until there was so much drag they seemed to be hovering. With the indicated airspeed reading sixty knots, the ground floated by at something under thirty, but still the Rover and the plane approached each other at a combined speed of close to eighty miles per hour. As Gable watched the car come nearer, he suddenly realized that the whole thing had inexplicably become personal, a trial of strength between him and the unknown adversary on the ground. His eyes ranged from the road to the instruments, from the instruments back to the road. Whoever gave way first, he knew it mustn't be him.

Flemming saw the plane just before nine. He tried to pull under cover, but it had already seen him, and came plummeting down like a bird of prey. The Australian sped on along the road, his mind churning. How the hell had Gould done it in the time? And where was the plane from? Sweat poured into his eyes, blinding him, and he drove desperately, a high-pitched stream of oaths fermenting from his mouth. The aircraft had levelled now, and was flying straight towards him on a collision course. Flemming kept his foot on the accelerator and gripped the wheel tighter until the Cessna leapt towards the windscreen. At the moment when collision seemed inevitable, his nerves, already strained to capacity, finally gave way. The road at that point ran steeply down beside a soda lake, and its brilliant surface stretched away into the distance like a sea of diamonds. Flemming felt a violent shudder shake the steering as he lost control, and with a savage wrench that nearly broke his thumbs the wheel spun to the right, and the Rover mounted the side of the trail and arched out on to the lake. The soda was firm near the edge, and then the wheels sank slightly, and the vehicle slowed. As though held by a giant magnet, it splashed to a halt and the motor died. Flemming looked back, and saw the plane making an approach towards the pan; whoever was flying it knew what he was doing. Then, clutching the Sterling, he flung open the door and started to run mindlessly through ankle deep soda towards the far side of the lake. He struggled along awkwardly, feet sinking through the frail crust. It was impossible to tell how far it was to the firm ground, three, maybe four hundred yards, and the glare was blinding, burning hot off the shallow alkaline liquid that mirrored only the sun. Exhausted, he reached a small island that had crystalized out, and his feet crunched in time with his laboured breathing, and the sky spun overhead, faster and faster, like a blue catherine wheel burning the edges off the world. When something hit him in the back and knocked him down he felt no pain, only a vague surprise that they had caught up with him. He fell with a splash, and lay there cursing weakly. Half mad with fear, he clutched the gun and tried to crawl away. It was then that he realized he couldn't move his legs. Under his ruined body the slow seep of blood made strange patterns in the thick alkali.

As the Rover swung away to his left Gable let the plane have its head, and they climbed rapidly, making a wide sweep to port. Chen spoke to Charlie, who in turn passed the message on.

'He said land on the lake.'

Gable looked quickly at the soda. To the right of the Land Rover there was a large white envelope of firm crystal, exposed like a sandbar at low tide. Further south, the ground was drier still, a featureless, starched tapestry, clean as a picked bone, hopeless in its relentless size, soda without end.

'Amen,' thought Gable, as he saw the tiny figure of Flemming starting to move with insect-like patience towards the firm ground lying to the south. With deft movements he lined the plane up.

'OK,' he said. 'We'll land.'

Priest and Gould saw the glint of sunlight on metal far in the distance as the plane turned. Priest looked again at the map on his knee, holding it taut as wind gusted through the hatch above his head. The radio was silent.

'We should be coming up to that soda any time now.'

Gould drifted the well-sprung truck round a long bend. The tyres shuddered quickly over baked corrugations in the murram, a legacy from the giant wheels of the long-distance buses.

'I'll get on to the soda as soon as I can if it's OK—that plane looked as if it was coming in to land.'

Dust marked their passage with a billowing ochre scarf, and the speedometer hovered round seventy five. Ahead, the road probed on into the arid country like an uncertain worm.

Charlie Soon leapt out of the Cessna and ran to the Land Rover. He flung open the back of the tarpaulin and looked in. Kalaba's eyes were wide and he tried to smile. Soon started to heave the man out into the sunlight and Gable gave Kalaba a water-bottle and whispered 'The others are on the way, if we can just slow things down a bit.' Kalaba drank hugely through swollen lips and nodded, his throat working convulsively as he swallowed. They were so engrossed that the sound of the shot came as a complete surprise. The three men started and looked up at the two Chinese. Uncomprehendingly Gable swung his gaze out over the soda. The sickening truth struck him—Flemming's slow-moving form had disappeared. They'd shot him in the back. He started forward, but Soon held his arm.

'No. They will kill you.'

'Kill me?' Gable was livid. 'No, chum, they need me to fly them out of here.'

There was a movement beside them, and Kalaba's deep voice came out strongly.

'No, they don't. That man is a pilot. He has flown me several times.'

Chen addressed Charlie, who nodded.

'He says get Kalaba in the plane.'

Together Gable and Soon went to help Kalaba to his feet, but he pushed them aside and stood up slowly on his own. For the first time Charlie realized how big the man was.

'I'm not going anywhere,' Kalaba announced, and leant against the Rover to take the weight off his bad leg. 'So unless it's part of your plan to bring me back dead, you'd better think about getting yourselves out of here.'

Charlie started to translate, but Chen held up his hand and moved forward. 'My orders are to bring you back in one piece. If you value the lives of your friends, you will get into the plane.'

Gable looked at the Chinese pilot and the rifle he held. 'The last bullet out of that gun killed Flemming,' he thought. 'And the next . . . ?' Suddenly he felt sick.

Kalaba shifted his weight and the soda squelched. For several seconds no one said a thing. Charlie stood without moving. The silence came to an abrupt end as Chen clapped his hands to-gether hard. The noise was like a gunshot, and Gable jumped in spite of himself. The Chinese laughed quietly. 'Then, Mr Kalaba, after we shoot your friends, we'll put a round through your bad knee, and carry you into the plane screaming. Come, you know I will do what I threaten.'

There was another silence and then, so faintly that it barely disturbed the air, the sound of an engine. For a second it came and went on the wind and the two Chinese looked out across the soda trying to locate its origin. For a second their attention lapsed.

Kalaba reacted with astonishing speed. He heaved himself

201

away from the side of the Rover and launched a tremendous kick at the arm holding the rifle. The gun flew into the air and the African overbalanced and landed flat on his back in the wet. The engine noise was constant now, and swelling in volume. Gable avoided the sprawled body of Kalaba and leapt towards Chen. His head crunched hard in to the man's chest and the Chinese went down with a splash. Simultaneously came the flat report of a pistol. Charlie saw Gable falling, his hands at his throat, and Kalaba frozen in the act of regaining his feet. He saw the Chinese pilot swing the pistol towards him, and Chen on all fours. Charlie backed off, and dived head first towards the Rover, rolling under the vehicle as he landed. An explosion of air came from one of the front tyres, and the truck dropped four inches, pressing him into the ground. By the time he wriggled around to see what had happened the two Chinese were on their way to the aircraft. He watched as they climbed aboard, and the sound of the aeroplane drowned out the approaching truck.

Somewhere in his mind Flemming supposed that he was dying, but the thought failed to alarm him. Perhaps he was already dead, floating in a sea of the warm juice from which all life was made, or blowing through the sky on a vast, white shroud. It was quiet out here, with nothing to disturb the peace except the minute organic gurgling from the soda, like bath water, or bath time, or just time running out. Gradually his sense of euphoria faded, and frightening waves of noise beat in towards him. Pain and fear came rushing back, and with them, aware-ness. They had lied to him, cheated him, shot him, and now—his mind reeled—they were coming to break him up in a plane, to stamp him out the way an elephant would stamp on lion remains, to break him completely. With a supreme effort he pulled back the cocking handle on the machine-gun, and squinted along the barrel. The air shimmered and danced, mock-ing his efforts to see, but he persisted. And when the dark, blurred shadow steadied and coalesced around the foresight the last thing he remembered to do was pull the trigger.

Priest said 'We're too late, they're off!' but even as he spoke the plane zig-zagged wildly and the tail lifted into the air. There

202

was a flurry of white as the prop scythed into the ground, and then the machine stopped moving altogether and perched there, nose down in the alkali, like a flamingo somehow immobilized in the act of feeding.

'What the hell ... ?' Priest asked, and Gould splashed to a stop near the Rover. Charlie Soon and Kalaba were standing there, soaked, and looking out at the Cessna.

'It was Flemming,' Kalaba muttered. 'Flemming did it.'

Priest got out of the car and ran forward. Johnny Gables's hands were still round his throat, and blood oozed thickly between his fingers. His face was without expression, as if he held no opinion at all about the way in which he had died.

Priest was reaching down to close Gable's eyes when Gould said 'Harry.' Something in his voice made Priest look up. What he saw was Charlie with the rifle dropped by the Chinese covering Gould and Kalaba. Slowly he straightened, feeling tremendously weary.

'You?' he said to Charlie. 'Just tell me why.'

The other man shrugged. 'Look at me,' he said. 'Why do you think?'

Priest shook his head. 'But we were nearly shot to pieces after the others took off. And you killed the guards ...'

Charlie moved the rifle impatiently. 'I am working for a man who represents factions unhappy with the leadership in Zanzibar. He suggested that I could do well for myself, much better than I stand to do with you. Not even Chen knew of this. And now he's finished I have no alternative but to kill you and take Kalaba back to the capital.'

The four men stood there motionless. The wind tugged gently at their hair and Charlie raised the gun. It was almost up when Gould yelled 'Get down!' and cannoned into Priest and Kalaba. The three of them sprawled out into the slush and Charlie lowered the barrel of his gun and backed away uncertainly.

'It makes no difference to me,' he started to say, but never finished the sentence. His body lurched forward as though pushed violently from behind and the rifle in his hands went off. Simultaneously, there was another more distant report. Soon's body fell with a splash.

Gould raised his head. Beside the fuselage of the crashed plane he could see a green-clad figure lining up another shot.

Quickly he slid forward and pulled the gun out from under Soon's body. A bullet splashed into the soda beside him, and he stretched out using the dead Chinese as a rest. The foresight came slowly up until the distant figure was sitting on top of it. Another shot rang out and there was a gasp of pain from behind him.

Gould squeezed the trigger. The green blob on the end of the sight hesitated, then rolled slowly to the side and out of sight. Gould knew. Warily he got up, his eyes still watching the plane for signs of life. Then he turned round.

'Who's hit?'

Kalaba got up slowly and straightened his bad leg. 'Priest.'

But Priest started to rise. 'In the back, Sam.'

Gould helped him up and looked at his back. The slug had plucked the cloth at the bottom of the rib-cage and scored a groove through material and flesh alike over a length of four inches. Gould widened the vent in the jacket and looked at the wound. It was clean and red, with blood just starting to well.

'You're a very lucky man,' he said.

Priest looked up at him and flexed his shoulder. There were only three of them left.

'I think we all are,' he said.

It was like a dream, Priest thought, like nothing on earth, nothing that he'd ever experienced. The sky was blue, the earth white, and these three men the last survivors of some terrible global devastation. The strange attitude of the plane, the minute, distant body of Charlie Soon, the stationary vehicles—all these added to the surreal quality of the picture, because distance was difficult to judge and perspective meaningless. His eyes dropped, and found the small patch of crystal that had been one of Flemming's last conscious objectives. He lay at their feet, face down in the slime. Around his body blood had stained the soda, but the bullet hole at the base of his spine was clean and neat. The figure looked absurdly young in shirt, shorts and boots. Slowly Priest knelt and went to turn him over, but Gould's voice cut across his thoughts.

'Don't do that.'

Priest was nonplussed, temporarily at a loss. He shrugged hopelessly. 'We can't just leave him here to be eaten by vultures.'

Gould's voice fell on him bitterly. 'Chemicals, vultures, what the hell's the difference? He was with me all the way until he realized he'd been used.'

Priest collected himself, and stood up slowly. 'Maybe you shouldn't have told him. Money's a strong motivation.'

Gould felt himself losing control. 'Motives! What the hell do you know about motives, you don't even understand your own.' Abruptly, he switched his attack to Kalaba. 'And what does it all mean? I'll tell you. It means a change of leader in an unimportant country in the middle of black Africa. And what does the change of leader mean to the people of that country? I'll tell you that as well.' He raised his voice to a shout, and for a moment Priest could actually see the words rolling away towards the hills, blown by the wind and sustained by their own despair. 'Nothing. NOTHING!'

Priest knelt again and extracted the gun from the dead man's grip. The right forefinger was still in contact with the trigger.

Kalaba raised his eyes and looked at Gould. 'What's your motivation, Mr Gould? To collect fuel for your self-pity? Your government was forced to listen to our cry for independence. Suddenly, the slaves were the masters. You had a choice of action then, all those years ago, but here you are still lamenting the loss of something that was never yours. You whites have been hard to tolerate, Mr Gould. You never learned to put up or shut up. You felt that granting independence to people like us was a joke, that life would go on the same as before, that whites would always be needed to supervise our hopeless attempts at government. You thought . . .' but Gould shouted him down.

'Government? You don't know the meaning of the word. Your whole bloody system is corrupt.' He struggled for words, the accumulated frustrations of years in Africa fighting to find expression in this one acrid, uncharacteristic outburst. But even before he spoke, he recognized that in an angry, fast-flowing argument he was out of his element.

'Your so-called ministers come to office knowing they have a job-expectancy of two years if they're lucky, so they set about collecting as much hand-out as possible in the time allowed. By graft. Whatever you thought of the British administration, it worked, and it worked honestly.'

Kalaba smiled tolerantly. 'Another pat on the back for yourselves, Mr Gould? You know, you're really very naïve. Do you imagine that we invented bribery as a system? That the British ran an empire without playing favourites? That Watergate never happened? You're an anachronism, my friend, alienated by your own bitterness. You have reached the stage where you can no longer judge people as individuals. You despise blacks because they are black, and judge us all by our worst performance.' He turned away. 'You have my sympathy. It can't be easy to live with so many regrets.'

Priest looked from one to the other. The African limped slowly back towards the vehicles, his back straight and proud. The silence was heavy until Priest broke it.

'Is he right, Sam?'

Gould looked round the horizon, his eyes slit against the startling brightness. He saw the long, curved skyline where blue and white struck up an uneasy empathy. He saw his own future offering little more than the desolation of these unchanging wastes. He saw that, in part, Kalaba had been right.

'Yes, he's right.'

It was the only time that Priest had ever felt sorry for the other man, and he knew he had to hide the feeling at all costs. He slung the Sterling round his neck and stooped to pick up the Australian's legs.

'You take his arms.'

'I'm sorry about Gable,' Gould told him. 'It seems we're running low on pilots.'

Priest forced himself to talk lightly, but his voice thickened with emotion. 'For someone, today's a lucky break. Dead men's shoes.'

Gould knelt by Flemming's arms.

'Come on,' Priest said. 'Let's move him into the Rover and later on we can get someone down here to do the decent thing.'

The two men lifted Flemming's body, which seemed surprisingly light. Neither one of them looked down at the red patch where he had lain.

'What now?' Gould asked as they started walking.

Priest adjusted his grip on Flemming's legs and found his eyes kept returning against his will to the blackened edges of the bullet hole.

'You'll be glad to know that our part in this is almost finished,'

206

he said, and noticed that the body was getting heavier as they progressed. 'You said earlier that I didn't understand my own motives. I'm not the only one. We're handing over to a man called Barratt.'

23.00, Friday, 29 March

In Kampala, the frightened populace awaited dawn. Fierce fighting on the Bombo road had brought the battle to within a few miles of the city centre, and the sounds of sporadic gunfire crept closer through the wet streets. At Entebbe, the international airport was already out of Omuria's hands. Troop carriers had landed with complete surprise on the sandy beach fringing the main runway, and swiftly fought their way over the tarmac, until the terminal was overwhelmed. The few passengers crouched terrified behind seats and covered their heads as troops swept through the building, and the roar of automatic weaponry overwhelmed the screams of hysterical women.

In room 512, on the fifth floor of the International Hotel, Max Ebert finished a Scotch and poured himself another. Radio Kampala had gone off the air abruptly at eleven in the middle of the national anthem, and now Jim Schreiber sat on a camera case toying unsuccessfully with the tuning of a nine-inch Sony portable.

Earlier in the evening, Ebert had climbed the service stairs to the roof, which commanded a view over the whole town, but the position was already taken by a platoon of soldiers and a field radio, and one of the former had escorted him back to the room at gunpoint. Ebert glanced at his watch again, but the hands hadn't moved at all, and he looked over at the bed where Mojo Peters slept soundly, as indeed he had slept through a dozen coups in the past. On the table, the tiny screen flickered uncertainly; it was like waiting for the results of a big ball game while the TV company showed a 'temporary fault' card. He was just reaching for his glass when the screen dissolved into a series of wavy lines and slowly from the confusion there resolved, fuzzily at first and then more clearly, the face of a man.

Even as Omuria sat in front of the camera he could hear the sound of small arms close at hand. His thin face looked pinched and strained, and in sunken sockets his black eyes bore a hint of madness. A last group of soldiers covered the studio doors and guarded his rear from attack. Shaking, the cameraman focused up on him and waited for instructions over his headphones. In the control room, two staff sat under the threatening presence of a soldier, and watched the picture on a monitor marked Cam 1. A black finger tapped a button, and the picture doubled, leaping sideways onto another screen marked TX. One of the men whispered a few words into a microphone and sat back. There was nothing else to be done. The President was on the air.

Omuria saw the red light flare on top of the camera and started to speak, but his voice was immediately drowned by gunfire. Behind him, the doors burst open, and one of his guards back-peddled ludicrously across the room. The picture swung wildly as the cameraman left his post and huddled in the corner of the room; then it steadied, feeding a shot of the door, passably framed and focused, to the transmitter. For a moment no one came or went, and there was just a confused cacophony of sounds to stimulate the viewer's imagination. Then, head down, capless, slumped in the arms of two soldiers, the unconscious body of Omuria was seen by all those watching as they dragged him away past camera.

07.00, Saturday, 30 March

The next morning dawned quiet, and Ebert dragged the crew out of bed early and down into the streets. The airlines were overflying, and he could neither cable nor telephone; but good footage this morning added to what they'd already got would make a nice package for charter to Nairobi and dispatch to London. The news on BBC's World Service indicated that little was known externally of recent events, and Radio Kampala had announced that representatives of the new régime would be making a midday address on television.

At eleven Ebert, Schreiber and Peters were on their way to the hotel to eat and watch the twelve o'clock newscast, when they passed the British high commission. Ranks of African soldiery thronged the front of the building, stretching right round to the side door that led to the passport office. Peters pulled in across the road and Ebert asked 'Got the gear ready?'

Schreiber nodded, and tapped the top of his Arriflex. Peters reached behind the front seat, and came up with the obscene, grey-frankfurter shape of a gunmike.

'OK, this looks like it could be important. As soon as whoever it is comes through that door we're into 'em.'

'Then you'd better be off with a mike of your own,' Peters told him.

Ebert opened the door of the Mercedes and swung his legs out. 'Stay with what you've got, we might never make it to first base.'

The three men moved quickly over the road, Ebert leading; predictably two uniformed Africans moved to bar their way, and he ignored them till the last minute, then flipped open a Press card. Inside, held secure by thumb and forefinger, a folded one hundred shilling bill showed a fringe of lettuce green. The first soldier took the card and showed it to his friend. When he handed it back, the money was gone.

Ebert smiled, 'Thanks boys!' and made to move on. But the Africans shook their heads in unison and began to unsling their rifles.

'Tricky that,' Peters said, jaws working rhythmically on a wad of gum.

'Yeah,' Schreiber added. 'Dishonest even.'

Ebert played for time. Out came a billfold, and he withdrew a crumpled piece of paper like a conjurer at an audition. It crackled as he opened it.

'Listen, boys, we're invited, see? Officially. By the ministry. You just read this and you'll see what I mean.' He spread the paper out, revealing a considerable screed in Arabic; stuck at the bottom was a postage stamp, and over it, in smudged ink, the legend 'Received with Thanks' in four languages. But before he could pass the paper over, the plate-glass doors of the commission opened and a group of men came out. Schreiber already had the film rolling, and the three men swung towards the building, Ebert doing what he could to protect the camera's passage. With a jolt he recognized two of them: the tall, tough-looking European was the man who'd called himself Barratt, and the African limping slightly at his side, ex-President William Kalaba. Still moving, he hissed in Schreiber's ear:

'It's a jackpot, Jim—the Ace of Spades at the front is Kalaba.'

Now they'd reached the soldiers, and Schreiber crabbed along the line hoping for a clearer shot before the group reached their car. Ebert called out loudly before they disappeared once and for all:

'Mr President? CBS News, sir. Could you tell us your role in the present situation?'

Kalaba stopped and turned; Schreiber stopped too, and pulled down on the zoom handle. Then he eased the shot into focus.

Kalaba said, 'There will be a broadcast on the national TV service at midday.' He glanced at his watch. 'That's in fifty minutes' time, gentlemen.'

He turned to go, but Ebert called, 'Do we understand that you have resumed your position of leadership, sir?'

The African opened the far door. 'Growing discontent in the country has necessitated a change of government. That change is now successfully accomplished.'

Schreiber kept rolling as the car doors slammed, then when it moved away he pulled out to a wide shot and cut. 'All right for you, Moje?'

Peters grinned and lowered the mike. 'Yeah, let's grab a bite to eat.'

The Mercedes started silently, and Peters shifted into first. 'That Barratt guy,' he mused. 'What the hell was he doing there?'

Ebert braced himself as they sped round the island outside the Grand Hotel. 'I guess we'll never know,' he said. 'But it'll be interesting to see who recognizes the new crowd first.'

Peters grinned. 'It won't be Peking!'

'Or Moscow,' Schreiber added.

Ebert thought back to his last assignment but one as they turned up the steep drive of the International. 'Or Libya,' he thought, and by that time the car had rolled to a halt.

11.00, Sunday, 31 March

Over Zanzibar there was no trace of rain: the sky was cloudless, and the sun making up for lost time. Tai Ling took a last look round, and felt no regret at all that he was leaving. He picked up a small leather case and walked across the courtyard. Seng was there by the car, and they got under way in silence, making for the airport, the sound of the motor rebounding in the narrow-walled streets, and once they had to wait while an old man explained the virtues of movement to a recalcitrant donkey. The car stopped, the driver got out to open the doors, first for Tai Ling, then Seng. By the helicopter there was an awkward silence. Tai knelt and opened his case, taking out a medium-sized box made from many woods of different colours; it was cleverly worked into the shape of an old temple set amidst flowering gardens. Then he shut the case and stood up, holding the box out to Seng.

'It's yours. Go on, take it. Then when I hear the Twittering of the Sparrows in Tunhwang I can think of Seng mixing the pieces and hoping for Imperial Jade.'

Seng accepted the Mah Jong gratefully. He hesitated, then :

'You were not happy here. I almost think that you have played the Game with us all, and now comes your final move— the Moon from the bottom of the Sea.'

Tai smiled, his mouth both sensitive and cruel; then he picked up the case and climbed up into his seat. 'I think perhaps that you too have been playing the game. There is a price we all pay for happiness: mine has been failure. Yours—who can say?'

Seng watched as the craft rose lazily into the air, and stray currents of wind plucked at his sleeve. He wondered what had happened to Soon and if Tai Ling knew of his reports direct to Peking. A recce aircraft had found only a crashed plane and an ancient jeep. Perhaps he would never know. Somehow, as the helicopter dwindled, he could still hear the abrasive voice, feel the power behind the hawklike Tartar face; and perversely, he felt empty and alone, the satisfaction of his own promotion fading away. Holding the Mah Jong tightly, he ducked into the car, away from the dust and heat.

But, unlike Seng, Tai Ling was on his way home.

13.00, Sunday, 31 March

Four hundred miles to the north, Priest was handling his goodbyes. It was not a moment that he relished, and this time was worse than most. In a way he was glad that McLoughlin was there, otherwise the whole proceedings might have got a bit emotional.

Katie was wearing a light yellow dress and a pair of high-heeled sandals, and Gould looked much as he always did, making few noticeable concessions to the fact that he was in town. Out on the baking tarmac, jet engines whined and moaned, and in front of the building an incessant conveyor belt of taxis and VW's poured human fodder to the check-in desks. Katie kissed him on the mouth.

'Don't leave it for ten years this time, Harry!' Her face laughed, but her eyes meant it.

Priest tried to respond lightheartedly. 'How can I compete with the Man of Iron here? Maidens rescued from the heart of UN held Congo ... you never actually told me, Sam, how you came to be fighting the United Nations?'

Gould chuckled. 'I was young and idealistic. You won't find me exposing myself to risks like that again.' The laughter went from his voice, and he stuck out a hand. 'Spare a few thoughts for the ones that didn't make it, Harry—they would've liked to be here.'

Priest took the hand, and thought of Flemming lying face down out there in the soda, and the premature death of Johnny Gable. He felt his mind clang shut against the familiar feeling of guilt, but still it was there, with tentacles that writhed beyond the threshold of his reason, insinuating themselves into every move he made, every word he said.

'Harry?' Katie's voice was concerned. 'Are you all right?'

Slowly his mind cleared, and the sunlight poured back in. 'Yes,' he said. 'I'm all right.'

Before he went through passport control he turned to Gould. 'What are your plans now, Sam?'

The man shrugged. 'I've offered to help Mac here sort a few things out, as you know. Then there's a man on foot down around the Rukuru who used to be on wheels till I turned up, and well, I said I'd take him some new transport.'

Priest raised an eyebrow. 'I never did meet that daughter of his. Well, if anyone feels like a holiday I should think your credit's pretty good in Uganda as soon as our friend gets things sorted out a bit. In spite of certain disagreements along the way. That goes for you too, Mac.'

He looked at the three of them, and said, 'I've got to go now, they're calling the flight. Thanks—all of you—for your help and friendship.'

He was almost out of sight when feet pattered up behind him, and Katie grabbed his arm. Her eyes were bright with moisture. 'Harry, I have to go to London in July—will you be there?'

Priest ran his hand lightly over her hair, and wondered just where the hell he would be in July. Emotional crises had never been his strong point, it always seemed better to sidestep them, and make a judgement later in the cold light of day. All his training, everything he'd learned, dictated that no rational decisions could ever be made in anger or in love. 'Love?' he thought. 'Has it really come to that?' The words sounded strange in his mind, and now the crisis was upon him and he was in the wrong place and ill-prepared to meet it.

Slowly, his hand reached and gripped hers. For a long moment they stood there as if there was all the time in the world, but when he turned away it was the most predictable thing that had ever happened, and she watched him out of sight.

She was still standing there with tears in her eyes, watching, when Gould came up and took her by the arm. With difficulty, he steered her through the crowds and out into the sunlight.

From his first-class window seat Priest saw the city dwindle. His ears popped as the plane continued to climb, and then a sign lit up over his head, and he took his hands off the arm rests and loosened the seat belt. Sun flared into the cabin and out again as they banked, and a smiling brunette took orders for the bar. Priest moved his watch back to match up with British Summer Time, and looked towards where Uganda was already sprawling to the west, vast, green and empty. Somewhere nearby ice clinked brightly on glass, and tomorrow was April Fool's Day. Priest felt whisky burn his throat and thought about goodbye.